Quinn's Family Tree

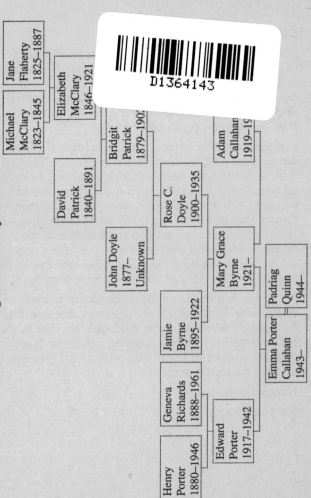

Michael McClary 1823–1845	Jane Flaherty 1825–1887

Elizabeth McClary 1846–1921

David Patrick 1840–1891

Bridgit Patrick 1879–190?

John Doyle 1877–Unknown

Rose C. Doyle 1900–1935

Adam Callahan 1919–19?

Mary Grace Byrne 1921–

Henry Porter 1880–1946

Geneva Richards 1888–1961

Jamie Byrne 1895–1922

Edward Porter 1917–1942

Emma Porter Callahan 1943–

Padriag Quinn 1944–

Dear Reader,

It's difficult to believe that this is the twelfth book in my Quinn family saga. When I began this series in September 2001, I never dreamed that it would become so involved. But many of you have written and even more have bought the Quinn books, making them a very popular family!

I've explored the original six Quinn brothers, their sister, three of their cousins and a good number of their ancestors, as well. And in *The Legacy*, I return again to Ireland to tell the story of a long line of women—the ancestors of Emma Porter Callahan Quinn, the mother of my three latest Quinn heroes, Ian, Declan and Marcus. The story begins in the months before the Irish famine of the 1840s and ends in America. And like the stories that came before it, it's a story of love and family loyalty.

I'm not sure if there will be more Quinn stories. It is a large family and there are many cousins. But for now, I'll leave you with this book. Be sure to look for new stories from me, coming out in the Blaze line. You can keep up to date with all my releases at www.katehoffmann.com.

Happy reading,

Kate Hoffmann

Kate
Hoffmann
THE
LEGACY

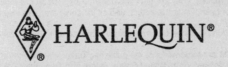

TORONTO • NEW YORK • LONDON
AMSTERDAM • PARIS • SYDNEY • HAMBURG
STOCKHOLM • ATHENS • TOKYO • MILAN • MADRID
PRAGUE • WARSAW • BUDAPEST • AUCKLAND

ISBN-13: 978-0-373-19855-9
ISBN-10:   0-373-19855-8

THE LEGACY

www.eHarlequin.com

Printed in U.S.A.

KATE HOFFMANN

has penned over fifty stories for Harlequin Books since her first release in 1993. She has enjoyed creating sexy heroes that her heroines (and her readers) can't possibly resist. Kate lives in a small town in Wisconsin with her three cats and her computer. She enjoys golfing, genealogy and gardening, and also volunteers with music and theater programs for young people in her community. Her favorite place in the whole wide world is her bedroom. Her second favorite place is Ireland, which is where the fairies worked their magic and put the Mighty Quinns in her path. The popular family saga now encompasses twelve books with the release of *The Legacy*.

For Marie Grace McDougall and
Jack Edward Parry, together again.

14 April 1845

Today is my wedding day. My name is Jane Flaherty—
now Jane McClary for I have married Michael McClary
this morning at our parish church. I begin this diary so
that I might look back in years to come on the early days
of my marriage, so that I might tell my children of the
tiny details of my life. And here I begin. This book was
given to me by the lady who employs me as a seamstress. Her name is Mrs. Grant and she tells me I am a
fine talent with needle and thread. She said it would be
useful to have a place to keep my household accounts,
and made of this small book, a wedding gift. But
instead, I will write my thoughts and my dreams on
these pages. It is for her kindness that I am able to write
and read at all, for she taught me when I first went to
work for her. And I will teach my daughters and they
will teach theirs. Then they may all see the world in the
pages of great books. My Michael has come home for
his supper and I must end here.

"AMERICA?"
Jane McClary slowly sank into the rough wooden chair,
placing her hands on the table. Her heart felt as if it had

dropped to the floor and she stared at her husband. His eyes were bright with excitement, a quality that had made her fall in love with him the very first time they'd met.

"Surely you see." Michael reached out and took her hands between his, the calluses rough against her skin. "Our future is there. There are jobs and good land to farm. People are leaving every day, from Dublin and from Cork. The boats are full to Liverpool and still more want to go."

"But, our home is here," Jane said. "Our families are here."

Michael shook his head. "But not our future." He glanced around the sod house. "I work until my back aches and my fingers bleed and we never get ahead. And you, you sew into the wee hours, your eyes straining to see the stitches, and for nothing more than a few shillings. How much longer can you do that, Jane? And what will happen when we have a family? It will be even more difficult to leave then. If we are to go, it must be now."

"But we can't afford one passage, how could we afford two?"

"We won't," he said. "It's three pounds ten. We have a bit saved and Johnny Cleary says that he'll loan me the rest for he's taken his entire flock of sheep to market just today. And when I get there, I will find work and send for you. Our babies will be born in America, Jane, and they will grow up fine and strong. They will have a future that they could never have here in Ireland."

Jane drew in a deep breath and let it out slowly. She had seen friends and relatives make the same decision, and though she'd heard harrowing tales of the dangers of crossing the Atlantic, all that she knew had arrived safely. And Michael was right. Ireland offered nothing to an ambitious man and he had always been that. A bit of a dreamer, too, she thought to herself. But how could she deny him this? She was his wife and bound to follow where he led, like Ruth from the Bible. It was her duty.

"When will you go?" she asked.

"In a week's time," he said.

"That soon?" Jane dropped her hands to her lap, twisting her fingers together nervously. They'd been married not yet three months and now he would leave her to live alone.

He reached into his pocket and pulled out a small piece of newsprint. "There. Read that. Johnny gave that to me. He says there'll be jobs waiting for us. Good jobs with good pay."

Jane picked up the paper and read the advertisement. "Strong Irish Lads Wanted," she said. "Railroad work. A dollar a day, room and board included. Call at 17 Carney Street, Boston, upon arrival." She glanced up at Michael. "And how long until I might join you?" she asked.

"They say the passage is six or seven weeks, eight if the weather turns bad. I will work through the winter and send for you in the spring. The time will fly by and you will barely know I'm gone. And during that time, you will sew curtains for our grand new house in America. I promise you, Jane, it won't be a dark and tiny stone cottage with a leaky thatch roof. It will be a grand house made of wood, with real glass windows and a marble fireplace to keep you warm at night."

Jane put her hand on her belly. The baby would be born in the spring, March if she counted correctly. She hadn't told Michael yet. She'd wanted to wait just a bit longer to be certain. But now, she would keep the secret from her husband, for if he knew, then he would never leave.

She pushed away from the table and walked to the dry sink, then pulled down the small butter crock from the shelf above it. Inside was their life savings, enough to buy a pretty dress, new pair of shoes and perhaps dinner at a fancy hotel in Dublin.

Jane crossed to the table and dumped the money on the scarred surface, then counted it out. "One pound, nine," she murmured. "We can sell the cow. You'll have to have food to eat, and a warm coat. I hear that winters are fierce in America and I won't have you getting sick for wont of decent clothing."

"And what will you do for milk and butter if we have no cow?"

"I will buy it in town. Mrs. Grant pays me enough to feed me. And Jack Kelly has always coveted this plot of land. He'll be happy to take it over after I harvest the crop. I can sell the potatoes you won't be here to eat and the garden will provide the rest. I will do quite well for myself," Jane said with a weak smile. "You married a clever girl, Michael McClary, and you would do well not to forget that."

Michael nodded, then rose to stand beside her. He wrapped his arms around her waist and pulled her against him, kissing her softly on the forehead. "We'll have a fine life in America," he said. "I've seen it in my dreams."

Jane closed her eyes and pressed her cheek against his chest. His heart beat, strong and sure, and Jane tried to memorize what it felt like to be held by him. There would come a night when she'd reach across the rope bed and he wouldn't be there. But she would be brave, for she loved this man and would follow him to the ends of the earth if he asked.

CHAPTER ONE
ROSE

Dublin, 1924

ROSE BYRNE STOOD IN THE protection of a church facade, staring out at the cold drizzle that had turned the cobblestone streets slick. The sky above was so gray she couldn't tell if it was morning or afternoon. She'd stopped listening to the chiming of the church bells on the hour. It only made the time move more slowly.

Rain had been falling for almost three days and the dampness had set into her bones and her lungs until she wondered if she'd ever feel warm again. She closed her eyes and tried to imagine a sunny summer day from her childhood, when she'd walked in the meadows around her Grandmother Patrick's Wexford cottage and lain in the tall grass amongst the butterflies and wildflowers.

Life had been so simple then, her dreams untarnished, her future full of promise. Though it had not been five years ago, it seemed like a lifetime now, so much had changed. She'd married at nineteen and traveled with her husband, Jamie Byrne, to Dublin where he'd found work at a mill. They'd lived in a small flat near the river, just two drafty rooms and a grimy window with a view of another tenement, so different from her grandmother's cottage. But it might have been scalp, a hole dug in the ground with sticks for a roof, for all she and Jamie cared.

Though the country was in turmoil and Dublin at the center of it, at first Rose and Jamie paid little attention to the politics that drove Irish life. Though Jamie worked hard, his pay never seemed to be enough to buy any more than the necessities. After a time, he became frustrated and spent his evenings at the pubs instead of at home.

Rose found work taking in laundry and sewing for a well-to-do Irish merchant and his family. And when she'd discovered herself pregnant after six months of marriage, she and Jamie had looked forward to the birth of their first child. But the baby had been stillborn just a month before it was due and a miscarriage followed that.

When she found herself pregnant again, she had begged Jamie to take her back to Wexford, to use the small inheritance from her Grandmother Patrick to build a new life where the air was fresh and she might have a chance to carry her baby to term. But Jamie had become involved in a patriot's cause, in a revolution that had been brewing for years in the pubs and factories all over Ireland. He refused to leave.

It was his duty to their unborn child, he'd argued. He wanted his children to grow up in a free Ireland, an Ireland that might promise a better future than the one he'd been dealt. But Rose was frightened she would bring a child into a world at war with itself and as her time grew near, she watched the conflict escalate and her husband take risks that put his life in danger daily.

Jamie had sworn his allegiance to the IRA, determined that Ireland become an independent and unified republic from north to south, east to west. But the Free Staters, willing to let the northern counties of Ulster go in a treaty with Britain, won out in the end.

His dedication to a lost cause had cost him his life. Jamie Byrne, husband of Rose Catherine Doyle, had been killed in October of 1921, when he and three other Republicans were ambushed on a country road outside of Dublin. He'd been buried by the government in an unmarked grave.

A cough wracked her chest and the child nestled against her body wriggled beneath the damp wool blanket, her wide, blue eyes staring up at Rose. "It'll be fine," she cooed. "We'll find a place to live with a warm fire and a solid roof. And we'll have hot food to eat and I'll feel better again."

"Sleep, Mama," Mary Grace murmured, reaching up to touch her mother's cheek.

Rose drew the blanket up around the child's face, then stared down at her dirty fingernails. Her hem had been soaked in so much muddy water, her white petticoat had turned grey. And her hair, once a vibrant auburn, was now limp and filthy.

Mary Grace Byrne had been born a week after Jamie was murdered, three years ago. Rose had almost expected the angels to take her, as well. They'd taken so many of the people she'd loved—her mother and brother, her grandmother, and her beloved Jamie. But though she'd come a month early, Mary Grace had inherited her father's dark hair, his indomitable spirit and his good health.

They'd lived on the inheritance for a time and money she took in for laundry and sewing. Rose had tried to find a job in a factory, but her health prevented her from working the long hours. Money soon became scarce and the landlord impatient. She'd been forced to sell the sewing machine that her grandmother had given her as wedding present. With it went any chance to make a living.

Three months ago, she and Mary Grace were evicted, tossed out onto the streets after she'd fallen behind on the rent. Now, she was forced to scrabble through the rubbish bins for food, joining the ranks of the poor and indigent who existed on whatever the streets of Dublin could provide. She knew to hide during the day and to forage at night, avoiding the authorities who might drag her off to the poorhouse and take her daughter away from her. And occasionally, a passerby would take pity and toss her a coin, enough to buy Mary Grace a bit of milk and bread.

She began to hum a tune, a lullaby that she remembered from her childhood, rocking her daughter against her. If only she'd had family she could turn to, Rose thought. Her parents were gone, her mother dead in childbirth with Rose's younger brother. Her father had put Rose in the care of Bridgit's mother, Elizabeth Patrick, and then left without a word as to his destination or his return. Rose could barely remember him. But when she fell in love with Jamie, she'd thought she'd found a man who would protect her forever. She'd been so terribly naive.

Rose shivered, hugging her daughter close. How much longer could they survive? Winter was nearly upon them and the weather was becoming so cold. She hadn't eaten in three days and if she didn't get out and find food for them both, she'd be forced to make a decision soon. To die with her child and join her family in heaven, or to leave the girl on the steps of St. Vincent's orphanage. Surely the sisters would take good care of such a pretty little thing.

She pressed her lips to Mary Grace's smooth forehead, then ran her fingers over the wavy dark hair on her head. "You're a strong little thing, you are. You come from a long line of strong women. We still have time, wee one. We'll find a way, I swear on all that's holy."

Rose reached into the bundle she carried, the sum total of her life tucked inside a tattered scrap of wool. She withdrew a leather-bound journal and carefully flipped through the pages of tidy script. Her family hadn't had much. No pretty heirlooms to pass down. But her grandmother had given her Jane McClary's diary, an account of the horrible years of the potato famine in the 1840s.

It had always been passed to the first-born daughter and when Rose had been married, her grandmother had handed it to her, tears swimming in her eyes. "You must keep the story alive now," she murmured. "This was my most treasured possession. I gave it to your mother on her wedding day and now, it is yours."

It wouldn't fetch much, Rose mused. Had it been a brooch or a bracelet, she might have sold it to buy food. But then, a previous generation might have done the same and there would never have been a legacy to pass along. But somehow, Rose knew that this was the way of it, that the words of Jane McClary had been written especially for her…to give her strength, to keep her alive when all hope seemed gone.

She opened to a random page and turned the book toward the feeble light. With the diary had come an education, for Jane had taught her own daughter to read and write, and Rose's grandmother, Elizabeth, had taught Rose's mother, Bridgit. And when the time came, Rose would teach her own daughter, Mary Grace, and she would know for herself that she came from a long line of stubborn, independent and courageous women.

10 August 1845

Michael is gone. Bound for Liverpool he is and from there will travel by ship to Boston, America. I made a brave face for his leaving, but my heart felt a terrible fear. The babe growing inside me must feel this too. There are whispers of a blight on the potato crop, but all seems well here. Michael will find work when he lands and then will send for me and our child. I pray for his safe journey and for the day we will see each other again.

Rose had read the diary over and over again since the day it had been given to her. And in the bleakest of times, it had provided courage and perspective. Jane had lived through a famine, nearly starving to keep her daughter, Elizabeth, alive. And Elizabeth had survived and given birth to seven children, including Rose's mother, Bridgit, and then had raised Rose. Elizabeth Byrne Patrick had lived to the age of seventy-five and died in her sleep six months before Mary Grace had been born.

All her living children had long ago left for America and there had been only one heir who remained to mourn her—Rose. Would she have a long life as her grandmother had? Would she live to marry again and give her daughter brothers and sisters to play with? Or would she leave this earth as her mother had, slipping away at a young age with barely a chance to live?

Rose pushed aside the wool blanket and reached beneath her daughter's rough linen shift. She withdrew a small gold medallion, then stared at the words written in Gaelic around the edge. "Love will find a way," she murmured. Jamie had given her the medallion as a wedding gift and he'd worn one just like it, the one she now wore around her own neck. The gold would buy them another week of life, perhaps two. Tomorrow, she would find a place to sell them both.

She closed her eyes, then slowly slid down along the rough stone wall until she sat with Mary Grace cradled in her lap. Drawing the blanket up over their heads, she closed her eyes and let sleep absolve her of her worries. Love would find a way.

The love she had for her daughter was such a powerful thing…it had to count for something.

LADY GENEVA PORTER SLOWLY walked up the steps to Christ Church cathedral. She made a point to visit the cathedral every time she traveled to Dublin, seeking comfort in the grandeur of the Gothic architecture and the beauty of the stained glass. Even on a gloomy day like today, she found warmth and light here.

She always came for the same reason. Her mother had once told her prayers said in a cathedral got to heaven faster than those said in an ordinary church. She'd always hoped that it were true. Reaching into the pocket of her cloak, she smoothed her fingers over the Bible she'd brought with her, then reached out for Edward's hand.

Her son was no longer at her side and Geneva turned, searching for the seven-year old. He'd wandered over to a large pillar and was staring down at a pile of rags, left in a sheltered spot.

"Edward, come along."

"Mummy, what's this?"

"Edward! Come away from there! It's probably just rags for the charity bin."

She watched as he kicked at the pile of rags with the toe of his boot. To Geneva's horror, it moved. Edward jumped back and she rushed over to grab his arm. "Come away, I said."

"Mummy! Someone's hiding under there!"

She pulled him along toward the door of the church, but a

child's cry stopped her in her tracks, the sound hauntingly familiar. "Lottie?" she murmured, pressing her hand to her breast.

Geneva turned around and slowly approached the source of the sound, stunned that someone would have left a child amongst a pile of rags. These Irish had no sense of responsibility, Geneva thought, anger bubbling up inside her. But when she reached the spot, she realized that the rags hid both a woman and a child.

"Is she dead, Mummy?" Edward asked, clinging to his mother's arm.

Geneva knelt and plucked at the filthy blanket wrapped around the woman's head and face. Once she'd brushed it aside, she found the child, resting in the woman's lap, whimpering, her grimy cheeks wet with tears. The little girl turned brilliant blue eyes up to Geneva and smiled through her tears. "Mama?"

Geneva felt the breath leave her body and for a moment, she thought she might faint. But then, her heart began to beat again and she reached out and touched the girl. "Edward, run and get Farrell. Tell him to bring the motorcar around."

"Why?"

"Just do as I say," Geneva snapped. She brushed dirty hair from the woman's face, stunned to see how young she was—and how deathly pale "Hello," she murmured. "Can you hear me?"

The woman stirred slightly, her eyes fluttering open for a moment. "My girl," she murmured. "Please help my daughter." With trembling hands, she tried to hold the child out to Geneva. "Keep her safe."

Geneva carefully picked the child up and set her on her feet. Compared to the mother, the child looked to be in relatively good health, although grimy from the soot and dust that hung in the air. From the child's size she'd judge her to be two or three years old, but children raised in Irish poverty were often smaller than those raised in the comforts of a good English home.

The girl stopped whimpering the moment Geneva helped her to stand and she held out her little arms and hands to Geneva as she tumbled into her skirts. "Mama," she said with a soft giggle. "Go home, Mama. Now."

"Charlotte?" Geneva whispered. Tears flooded her eyes as she remembered the first time she'd held her own daughter, all red and wrinkled, the doctor proclaiming the first Porter child to be in excellent health.

Geneva hooked her finger beneath the child's chin and examined her face more closely. "You are Charlotte, aren't you?" Geneva said, her voice trembling. "You called to me and I came. I knew I'd find you again." She hugged the child fiercely and the girl gave a tiny cry of surprise. "I never stopped looking. Never. I'm going to take you home, Charlotte."

She felt a hand on her shoulder and she turned to find Edward standing behind her. "Mummy, are you all right?"

Geneva brushed the tears from her cheeks and forced a smile. "Of course, darling. Did you find Farrell?"

Edward nodded. A few moments later, Farrell joined them, dressed in a finely pressed uniform. "Help me," Geneva ordered. "Farrell, we need to get this woman to the car immediately."

"Lady Porter, I beg your pardon, but you can't possibly mean to—"

"Farrell, you heard what I said. We are going to take this poor thing and her child home and you will help me or I'll drive the bloody motorcar myself. Now get her to her feet."

Grudgingly, Farrell reached down and pulled the woman

up to stand. When her knees buckled beneath her, he cursed softly, then scooped her into his arms and carried her.

"I'll fetch her things," Edward offered.

"Don't be silly," Geneva said. "She can't possibly have anything of value." But her son didn't listen and gathered the blanket and a small bundle into his arms. A book fell out of the bundle and he picked it up and tucked it beneath his jacket. "Mummy, she has a book."

The boy crawled into the front seat of the touring car while Farrell helped Geneva and the woman into the rear. Geneva nestled the child in her lap, wrapping the girl in her cloak and trying to warm her little limbs with her body. But there wasn't much she could do for the young woman. She looked as if she were half dead of starvation. And who knows what fever she might be carrying?

Geneva had been sorely tempted to leave her there, to take the girl to safety first and then come back and look after her mother. But it would not have been the Christian thing to do and Geneva prided herself in her adherence to a strict standard of moral behavior.

Farrell pulled the car out onto the street and headed west out of Dublin. "Drive quickly," Geneva said, "but not too quickly, for the wind can be bitter cold back here." She adjusted her hat pin, then wrapped the trailing ends of her veil around her neck. It was at least a thirty-minute drive back to Porter Hall. "Hand me that lap robe, Edward," she shouted.

Then little boy crawled up onto his knees and shoved the heavy fur robe over the back of the seat. Geneva clumsily covered the young woman. "What is your name?" she asked, shaking her awake.

The woman moaned, then looked at Geneva through glazed eyes. "Where am I?"

"What is your name?" Geneva repeated.

"Rose," she said. "Rose Byrne.

"And the child?"

"Her name is—" A fit of coughing interrupted her and she pulled the lap robe up to her mouth. When she'd finally regained her voice, she sighed softly and closed her eyes again. "Her name is Mary Grace."

Geneva looked down at the child. Mary was such a common name among the Irish. Every other girl in the countryside was named Mary. But Grace was a fitting name for a child found outside a church. "Grace," Geneva murmured. She tickled the girl's cheek. "You are Grace."

The rest of the drive passed relatively quickly. Rose slept the entire route while Edward rested his chin on the back of the front seat and watched the scene before him. "What are we going to do with that girl?" he asked.

"Her name is Grace. Her mother is Rose. And I suspect we will take care of them until they are both well and then we'll send them on their way. It is an act of charity to help those less fortunate, Edward, and this is a lesson you would do well to remember. We were sent to that church for a reason today. It was God's will."

When they reached Porter Hall, Geneva ordered the car taken around to the kitchen entrance. Farrell carried Rose inside with Geneva and Edward trailing along behind, the little girl toddling between them. The two kitchen maids and Cook were left speechless by their unexpected entrance, but Geneva wasn't about to make any long-winded explanations to the help.

"Warm some soup," she ordered. "Farrell, take Rose upstairs and put her in the yellow room, across the hall from my chambers. Betsy, heat some water so that we might wash the grime off of her and the child. I want blankets and a clean nightgown brought up. And we must feed them both, perhaps some warm milk and porridge to start." The servants stared at her, unsure of what to do, and Geneva cursed softly. "Don't stand there with your mouths agape, do as I say. Now!"

With that, she picked up the little girl, resting her on her hip, then she walked out of the kitchen and up the rear stairway to the bed chambers on the second floor. Farrell had already settled Rose in the yellow room and Geneva set the little girl at the foot of the bed.

"Shall I fetch Lord Porter?" Farrell asked. "He's at the mill today."

"What could he possibly do to help?" Geneva asked. "You will go for the doctor and I will inform Lord Porter of this myself when he returns home."

Geneva bit back an oath. Ever since Charlotte's death three years ago and Geneva's subsequent breakdown, the servants had been particularly watchful. She suspected they'd been ordered to report any unseemly activity or behavior to her husband, for though they were deferential to her, Lord Porter paid their wages.

Surely this latest incident would call her sanity into question, but Geneva had already begun to formulate a plan to keep Rose and her daughter at Porter Hall. Once the young woman had recovered, they would offer her a job. There were always scullery maids coming and going. She could start there and work her way up. And then, her child could take on some simple duties once she was old enough.

Geneva looked down at the little girl's face, wondering at how a child of such common birth could be so pretty. Perhaps Geneva would take Grace under her wing, as she had her own daughter. Charlotte had just begun to appreciate fine music and art when the angels had come for her.

The spiritualist Geneva had visited in London just last month had assured her that Charlotte would return, that she would make her spirit known to Geneva before the third anniversary of her death. And now she had come again, reborn in this beautiful little girl. Geneva dared not believe it was true, but it had to be. All the signs were there, just as the spiritualist had told her.

She examined the child closely. The girl wore nothing more than a rough linen shift with ragged underclothes beneath. She stripped them off, carefully examining her before counting her toes and fingers. "Well, Grace, you don't seem to be in such bad health for such a horrid beginning in life." The girl watched her silently. Though she was small, her arms and legs were still plump. "You're quite a lovely little thing now, aren't you?" She wrapped her in a blanket, then picked her up and carried her over to the fire that burned in the grate.

"What is that?"

Geneva glanced over her shoulder to see her eldest son, ten-year old Malcolm, standing near the door. "It's a child," she cooed.

"Not that," he muttered in cold voice. He pointed to the bed and Rose. "That. Father will be furious when he sees what you've brought home. That filthy wretch should go back to the gutter where she belongs with the rats and the lice and the other Irish rubbish. And she can take her ugly Irish child with her."

Geneva found it difficult to believe that she'd given birth to both Malcolm and Edward. Edward was sweet and caring and Malcolm was the exact opposite, spiteful and foul-tempered. Edward had inherited Geneva's compassionate streak and Malcolm had taken after his cold and ruthless father, a man who never passed up a chance to give voice to his prejudices. "The Bible tells us to be charitable to those less fortunate," Geneva murmured as she pressed a kiss to the girl's forehead.

Malcolm scoffed. "Is that what you call this, Mother? Charity? Or are you just trying to replace Charlotte again? It didn't work last time and it won't work this time."

"No one could ever replace your sister," Geneva said.

It was obvious Malcolm was fully aware of the incident that had sent her to the hospital just six months after Charlotte's death. She hadn't meant to just walk off with the little girl in the park, but she'd looked so much like Charlotte and Geneva had become confused. When they'd arrived home, the authorities had been called and money paid to silence the parents of the little girl.

"She's dead," Malcolm screamed, "and she'll never come back and it's all your fault. Papa told you not to take her with you to London. He said there was sickness there. But you never listen to him. You're the one who took her away." He rushed over to Geneva and grabbed the girl's foot, giving it a vicious yank.

"Ow," Grace cried. "Bad boy!"

"Charlotte was the only one in this family who loved me and you took her away."

Geneva felt the emotions well up inside her and she turned on her son, slapping him across the face. She had said the same words to herself over and over, every hour of every day for the past three years. It had been her fault. They would have been safe in Ireland, but there had been a new exhibit at the National Gallery that she'd been certain Charlotte would enjoy, so they'd traveled together.

"I am your mother and you will not speak to me in that manner again."

Malcolm laughed. "No great loss, Mother. You've gone so far 'round the bend that you don't understand half of what's said in this house anyway." He stalked out of the room, brushing by Edward, who had taken up a spot at the door.

Geneva sent her youngest son a wavering smile and he immediately returned it, then came rushing toward her. "Don't listen to him, Mummy. I think you did a very fine thing bringing the poor lady and her little girl home with us. We'll make them both better."

"We will, won't we," Geneva said. "Now, you run and see if you can find Mummy's maid. Ask her to go to the nursery and see if she can find one of Charlotte's old nightgowns in the chest. I believe I saved a few just to have around for my grandchildren."

"I'll go look for them," Edward offered.

Geneva had only one ally in the house and that was Edward. He'd always tried his best to make her happy, to take her mind off the dark thoughts that seemed to plague her daily. If it came down to it, Edward would stand up for her against her husband and her older son. Though he was only seven, he was wise beyond his years and knew exactly how to get what he wanted. And that was usually no more than the means to make his mother smile.

"You're a good boy," she whispered as she watched him run out of the room. "And I will always love you the best."

CHAPTER TWO

"IT'S TIME FOR YOU TO WAKE up now."

Rose drifted toward consciousness, following the voice of the child. Was it Mary Grace who was speaking to her? Mary Grace hadn't learned to string many words together yet. And she didn't speak with an English accent. Had she died and gone to heaven? Was it an angel's voice she was hearing?

"Open your eyes," the child whispered.

She felt fingers touch her face and Rose willed herself to do as she was told. Her eyes fluttered open and she found herself staring into the face of a young boy, his dark hazel eyes ringed with jet black lashes. She opened her mouth to speak, but nothing came out.

"Would you like a drink of water?" the boy asked.

Rose nodded and he held a cut-crystal tumbler up to her lips. She sipped slowly at the cool liquid, letting it slide across her parched lips and tongue. And when she could drink no more, she fell back into the down-filled pillows. "My daughter," she murmured. "Where is she? Is she all right?"

The little boy nodded. "Mummy has put her to bed in the nursery."

"She's alive?" Rose asked.

The boy frowned, then nodded. "Mummy was feeding her and then she fell asleep. She ate a little bowl of porridge and her belly got very fat." He held out his hands in front of his stomach.

Rose closed her eyes and smiled. Mary Grace was alive and so was she. Somehow, she'd ended up in a beautiful room, in a comfortable bed, watched over by the young boy. And her daughter had been given a meal. God had finally answered her prayers.

"There's food," he said. "Would you like something to eat?"

"Yes," Rose replied. As she tried to sit up, she realized how weak she was. Her head spun and her arms were barely strong enough to support her weight. The little boy helped her tuck a pillow behind her back, then set a tray beside her on the bed.

"The porridge is cold. So is the tea. But there is bread and butter and some of the ham we had for supper last night. I'll fetch you something to drink. Would you like that?"

"Stay here for a bit," Rose said. "Tell me who you are and where I am. How did I get here?"

The boy sat down on the edge of the bed. "My name is Edward Porter. I'm seven years old. My father is Lord Henry Porter and my mother is Geneva. And I have a brother named Malcolm." He glanced around. "This is my house, Porter Hall. My sister, Charlotte, used to live here but she got a fever and died and now she's gone to heaven."

"I'm so sorry," Rose said.

He shrugged. "Everyone says that."

"Do you miss her?"

"Oh, yes. Terribly. But Mummy says she's with the angels in heaven and she watches over me. Sometimes at night, she comes into my room and talks to me."

Rose nibbled at the bread, taking small bites until she felt the food begin to fill her stomach. "How did I get here?"

"We found you at the church," Edward explained. "And we put you in our motorcar and brought you home."

"Have I been here long?"

He shook his head. "It was morning and now it's evening. Papa will be home soon and he will be very cross with Mummy. Malcolm says he'll send you to the poorhouse. But you mustn't be scared."

Rose pushed the tray aside, then slipped from beneath the bed covers and swung her legs to the floor. She stared down at herself, surprised to find that she'd been dressed in a lacy nightgown and her hands and feet were clean. "I have to leave then," she said. "Will you help me find my clothes?"

"No," Edward cried. "You must stay. Mummy will make it right, you'll see."

"What is going on in here?" A woman, wearing a beautifully detailed afternoon dress, bustled into the room. Her pale hair was pulled back into a tidy knot. Her lovely face was marked by delicate and refined features. Rose had a vague memory of her voice. This must be the little boy's mother—and Rose's savior.

"Get back into bed," she ordered, her words spoken in aristocratic English. "You are far too weak to be walking about. Edward, I asked you to look after our guest."

"This is my mummy," Edward told Rose.

Rose tried to stand, but her legs were weak and her knees buckled. She sat on the edge of bed, a bit dizzy with the effort. "Thank you so much for your kindness, ma'am. But I wouldn't think to impose on you and your family any longer."

The woman frowned, her arms hitched on her waist. "You're educated," she said. "You don't speak like a common Irish girl."

"I know how to read and write," Rose said. "My grandmother taught me when I was just six years old, so that I might—" Rose stopped and glanced around the room, a sudden panic gripping her. "Where are my things? The bundle that I had with me? I must find it." She tried to rise again, but Edward skipped over and handed her the leather-bound diary.

"Is this what you want?" he asked. "I put it in my pocket to keep it safe."

Rose took the diary and clutched it to her chest. "Yes," she murmured. "Thank you. I couldn't bear to lose this." She sighed. "I'd like to see my daughter. Could you take me to her, ma'am?"

"You may call me Lady Porter," the woman said. "And before we do that, you and I must speak. My husband will be home soon and we must prepare a good story for him. Have you ever worked in a house like this?"

Rose shook her head. "No. But when I first came to Dublin, I worked for a well-to-do Irish family. The Dunleavys. Mr. Dunleavy owned a dry goods store."

"And what did you do for them?"

"I was a laundress. But I also did sewing for Mrs. Dunleavy and her daughters. I made them gowns and I mended their clothes. I'm very good with a needle and thread and I can operate a sewing machine. My grandmother taught me well. I can make a dress from any fashion plate you might show me. And I do fine embroidery." She pointed to Lady Porter's gown. "Like that."

"Then when you have recovered from your ordeal, you will work for me as a laundress and a seamstress. That way, you can watch your daughter while you work. We will find a room for you above the carriage house where you might be…out of the way."

Rose stared at Lady Porter, unable to believe her good fortune. "Oh, ma'am, that is far too kind. You've already done enough."

"Nonsense. It becomes more difficult daily to find good help and you're motivated to work hard. You've had an education of sorts, which recommends you as well. And both of us know you would never last another week out on the streets. Now, your wages won't be much, since we will also be supporting your daughter."

"I don't need wages, ma'am. I'll work for food and a warm place to sleep."

"We'll discuss this when you're well. Now, there is one other thing. And you must be truthful about this. The child. Was she born out of wedlock?"

"Oh, no," Rose replied. "No, I was married. My husband was—" She paused. If they knew the truth of Jamie's political activities, the Porters might not be so glad to have the wife of an IRA sympathizer working in their very English household. "He died. Three years ago. It was an accident. He fell while he was helping a friend to repair a roof." She promised herself to say a rosary for the lie.

"How tragic," Lady Porter said. "And how long were you on the street?"

"Three months," Rose said.

"You must have been quite resourceful to have survived that long. That quality will serve you well in this household." She held out her hand. "Lie back now and finish eating. You need a good night's sleep. You can see Grace in the morning."

"Mary Grace," Rose corrected. "Her name is Mary Grace."

"Yes, well, I'm sure she'll be quite happy to see her mother in better health. But she's sleeping now herself and it wouldn't do to wake her."

Lady Porter took Edward's hand and led him to the door. "Come, let's leave Rose to rest. We must see if we can convince Malcolm to take our side in this matter before your father returns."

When Rose was alone, she tried again to stand, holding on to the bedpost for support. She took a few steps, then a few more, feeling her strength beginning to return. She grabbed a small blanket from the end of the bed, and wrapped it around her shoulders, then slipped out of the room.

The hallway was dimly lit and quiet. Her bare feet brushed against the soft wool carpets and she peered in each door, searching for her daughter. When she found what looked to be a nursery, she stepped inside, then realized she wasn't alone. Lady Porter sat in a rocking chair near the window, Mary Grace in her arms.

"Aren't you my pretty girl, Lottie," she cooed. "You've come home to me at last. And this time, I'll never let you go."

Rose stepped inside the room, ready to correct her. Why was she having such a difficult time remembering Mary Grace's name? And why did Lady Porter insist that Mary was napping when she wasn't? But as she watched Lady Porter, Rose began to realize that all was not right with the woman. She continued to talk to the child as if she were much older.

In then end, Rose returned to the hallway, an uneasy feeling settling over her. For now, she'd accept the Porter's hospitality and her hostess's odd behavior. She didn't have any choice. The dangers out on the streets of Dublin were far worse than any danger she and Mary Grace might face inside the walls of Porter Hall.

"GENEVA, THIS IS ABSURD. You cannot bring home an Irish peasant and her brat like they were stray animals. This behavior only proves you still haven't recovered fully."

Edward stood in the hallway outside his father's library,

hidden in the shadows as he listened to his parents' conversation. Though he knew it was wrong, eavesdropping was the only way he ever really discovered what was happening inside Porter Hall. Most of the servants paid him little heed, for they assumed he didn't comprehend most of what was being discussed by the adults. And Malcolm took great delight in keeping the secrets he'd been privy to.

There was only one thing Edward truly didn't understand and that's why he continued to listen. Something was not right with his mother, but no one would say what it was. She'd had to go away after Charlotte had died and though he wasn't sure exactly how long she'd been gone, it had been a long time. If she was going to be sent away again, this time he wanted to know why.

"What was I to do?" she asked. "Let them both die? That poor child needed my help. At least there was something I could do."

"They're Irish. They have their damn free state now. Let them take care of their people the way they always wanted to."

"Don't be ridiculous," Geneva said. "She was close to death. How was she supposed to care for that little girl?"

"Do you have any idea what's going on outside this house, Geneva? Have you any conception what this family has had to face in the past ten years? With the uprising and the civil war, we have been teetering on the edge of ruin. It's been all around you and you've been completely oblivious."

"I read the papers, Henry. I'm aware of the political climate in Ireland."

"Well, let me give you a better account of it, just to be certain. We used to have a good life here. A prosperous life, a life that my father blessed us with when we married. I was happy to take over the enterprises in Ireland. But now, we live here in—in exile."

"That's not true, Henry."

"Oh, no? When the troubles started, my brother and father didn't hesitate to sell anything that might fetch a good price. They left me with the mills and the mines they couldn't get rid of. Let Henry have them," he muttered. "He'll be grateful for that much."

Edward's father stood and walked over to the whiskey decanter, then poured himself a drink. He took a long swallow, then turned back to his mother. "Now that this country belongs to the Irish again, our property is worth only what an idiot Irishman might pay for it. We're trapped here, Geneva, with no way out."

"The uprising was put down. The civil war is over," Geneva said. "You employ hundreds of Irish workers who want to work. I can't see how we're headed for ruin, Henry."

"I served in parliament, I helped run this country. And now, suddenly I have no say in how this government treats my interests. That's decided by the Irish now and their damned Diál Eireann. And with them in charge, this country is doomed to fail."

"Irish, British, free state, republic, Catholic, Protestant, what does it all matter? We have a home and you have a livelihood. You make a comfortable living. You're a smart man, you can make what you have a success. The terrible times are ended. We have two sons and we must make the best of it."

Edward peeked into the library and watched as his father stared into his glass. "The terrible times have only just begun, Geneva," he muttered. "As long as Ulster is under control of the British, the people in this country will never rest. Another civil war is just around the corner."

"Then perhaps we should stop thinking of ourselves as English and consider ourselves Irish. We've lived here through all the troubles, for nearly fifteen years. Our future is here. This is our home and we are not visitors in this country."

"You are mad," Henry muttered.

Geneva shook her head, her voice quivering. "I—I am not mad. You live in your world of comfort and wealth, you employ these people in your mills and mines and take advantage of them every day. But you never look at them, you never see them. They're good people. They survive on nothing, trying to support their families on pay that isn't enough for one, much less seven or eight."

"And you live in the same world with me," he said, his voice angry and accusing. "My money buys those beautiful gowns you wear and pays for your trips to London and for your spiritualists and fortune tellers." Edward's mother gasped. "What? You didn't think I knew about them? Those charlatans preying on your grief." He cursed, then sat down behind his desk.

Everyone in the family had changed since Charlotte's death, Edward thought. Malcolm had become mean and nasty, deliberately inflicting pain on his younger brother whenever he could. His father stayed away from home as much as he could and when he was home he was cold and unapproachable and often drunk. And his mother… Edward drew a ragged breath. Some days she was just like she used to be, happy and lighthearted, laughing at the silly stories he told. And other days, she wouldn't come out of her room, caught up in the midst of one of her black moods.

"We cannot keep her or her daughter in this house," he said. "I won't have it."

"She's worked as a domestic before and she claims to be an excellent seamstress."

"Let's be candid with each other, shall we, Geneva? You don't need a seamstress. You want that child."

Edward watched as his mother's face grew pale. She slowly

rose, her hands clutched in front of her. "Why can't you do this one thing for me?" she asked in a strangled voice. "Just let me have what I need. I will make my way through this, I promise. But I have to deal with this in my own way."

"This child is not yours," he warned. "And if I see you becoming too attached, I will force them out of this house. And if I see any strange behavior from you, then you will return to the hospital until you are able to comport yourself in a proper manner. Is that understood, Geneva?"

His mother nodded. "Yes, Henry."

"This will not become an obsession, or I will call an end to it."

"I understand," she replied.

He picked up a ledger from his desk and opened it, focusing his attention on the columns and rows of numbers. "That is all."

Geneva circled his desk, then placed a dutiful kiss on his cheek. "Thank you, Henry." With that, she swept out of the room, her head held high, her eyes watery with tears. She didn't even notice Edward standing outside the door, brushing right by him, her skirts rustling.

A few moments later, Edward walked into the library, his footsteps silent on the thick Oriental carpet. He stood in front of his father's desk, his heart slamming in his chest. When his father finally looked up, there was an expression of impatience etched across his face. "What is it?"

"Are you going to send Mummy away again?"

"That is none of your concern," he said.

"Please don't send her away," Edward begged. "I promise, I'll watch over her."

Henry Porter stared at his son for a long moment. "And will you tell me if she begins to confuse this Irish urchin with your sister Charlotte?"

Edward nodded, crossing his fingers behind his back to lessen the lie. "I will, Father," he said.

His father nodded slowly. "You're a good boy. And I think you understand how important it is that your mother keep her wits about her. She has been very emotional lately and that's not good for anyone. You must try to distract her from her worries."

"I will. I'm good at that."

"Very well," his father said. "I'm glad you see things my way. Run along now, Edward, I have work to do."

Edward hurried out of the library and when he reached the safety of the hallway, he uncrossed his fingers and asked God to forgive him for the lie. It wasn't really a sin to lie when he was just doing it to make his mother happy, was it? She'd suffered so much over the past few years. And if Rose and little Grace were the key to her happiness, then Edward would do everything in his power to make them both stay, his father's wishes be damned.

"What are you doing out here?" Malcolm strode down the hall and gave Edward a hard shove, sending him back against the wall. "I thought you'd be in the nursery playing with that little brat Mother brought home."

"She's not a brat," he said.

Malcolm sent Edward a look of utter disdain. "That brat is going to steal every minute of Mother's time. She won't pay attention to you anymore. She won't even see you, just like she doesn't see me. Get used to it, Edward. It's only a matter of time before she loves you less than she loves me."

"Maybe if you'd be nicer to her she'd love you again," Edward accused.

"I don't need her," he replied. "Neither does Father. You're the only one in this family who still cares for her and that's because you're still a baby."

"I am not!" Edward shouted, lashing out at Malcolm. He shoved against his chest, but Malcolm had three years on him and considerable strength.

Malcolm grabbed Edward's arm and twisted it behind his back, then pushed him up against the wall. "Don't ever touch me again," he muttered, his breath hot against Edward's ear. "If you do, I'll just find a way to take it out on that little Irish girl you're so fond of."

He gave Edward's arm a final twist, then pasted a smile onto his face and walked into the library. As Edward stood outside, he listened as his older brother spoke with his father, the conversation relaxed and friendly.

The lines of loyalty in the Porter house had been clearly drawn since Charlotte had died. His older sister had held them together as a family, but they were on different sides now—Malcolm and Henry against Edward and his mother. Even though Edward was younger, he wasn't afraid of his brother. Malcolm may be stronger and taller, but Edward was far more clever. He would do what it took to protect his mother, even if that meant destroying Malcolm in the process.

CHAPTER THREE

ROSE SAT AT THE WINDOW in her room above the coach house, sunlight spilling onto her lap and illuminating the mending that rested there. She rubbed her eyes, trying to wipe away the fatigue that seemed to descend upon her in the early afternoon.

Though it had been three years since she'd been rescued from the streets by Geneva Porter, her health hadn't fully returned. Her lungs were often congested and her eyesight had begun to falter. Though she was strong enough to work, she was left with far too little energy to raise a rambunctious daughter. She tipped her head back and closed her eyes, remembering the first months of her stay at Porter Hall.

It hadn't taken long to understand the strange dynamics of the Porter family. Geneva's "illness" wasn't an illness at all, but a chronic melancholy that seemed to grip her without warning. She'd visited countless doctors and taken just as many remedies, but the only thing that drew her out of her depression was Mary Grace.

The little girl, now six years old, had became a balm to Geneva's spirit and whenever she felt her mood darkening, she'd come to the carriage house to fetch Mary Grace and spend the afternoon in the garden, watching her chase butterflies and pick flowers.

In the beginning, Rose hadn't minded. She believed a strong bond between the two would only help her position in the household. But it had also caused some jealousies with the other, more senior, staff members. Geneva's maid, Ruth, had distrusted Rose from the start and jumped on any opportunity to drive a wedge between Rose and the mistress of the house. Cook was chilly and aloof, perturbed that she was expected to deliver meals to the carriage house for Rose and Mary Grace, while the rest of the staff took their meals in the kitchen. And their quarters had been decorated with many little luxuries from the attic, so different from the cold and sterile servants' rooms on the third floor of the manor house.

But Rose wasn't going to feel guilty for her position with Geneva Porter. If Geneva's affection for Mary Grace would keep them warm and well-fed, then who was she to deny her mistress anything? Or her daughter? She glanced over to the corner and watched as Mary Grace bent over an old wooden box she'd found.

"What are you doing, my girl?" Rose asked. "What do you have there?"

Mary Grace picked the box up and carried it over to her mother. She opened the top to reveal a variety of wood-carving tools. "Where did you find these?" Rose asked.

"In the stables. Under a pile of hay."

"Do you know what they are?"

Mary Grace shook her head. "I'm going to give them to Edward. He'll know what they are."

"They're wood-carving tools," Rose said. "And I think Edward would like these. He's always carving with that little knife of his. He'd do much better with a fine set of tools like these."

"I'll give them as a gift. Maybe for Christmas," Mary Grace said. "Or Edward's birthday. He'll be ten years old in…" She screwed up her face as she tried to remember. "Soon."

Rose smoothed her hand over the top of the box. "Why, we could find some paint and put his monogram on the top. That would make the gift very special."

"What's a monogram?" Mary Grace asked.

"Edward's initials. Fancy folk put their initials on everything they own. That way everyone knows who it belongs to."

A box of old tools was little to offer in return for what the Porter family had given Mary Grace. Clothes had magically appeared in the wardrobe and new dolls would find their way into the old chest at the foot of the bed. Books full of beautiful, hand-tipped drawings were stacked on the table beneath the window and nearly every day, Mary Grace would return from the house with some tiny trinket, an old piece of jewelry or a hair ribbon.

Even if Jamie had lived, he never would have been able to provide so well. But Rose knew all the lovely luxuries came at a price. She just hadn't been asked to pay it yet. Whatever it was, she'd simply remember that her daughter was happy and healthy and that was worth more than anything in the world to her.

A soft knock sounded on the door and Mary Grace jumped up to answer it. To Rose's surprise, Geneva stood on the other side. Lady Porter had never been to Rose's rooms. When she'd wanted to speak with her, she always sent someone to fetch her and they talked in her parlor. And now she was here with tea, all laid out on a silver tray.

Mary Grace jumped up from her spot and ran over to Geneva. She helped her lay the tea service out on a small table as if she'd been doing so for years. Rose watched them make the tea, then realized that they'd probably had tea together often. When they finished, Geneva pulled a hard candy from her pocket and placed it in Mary Grace's palm. "Run along now, Grace. I need to talk to your mother."

"Thank you, Lady Porter," the little girl said with a curtsey.

"Edward is out in the garden. Why don't you go visit with him."

They both watched as Mary Grace skipped through the door, her pretty skirts flying out behind her.

"I hope I'm not disturbing you," Geneva said. She handed a cup of tea to Rose. "There's sugar and milk. Do you take either?"

Rose shook her head, unsure of how to respond. It wasn't the choice of sugar or milk, but the fact that her mistress was waiting on her. "Is everything all right?"

"Yes, of course." Geneva poured herself a cup, then grabbed a chair from the table and set it in front of Rose. As she sat down, she smoothed her hands over the skirt of her elegant frock, then crossed her ankles. "There is something I've come here to discuss with you. It's about Grace."

"Has she caused some trouble? I try to keep a close eye on her, but sometimes she does wander off."

"She's six years old and I know that you plan to send her to the parish school in the village when the term begins next month. I'm sure you're aware that she's a very bright child." Geneva cleared her throat. "You're also aware that I've grown quite fond of her since you've both come to live here."

"Yes," Rose replied. "And I thank you for everything you've given her. You don't know how much it means to me to know that she's safe and healthy."

"But that isn't always enough," Geneva said. "There will come a time when Grace will have to make her own way in

the world and to do that, she must be educated. I would like
to take responsibility for this."

"But I'm certain she'll learn everything she needs to know
in school," Rose said. "And I'd prefer her to have a religious
education."

"I don't think sending her off to a parish school will really
serve her well," Geneva said. "I'd like to provide her with a
tutor. That way, she can get the very best education. And,
when she's older, if she wants to have a profession, then she'll
be prepared."

"But the parish school would—"

"The parish school will teach her just enough so she can
keep house and cook meals and raise children," Geneva
said. "I'm talking about more. French and art history and
literature."

"Why would she ever have need of that?"

"Maybe she won't," Geneva said. "But it will expand her
mind. It will make her want more for herself than what most
Irish girls do."

"It will make her yearn for things she can never have," Rose
countered stubbornly. It was the wrong thing to do. Every
ounce of sense told her that the more Mary Grace came to
depend on Geneva, the more she'd be hurt when she realized
this fine life was far beyond her reach. Perhaps this was the
price? Her daughter's broken heart?

And if she turned Mary Grace over to Geneva's care, then
what part would she play in her daughter's life? Mary Grace
had already become accustomed to the luxuries of life at
Porter Hall. Rose wanted to believe that the time they spent
together as mother and daughter would form the woman she'd
become. "It is too generous," she said. "I'm sure Lord Porter
would not approve."

Geneva's eyebrow shot up and she gave Rose a cool look. "My husband would have you both out on the street again. It is only my generosity and affection for Grace that keeps you here."

In that single sentence, Rose knew the decision wasn't hers to make. She could either chose to fight and lose, or surrender immediately. "I see. And what say will I have in my daughter's life?"

"You know you are ill," Geneva said, her voice suddenly conciliatory. "You grow weaker by the day. Consumption is not a disease that one recovers from, my dear."

Just the word sent a shiver down Rose's spine. She suspected that her bouts with lung fever were more than just a passing illness, but hadn't wanted to admit there was something more serious affecting her health. And if she admitted it now, then surely she would be put out. "It's not consumption," she said. "My lungs were weakened by fever while Grace and I were living on the streets. It hasn't affected my work. And I will recover."

Geneva stared at her for a long moment, then smiled. "Of course you will. But the more time she spends at the house with me and her tutors, the more time you have to rest and recover."

"I—I suppose you're right," Rose said.

"Of course I am. We are agreed then." Geneva stood and smoothed her hands over the waist of her frock. "I'm so glad we had this little talk. I'll see to hiring a tutor for Grace. And she'll begin her studies next month."

Rose got to her feet and gave her a curtsey. "Thank you, Lady Porter. For your generosity. I'm sure that my Mary Grace will do her best to please you."

Geneva nodded, then walked out of the room, closing the door softly behind her. Rose immediately went to the wardrobe and grabbed an armful of clothing, tossing it on the bed. They couldn't stay. They would leave tonight, sneak off while the family slept. She'd be able to find another position, perhaps not one as comfortable as this, but certainly with her experience and— A fit of coughing overtook her and Rose bent forward, her hands braced on her knees, gasping for breath.

When she regained her composure, she sat down on the window seat and pressed her palm to her chest. There would be no references. And without references, there would probably be no job. Who would hire her? Geneva was right. She was sick. And she had a daughter who wasn't yet old enough to take care of herself. Her choices were no better than they had been that day when Geneva found them on the front steps of the church.

The money she'd saved would last them three or four months at the most and after that, they'd be right back to where they began. There would have to be another way to hold on to her daughter. Rose took the clothes back to the wardrobe and carefully hung them up, then noticed the diary sitting on the top shelf.

She closed her eyes and hugged it to her chest. This would be the way. Since she'd arrived at Porter Hall, she rarely opened it. But now, she'd begin reading it to her daughter. And if the day came when she was no longer in this world, then her daughter would know where she came from. And she would remember.

She opened the leather-bound book and began to read a passage, the words coming back to her, renewing her strength. She would go on one more day, and after that, another. And no matter what disaster or tragedy befell her, she would carry on for as long as God let her live on this earth.

13 September 1845

I know not where to begin. Michael is gone a month already and I imagine him standing onboard a wonderful sailing ship, on his way to America and a new life for us both. But life back here in Ireland has grown troubled. We've begun to dig the crop and a terrible thing has happened. After but a day or two out of the earth, the potatoes begin to putrefy. None are fit to eat and I am forced to take what is left from the rest of our garden patch. Without the cow to provide milk, my belly is hungry most of the time. I pray that Michael will send for me as soon as he arrives in America, for our life—the baby's and mine— becomes more fragile with each day that passes.

"IT'S BEAUTIFUL. LOOK AT ITS little ears. Oh, Edward, it looks so real."

Edward held a tiny carved rabbit up on his palm and Grace studied it more closely. "I like it better than the turtle I made for you," he offered.

"I think all your animals are wonderful," Grace said.

"What would you like me to make now?" He spread the carving tools in front of him and picked up a small piece of wood that Dennick had brought him. "I've wanted to try a horse, but I think the legs would be hard to carve."

Grace lined up her small menagerie, rearranging the animals on the blanket that they'd spread on the grass. He hadn't many friends, but he could count Grace as his best. Sure, she was only six years old, but she was a lot like Charlotte, always interested in what he was doing and thinking. In truth, since she'd come to Porter Hall, Edward had nearly forgotten Charlotte and all the sadness that had followed her death.

His mother had been happier than he'd seen her in a long

time, her dark moods coming only occasionally now. And though Malcolm barely tolerated Grace, he'd become too busy with his own school chums to care much about what either of them did. In truth, it had been a relief when Malcolm had decided to continue his studies at a private school in Dublin. He left early each morning and returned right before supper, then spent the rest of the evening working on his studies.

Edward's father had insisted that Edward be enrolled as well, the argument going on for days before a final decision was made. In the end, Geneva had won out and Edward continued on with his tutor. But the fight had caused the two factions in the Porter family to become even more distant. Edward was Geneva's son and Malcolm belonged to Henry and decisions would be made accordingly.

He wanted his father to love him as much as he loved Malcolm. But there were qualities in his father and brother that he could never understand—or accept. They were both self-centered and cold-hearted, with a cruel streak that ran deep. And they considered themselves above others, especially the Irish. Edward had never been able to understand their hatred of a people that he found warm and charming and kind-hearted.

"Oh, make me a kitten," Grace said.

He picked up the block of wood. "Are you sure? Wouldn't you like a jungle animal? I could try a lion."

Grace nodded, a wide smile on her face. "Yes. A lion then." She continued to play with the little animals, walking them across the blanket and talking to them. When she'd made a gift of the carving tools, he'd realized how well Grace knew him. There was no one in the world who knew him better.

"What do you have there?"

Edward turned around to find Malcolm standing over them. He was thirteen now and had grown so much bigger since his last birthday. But he'd also become lazy and unkempt, unconcerned with his appearance. He wore his school uniform, the jacket rumpled, as if he'd slept in it, and the trousers were stained with mud. It looked like he'd been in another fight at school.

"Wood carvings," Edward muttered, turning back to Grace.

"Wood carvings," Malcolm mimicked in a high-pitched voice. He bent over Grace's shoulder and plucked the rabbit off of her palm.

She jumped up and tried to get it back, but Malcolm grabbed the wooden animal by the ears and pulled, then let the pieces fall to the grass. A tiny cry slipped from Grace's throat and she knelt down to pick up the broken rabbit.

A blinding anger filled Edward's head and with a primal growl, he tossed aside the tool and hurled himself at Malcolm's legs, driving his older brother to the ground. The tackle caught Malcolm by surprise and knocked the wind out of him, giving Edward time enough to land a few decent punches to the face. When he bloodied his brother's nose, Edward sat back on his heels.

"You ugly piece of shite," Edward muttered, twisting his brother's arm around his back. "What would you do that for? Why would you hurt her feelings like that?"

"Get off me!" Malcolm shouted, twisting beneath him. But no matter how he struggled, Edward kept hold of him. Though he'd fought with his brother in the past, the fights had always ended with one of their parents stepping between them or with Edward surrendering. But he had an advantage now and he wasn't going to give up.

"Apologize," Edward demanded.

"Get off," Malcolm shouted, kicking and punching at Edward. Though he landed a few hard jabs, they didn't hurt, the anger coursing through Edward dulling the pain. This time had been coming for a long while, the chance for Edward to stand up to his brother's cruelty, the chance to stand up for Grace. But Edward knew that he'd only bested him through a surprise attack. He was still far too small to do so on a daily basis.

"Stop," Grace begged, trying to pull the two of them apart. "Please, Edward, stop. You can make me another rabbit."

"No," Edward growled. "Not until he apologizes." Edward twisted Malcolm's arm again and his older brother cried out in pain.

"All right," he muttered. "I'm sorry. I'm sorry I broke your bloody bunny. Now let me go."

Edward released his hold and rocked back on his heels. Malcolm scrambled to his feet, then gave his younger brother a shove, sending him back into the grass. "Don't you ever put your hands on me again," he threatened.

"Then stay away from Grace, and stay away from me."

Malcolm brushed the grass off his trousers, then strode back toward the house. Grace bent down beside Edward and placed her hand on his shoulder. "Why does he have to be so mean?" she asked.

"I don't know," he replied. Before Charlotte's death, Malcolm had been so different. They'd all cared about each other, protected each other. But now, he had an anger inside of him that grew stronger every day. And he seemed to delight in taking it out on the nearest vulnerable target. Usually that was their mother, often it was Edward. But now, he preferred Grace as his object of torment.

"If he bothers you, you have to tell me," Edward said. She was so much weaker, unable to defend herself against a bully who was seven years older. As he'd done for his mother, Edward would now try to protect Grace.

"Don't tell your mother," she whispered. "She might want to send me away."

"No," Edward said, taking her hand. "She'd never do that. She loves you." He smiled. "I love you, too, Grace."

She returned the smile. "And I love you, Edward."

"What is going on out here?" Rose approached, her skirts rustling as she walked toward them. "I heard shouting. And Malcolm has a bloody nose."

"Nothing," Edward said. "Malcolm fell out of the tree."

She held out her hand to Grace, then pulled her to her feet. "Come along, Mary Grace. I need you to help me with the ironing. You mustn't bother Master Edward."

"She's not bothering me," Edward said. "Grace is my friend."

Rose hitched her hands on her hips. "No," she said. "Mary Grace is a servant in this house. She works here along with me. There will be no friendship. You are not equals."

With that, Rose turned and pulled Grace along behind her. Edward watched them leave, puzzled by her statement. Though he understood Rose's position in the household, he'd never thought of Grace as a servant. His mother treated her like a daughter, dressing her in Charlotte's old clothes and making gifts of Charlotte's books and toys.

But perhaps that was Grace's job in the household, to keep his mother happy, to stave off the dark moods that always accompanied Geneva's grief over Charlotte's death. Though he was only ten years old, Edward understood the difference between servants and their masters. He'd seen his father turn out kitchen maids and gardeners without a second thought as to how they might survive without a job.

He gathered up the tools and Grace's animal collection,

then walked back to the coach house. Though it was a simple fact, Edward still couldn't think of Grace in that way. It wasn't proper to love a servant, not the same way he loved his sister. But his feelings were his own, and as much as Malcolm hated Grace, Edward loved her even more.

The door to the coach house opened and Grace emerged with a small wicker laundry basket filled with linen napkins. She struggled to get it out the door and Edward jumped up and grabbed it from her.

"Don't," she said.

"I'll help you."

Grace shook her head. "Mama says we shouldn't be friends. She says it's not right."

"No," Edward said. "She's wrong. My father is the master and she's the servant. That's nothing to do with us."

"She says someday I'll work for you. That I mustn't love you like my brother. I must respect you like my master."

Edward wrested the basket from her arms, the napkins tumbling onto the grass. "No! I won't have it. If I'm your master, then I order you to be my friend."

She fell to the ground and began to pick up the table linens, carefully refolding them and putting them back into the basket. "I—I want to be your friend, Edward. But we'll have to be secret friends."

"Yes," he said. "We can do that. We will swear an oath. Where shall we meet?"

"In the stable," Grace said. "In the afternoon, while Mama takes her nap and Lady Porter writes her letters. No one will find us there."

Edward nodded, then picked up the basket and placed it in her hands. He set the animals on top, wrapping them up in a napkin. "We will meet tomorrow."

Grace nodded, then hurried along to the kitchens. Edward sighed softly. Grace had been his from the moment he'd first found her at the church. She was the only person in the world who loved him for who he was, the only person who mattered to him. There were times when he believed what his mother believed, that Charlotte had come back in Grace's body. He saw it in her delicate features, in her sweet nature and her unbending loyalty, in her sparkling blue eyes and raven black hair.

They were best friends, though he knew better than to admit it out loud. Boys his own age, from proper Dublin families, ought to be his best friends. That's what his father had said. But he and Grace shared a special bond, one that would never be broken. And if that was wrong, then Edward didn't care. For in his heart, it felt right.

CHAPTER FOUR

"*Bonjour, Monsieur Professeur. Comment allez-vous aujourd'hui?*"

"*Trés bien, merci, Mademoiselle Grace.* I see you are anxious to begin your lesson for today."

Grace smiled at her tutor. Professor was so simple to please. Though he'd been a bit chilly to her at first, she managed to charm him after only a few weeks of lessons. She'd suspected he'd felt it beneath his station to tutor an Irish Catholic girl, considering his proper British breeding. But Geneva had stepped in after only a few lessons and made certain that he was giving his full attention to their work together.

"I've studied my verbs," she said. "Would you like to hear them?"

"Very well. The future indicative of 'to have.'"

"*J'aurai, tu auras, il aura, nous aurons, vous aurez, ils auront.*"

"*Très bien, mademoiselle.* We have worked together for how long now?"

"Since I was six," Grace said. "Four years now, Professor."

"I will tell you, you have far surpassed Master Malcolm in your studies." He leaned closer, as if to impart a very interesting secret. "I helped him study for his entrance exams to university and he is a rather unremarkable student. His Latin is atrocious, his penmanship is illegible and he can barely cipher. Master Edward, however, is the opposite. Since I've been teaching him, he has embraced his education. He will always excel, I am sure of it."

"Grace!" Edward burst into the room, his color high, his dark hair tousled. He was growing into a very handsome young man, Grace mused. Nearly fourteen years old. If she didn't consider him a brother, she might actually fancy him—when she got a bit older. "You have to come. Right now."

"Miss Grace is having her French lesson," Professor said. "And when she's done, you and I have a rendezvous with your mathematics book."

"This is much more important." Edward crossed the room and grabbed Grace's hand, then dragged her to her feet. "We have to go now. Lesson over."

They ran out of the room, Grace's hand clutched in Edward's. He led her out the back door, then across the court-yard toward the stables. The old stone building was a fair distance from the house and by the time they reached it, Grace was out of breath. She bent over and placed her hands on her knees, gasping. "What is it?"

"Lily has had her colt," he said. "Rawley came up to the house to tell me and I wanted to show you." He pulled open the heavy wooden door of the stable and they stepped inside. The interior was dark and dusty and Grace crinkled her nose as they walked down the row of stalls.

When they reached the end, Edward jumped up on the gate, then held his hand out to her. "She's in here," he said.

Grace climbed up beside him and stared down at the newborn colt, curled up in a pile of straw in the corner. Like its mother, it was a rich, chocolate brown with a white blaze on its forehead. "It's a girl?"

Edward nodded. "And it's yours," he said.

She gasped. "Mine? Whatever will I do with a horse?"

"You'll learn to ride. You're a young lady and Mother said Lily's colt was to be a Christmas gift for you."

"Isn't the colt a little small to ride?"

Edward gave her a playful punch to the shoulder. "Don't be a ninny. Of course, you can't ride her now. You'll ride a pony first and then one of the gentler mares. And by the time she's old enough to ride, you'll be an expert."

"What will we call her?" Grace asked.

"That's up to you," he said. "Mother asked that you name her."

Grace thought about it for a long time, trying to come up with the perfect name for the baby horse. The colt's mother was called Lily, so perhaps she ought to be named after a flower as well. "How about Daisy?" she said. "Or Violet. I like Violet. Or maybe Sweet Pea?" She sighed. "How am I supposed to decide?"

"You don't have to decide now," he said.

"No, she should have a name. She's been born and everyone gets a name when they are born. It will be Violet. Violet is her name."

Edward grinned. "It's a fine name. The one I would have chosen." He jumped off the gate and held out his hand to her. "Come. Mother asked that I bring you to her after you'd seen the colt."

"I should go back to my French lesson."

"Bugger your French lesson. She has a surprise for you."

They walked back to the house, Edward chatting about riding lessons and saddles and stirrups. She'd never thought to learn to ride. It didn't seem of much use, considering most people were replacing their horses and carriages with motorcars these days. "You know, I'd much rather learn to drive than ride," she said. "How old must I be to drive?"

"You want to drive a motorcar?" Edward laughed. "Don't be silly. We have a chauffeur. If we drove ourselves, we'd have no use for Farrell."

"But wouldn't it be fun?" she said. "We could fly down the road as fast as the car would take us. You will teach me how to drive, won't you Edward? Just as soon as possible."

"Only after you learn to ride," Edward said.

When they entered the house, they went straight to Geneva's parlor. She was sitting where she did most mornings, at the pretty desk in the corner by the window. Her correspondence was stacked around her and when Grace stepped up to the desk, she looked up and smiled.

"And what do you think of your gift, Miss Grace?"

"Thank you, Lady Porter. It's a wonderful gift. But I'll have to ask Mama if it's all right to keep it."

"One does not turn down a gift like that," Geneva said. "It shows bad breeding. You will graciously accept and tell your mother I will hear no complaints about it. Is that clear?"

"Yes, ma'am," Grace said. "Now, I must go back to my studies. The professor is waiting for me."

"No, you should come back to the stables," Edward said. "I'll introduce you to your pony and then I'll give you your first riding lesson. Can we, Mother? Surely Grace can leave her studies for one day."

Geneva glanced back and forth between the two of them, an odd expression on her face. But then it passed, and she nodded. "I'll let him know you're taking a short holiday from your books." She set her pen down on the desk and stood. "Come. If you're going to ride, you'll have to have proper clothes."

Grace followed Geneva upstairs to the room that had once

been Charlotte's. The door had always been closed whenever Grace was in the house. The servants had warned her that the only person allowed inside was Lady Porter.

"My daughter had a lovely riding costume," she said. "It would probably fit you perfectly. She was nine when we bought it, but you're a bit smaller than she was."

"I couldn't think of wearing—"

"Nonsense. There is plenty of wear left in it."

Lady Porter opened the door and walked inside the room, but Grace hung back, waiting to be invited in. "It's a lovely room," she murmured.

Lady Porter turned around. "Yes, it is. I took great care in decorating it."

"You must miss her terribly."

Her expression grew wistful. "Every moment of every day. A daughter is a precious jewel, a reflection of all the dreams that I had as a young girl. Sons belong to their fathers, until they go off and make a life of their own. But there is a connection between mothers and daughters that can never be broken." She forced a smile, then turned back to the wardrobe.

The wide cabinet was filled with clothes but Geneva found the blue velvet habit right off. She held it out in front of her, slowly stroking the fabric. "I remember when we bought this," she said. "Charlotte was so pleased with the way she looked." Geneva held it out. "Go ahead. Try it on."

"Now?"

She nodded. The look in her eyes was so hopeful, so melancholy that Grace was afraid to refuse. She slowly stripped off her dress until she stood in her chemise and pantalets. Then, she pulled the skirt up over her hips and fastened the buttons at the waist. A fine linen blouse with ruffled cuffs came next, followed by a matching velvet jacket. Grace turned her attention to the buttons and when she was finished, she looked up to find Geneva staring at her with a frightened look in her eyes.

"Lady Porter? Are you all right?"

Slowly, the woman sank to her knees, her hands clutched against her chest. A low moan slipped from her throat and a moment later, she bent forward and began to wail. Grace glanced around the room, uncertain of how to react. She reached out and touched Geneva on the shoulder, but the woman was so distraught that she didn't notice.

Grace backed out of the room, then raced downstairs to find Edward. He was in his father's library and when she entered, he knew immediately that something was wrong. "It's your mother," Grace said.

They hurried upstairs to Charlotte's chamber and Edward immediately dropped to the floor next to his mother. He held her elbows, forcing her to sit up, and when he'd caught her gaze, he spoke to her in a soft but firm voice. "Stop. Mother, you must stop now. Listen to me. If you don't stop now, you won't be able to stop later."

"I can't do this," she sobbed. "Everywhere I look, I see her. She's crying out to me and I can't reach her."

"If you don't control yourself, Father will send you away again. And I won't be able to rescue you. Please, Mother, try to stop."

"Where is she? Where is Charlotte?" She glanced up at Grace and through her tears, a smile broke across her face. "There you are, my darling." She held out her hand and it trembled.

Grace looked to Edward for guidance and he shook his head. But Geneva was insistent and finally, Grace bent down on the other side of her and took her hand. "You have to stop now...Mother," she murmured. "Listen to Edward. He knows what's best."

"Oh, my darling. Look how pretty you are. That color suits you. It always has."

"Let's get her to her bedchamber," Edward said.

They both took an arm and drew her to her feet, then walked her down the hall to her room. When they got inside, Edward settled his mother on the bed, then picked up a small bottle from a tray beside the bed. "This always seems to calm her," he said, mixing a spoonful of the medicine with a glass of water. He handed it to Grace. "You do it."

Grace drew a deep breath and held the glass out to Geneva. "Here, Mother, drink this. It will make you feel better."

She gulped the liquid down, then slowly lay back on the bed. When she closed her eyes, Grace moved away from her, her own hands trembling. There were times when life seemed so good at Porter Hall, the days so bright and carefree. But then something would scratch the shiny surface and expose the darkness beneath. They were all teetering on the edge of disaster. And Grace felt as though she was the only one who could hold them all together.

"Do I resemble her?" she murmured.

Edward shook his head. "Charlotte was fair, like my mother. She had light brown hair." He looked at her. "Your eyes are the very same color, though. I don't know why she doesn't see the difference." He took a ragged breath. "She frightens me sometimes."

Grace took Edward's hand and held it tight. It was such a burden to carry for a young man of fourteen. And even more so for Grace, whose own loyalties seemed to be tested at every turn. She'd found a home here with the Porters and though she didn't remember a life before this, she knew from her mother that it had been desperate.

She would do whatever was needed to keep her place at Porter Hall. And if that meant pretending to be Charlotte Porter on occasion, then she'd learn to play the part well.

GENEVA'S HEAD THROBBED. She pressed the cool cloth to her brow and sank back into the pillows. It had been nearly a week since she'd ventured out of her bedroom, but gradually she was beginning to drag herself from her stupor.

She'd grown accustomed to the drugs she took and as of late, it required more and more of the tonic to make her mind go quiet enough for her to sleep. And then, when her thoughts were finally silenced, it took longer to recover.

The bottle of medicine sat on a silver tray next to her bed and she reached out for it. But her hand shook as she tried to grab it and Geneva closed her eyes. She couldn't allow herself the luxury of sleep any longer. The rational part of her mind told her that there was a limit to her husband's patience and it was usually reached after a week in bed.

Edward had spent most of his time watching over her, making sure she was protected from the prying eyes of the servants. He brought her meals, gave her medicine and read to her from the poems of Keats and Browning. And when he wasn't reading, he spoke to her in soft tones, drawing her back to a world that had become so difficult to face. It was more than a boy his age ought to bear, but Geneva had no one else to depend upon.

A soft knock sounded on the door and she called out, expecting Edward to come in. But Rose stepped into the room and softly closed the door behind her. She wore the plain gray uniform that all the servants at Porter Hall wore and her dark hair was drawn back into a severe knot at the nape of her neck. She looked thin and very pale.

"Lady Porter, I've brought some fresh linens. Master Edward asked that I bring them right up."

"Leave them on the chair," she said, her voice filled with all the exhaustion she felt.

"And I've also returned the riding habit you gave to Mary Grace. I don't think it's a good idea for her to learn to ride. It's so…dangerous."

Geneva stared at her for a long moment, trying to make sense of her words. "Riding habit? What riding habit?"

Rose cocked her head, confusion marring her somber expression. "I'll—I'll just put the linens here." She set the bedsheets on the chair, then turned back to the bed.

"How are you feeling? Mary Grace has been very worried." She paused. "Sometimes grief is a terrible thing to bear. Especially the grief of a mother."

Geneva closed her eyes. She felt so numb, as if every ounce of emotion inside her had evaporated. This was the way it went, the lows and then the highs, the plummeting descent and the slow, gradual rise back to happiness. "A mother should never have to watch her child die."

"Do you not believe she's in a better place?" Rose asked.

"How can I think any place is better than her home, with her mother and her father?" Geneva sighed. "Is your faith that strong?"

Rose shook her head. "Not all the time. In the middle of my own grief, when I needed it most, it seemed to vanish. But then, I realized that I was not grieving for my husband or for the life he might have had. I was grieving for myself, for everything I'd lost."

"And I suppose you'll tell me that it was God's will that my Charlotte died? That he was the one who struck her down with scarlet fever? I cannot believe in a god who would take such a precious child from this world. From me."

"I lost two babies before I gave birth to Mary Grace," Rose said. "The first was stillborn, a son, a beautiful child with the face of an angel. I would like to think they're all in heaven with Jamie, though my priest tells me they are not."

"You don't believe dead babies go to heaven?"

"They weren't baptized. Babies who aren't baptized remain in limbo, in neither heaven nor hell. Since they cannot be baptized, they cannot be cleansed of their original sin."

"So their souls just float there forever."

Rose nodded. "It is a difficult thought to bear and one I struggle with. But I try to think of limbo as a place that's pure and simple and innocent, where the babies know nothing of God or heaven, so they can't know what they're missing."

"Believe what you need to believe," Geneva said, flopping back into the pillows and throwing her arm over her eyes.

"At least you know she's in heaven," Rose said. "There must be some comfort in that."

"I'm tired," Geneva muttered. "Leave me now."

Rose walked to the door, but she didn't leave. "You can't have her," she murmured. "She's all I have. I've lost everything."

Geneva pushed up on her elbows. "What are you babbling about?"

"Mary Grace. She's my daughter, not yours. Nothing you do for her, nothing you give her, will ever change that."

"Get out!" Geneva screamed. "Get out! You have no right to speak to me that way." She sat up and a blinding pain shot through her head, turning everything around her black. Geneva swallowed back a wave of nausea. "Pack your bags," she muttered. "I'll give you a month's severance. But I want you out by the end of the day."

Rose stared at her for a long moment and Geneva waited for her to plead for her job, knowing the satisfaction she'd take in putting Rose Byrne in her place. Since the day she'd brought Rose and Grace to Porter Hall, the woman had always been just a bit too proud and haughty for a servant.

But to Geneva's surprise, Rose didn't rise to the bait. She simply tipped her chin up and nodded. "I think that would be for the best, Lady Porter."

She turned and walked out. A few moments later, Edward came in, carrying a tea tray. He glanced back over his shoulder, then studied Geneva for a long moment. "What is it?"

"Nothing," Geneva said, straightening the bedclothes over her lap. "I—I just sacked Rose."

Edward gasped. "What?"

"You heard me. She was getting entirely too comfortable here. She had the audacity to imply that I wasn't grieving Charlotte's death in a proper way. That I ought to be happy that she's in heaven and not here with me."

"What have you done?" Edward accused. "You can't send them away."

"I have every right to do just that. I'm in charge of the household staff. I hired her and I can sack her."

"You're just tired," he said. "I know Rose speaks her mind, but she's a proud woman. And there are times when you do treat Grace more like she's yours than Rose's. Mother, please. Let me go to her, let me try to convince her to stay."

"I will not be spoken to in that way," Geneva said, her anger growing.

"Then you will put Grace out on the street," Edward said. "And they will wander about until they both get sick and die.

You'll allow Rose's daughter to die, simply to make you feel better about Charlotte. Where is your Christian charity, Mother? Does it disappear simply because you have a headache or you've taken too much of your tonic?"

Geneva opened her mouth to speak, but then snapped it shut. Emotion welled up inside of her as the reality of what she'd done sunk in. She'd managed to keep herself on an even keel since Grace had arrived. The dark moods were far less frequent and she felt as though she was beginning to climb out of the depths of her grief.

Was that because time had passed or was it because she'd had Grace to raise? For that's what she was doing, behind Rose's back. She'd given Grace everything that had been meant for Charlotte, all the womanly wisdom that she possessed. And had Rose Byrne been any other mother, she might have had a right to be jealous.

But Geneva had saved their lives. She'd picked them up off the street and given them a place to live, fed them and clothed them and even educated Grace at no small cost. Rose at least owed her a little understanding and gratitude. Unbidden tears began to roll down her cheeks and Geneva found it difficult to breathe.

"Bring her here," she said in a strangled voice. "Tell her I must speak with her again."

She closed her eyes and laid back, drawing in slow, deep breaths to try to quell the pain that was now pounding in her brain. There had been a time, in the not too distant past, when her life had been so right, when she'd had everything she'd ever wanted. Now, it was filled with confusion and regret, fear and loss. Would she ever feel happy again?

CHAPTER FIVE

EDWARD DRAGGED THE TRUNK INTO his bed chamber and left it at the foot of his bed. His mother stared at it critically, her hands hitched on her waist. "We really ought to buy a new trunk for you. It wouldn't do to have you arrive at Harrow with that tatty old thing."

He shook his head. "Mother, it doesn't need to be all shiny and new. This trunk has seen a lot of the world. I'd prefer it. It will make me appear well-traveled."

"But Malcolm had a new trunk when he went to off to school. You should, too."

"Malcolm has always been more concerned with appearances," Edward murmured. When his brother had left for university last fall, he'd required an entirely new wardrobe, including six suits, eight pairs of shoes, three hats and a cashmere overcoat. And not one trunk, but two. Edward assumed the fine clothes were to make up for his brother's lack of academic acuity.

He ran his hand over the scarred surface of the trunk, examining the stickers that told the trunk's history. "When did you go to Istanbul?" he asked.

"Your father went there when he was just out of university. He did the grand tour. My parents only allowed me Italy and France. And here is our honeymoon," she said, pointing to another sticker for New York. "We went to America on the maiden voyage of the *Olympic, Titanic*'s sister ship. Your aunt Fanny and uncle Richard lived there before they moved to California. I was seasick the entire way, but it was a wonderful trip. Your father nearly decided to stay and find his fortunes there. Just think, you could have been born an American."

Geneva crossed the room to the wardrobe and flung open the doors. She studied the contents, kept tidy by the upstairs maid, then shook her head. "This will never do. You'll need new clothes." She turned and faced him. "We'll just have to leave a bit early and do some shopping in London before we deliver you to school."

"We could always just go to Dublin and find what I need at Clery's."

"At a department store? No matter how much your father complains, our family fortunes have not sunk so low that we are forced to shop at a Dublin department store for your wardrobe. Your father will take you to his tailors on Savile Row, and have suits made for you. We can have them delivered to you at school when they're finished."

Edward forced a smile. "I don't think Father will have time for a trip to London."

His father had been even more preoccupied with business since the spring elections and Edward doubted that he'd accompany them. De Valera was now in charge of the government and he advocated a complete break with Britain and a sovereign Irish nation including those counties in the north. He abolished the oath of allegiance to Great Britain and withheld British land annuities. In turn, Britain imposed a twenty-percent duty on all Irish imports—including wool. The coal business still flourished, however, since Ireland had in turn imposed a tariff on the imports of English coal.

"And I certainly don't need a new wardrobe. One or two suits will do. We wear uniforms most of the time."

They hadn't traveled to London for years, not since his mother had been caught up in the world of spiritualists and psychics. Once Grace had come to live with them, Geneva had seemed content to remain at Porter Hall.

She pulled a jacket out of the wardrobe and held it out in front of her. "There is an exhibit of French paintings at the National Gallery that I'm wild to see. And, of course, we must attend a concert or two. We'll do some shopping and—" She smiled as if struck by a sudden idea. "Since your father won't go, we'll take Grace. Oh, it will be a wonderful trip, the three of us. Edward, go fetch her. Now. We'll tell her all about it."

"Mother, I'm not sure that Rose would agree. You know how she can be." His mother had been much more careful with Rose's feelings since she had nearly walked out two years ago and taken Grace with her. But lately, Geneva had become obsessed with Grace again and Edward sensed that another confrontation was just on the horizon. He had hoped it might happen before he left for school. That way, he would have the chance to smooth it over and soothe hurt feelings before either party took drastic measures.

"She agreed to let me hire a tutor for Grace, didn't she? This is just another educational experience. Every young lady should see the great capitals of the world. And Dublin does not count," she added, wagging her finger at Edward. "Now go. And bring her back. I want to give her the good news myself."

Edward wandered out of the room, convinced that he wouldn't be able to change Geneva's mind. When it came to Grace and what she believed the girl needed, Geneva could not be dissuaded.

After the last row, it had taken nearly a year for Grace to

feel comfortable again at Porter Hall. Her mother had gone so far as to pack their belongings and convince Farrell to drive them to Dublin. Grace had been hysterical, begging her mother to relent. It had taken Edward an entire day of pleading before Rose had finally accepted Geneva's apology and agreed to stay—with a substantial raise in pay.

Taking Grace to London was a bold move. Unless… Edward smiled. Unless the invitation came from him. Perhaps if he presented his case, then Rose might agree. And since he was going away to school, it would be a chance for the two of them to have one last adventure together.

He found Grace in the yard, hanging bedsheets to dry in the warm breeze. Her dark hair was pulled back and tied with a ribbon and she wore a simple cotton dress. "I know my love and well he knows," she sang softly. "I love the grass where on he goes." She continued to hum as she reached into the basket and withdrew another sheet.

He snuck up behind her and grabbed her around the waist, causing Grace to scream in surprise. She turned and punched him in the shoulder. "I'll die of fright one of these fine days," she said. "And you will stand at my grave and weep, Edward Porter."

"I will not," Edward teased. "I'll be glad when you're gone. You're a right pain in the arse, Grace Byrne. And I haven't a clue why my mother would even consider taking you to London."

She blinked in surprise, her mouth hanging open. Edward reached out and hooked his finger beneath her chin to close it. "Well?"

"London? Your mother wants to take me to London?" Her bright expression slowly faded. "I—I don't think my mother will allow me to go," Grace said. "And I can't leave her. There's so much work and she needs my help."

"She can do without you for five or six days. And Mother will make sure she has help with the laundry and the mending while you're gone."

"I suppose I could ask," Grace said.

"Now, there's the tricky part. You must say it was my invitation, not my mother's. Do you understand? That way, I'll help to convince her. I will say it does you no good to study art history and then never visit a museum, or to study piano and never hear a great concert. It's my wish that we have one last adventure before I go off to school. And she will agree."

"Then let's go ask her now," Grace said anxiously.

Suddenly, the trip seemed so much more exciting. To explore a city as grand and as wonderful as London with his best friend would be an adventure to remember for a lifetime. He'd shown her all the pictures in the books, told her stories of his previous trips, the museums, the parks, the shops. But it wouldn't be the same as experiencing it together.

When they reached the carriage house, they found Rose sitting near the window, darning stockings. She was hunched over her work, trying to see the tiny stitches through a pair of spectacles she'd purchased from a passing tinker. She looked up as Grace crossed the room. Edward waited by the door for an invitation to enter.

"Are you all right then?" A frown furrowed Rose's brow. "You look as though the devil has been chasing you."

"It's the most wonderful news," Grace said, trying to catch her breath. She glanced back at Edward and motioned him inside.

"What is it?"

"I've been invited to go to London. With Edward and Lady Porter. Isn't that wonderful, Mama? I'm to see London."

Rose's expression turned cold and she stared down at her work, her fingers nervously toying with the needle and thread. "No," she murmured. "I won't have it."

"But why?"

"I just won't. You'll not leave Ireland, not as long as I have breath in my body."

Grace took a step back, as if stunned by the anger in her mother's voice. "But why?"

Rose stood, tossing her darning to the floor, then crossed the room. She grabbed a linen towel and folded it smartly, then grabbed another. "You don't think I know what Geneva Porter is about? She thinks she's very clever, sending her son to convince me. But I see through her ways."

"Mama, I don't understand."

"Tell her, Edward," Rose said. "Tell her why your mother spends so much time and money on a servant girl."

Edward shook his head. "I don't know what you mean," he replied, refusing to rise to her challenge. This battle for Grace's soul had gone on since the very first day Geneva had held Grace. And it would continue until his mother or Grace's departed this world.

"She has found a replacement for her dead daughter," Rose continued. "And now, she's decided to turn you into her daughter. The lessons and the clothes, the gifts. And now London. They're all given at a price, Mary Grace."

"She's just generous," Grace said. "It wouldn't do to refuse. It would show that I have bad breeding."

"Bad breeding?" She shook her head. "Tell me your name," her mother demanded. "Say it. Say your name to me now."

"Grace," she replied. "I'm Grace Byrne."

Tears flooded her mother's eyes and she shook her head. "No. You're Mary Grace Byrne. Mary is your given name. But because Lady Porter preferred Grace, I allowed you to be called that. But I won't have her putting all these fancy ideas in your head. You're a simple Irish girl who doesn't need to be puffed up with silly dreams."

"She doesn't do that!" Grace shouted. "You're lying."

"I am your mother, Mary Grace. And you'd do well to remember that. Lady Porter isn't interested in you. You remind her of her dead daughter and she'll live off that fantasy for as long as she needs to grieve. When she's finished, she'll toss you aside."

"Do you think I want to be a servant my whole life? Maybe I want something better. Lady Porter can give that to me."

"You will be servant in this house, or some other house. Mark my words. If you think the Porters will ever accept you as their own, then you're a bigger fool than I am, Mary Grace Byrne."

"I'm going to London," she said. "And you can't stop me."

Her mother stared at her for a long moment, then turned away. Edward watched as Rose's shoulders slumped. For a moment, he thought she might collapse. But then she straightened her spine and lifted her chin. "Go then. You'll make your own mistakes, you will. And when your heart is broken, then maybe you'll finally know that I'm the only mother you'll ever have."

THE TRIP WAS MORE THAN Grace could have ever imagined. They'd taken the *Lady Leinster,* a night express steamer ship, across the Irish Sea from Dublin to Liverpool and then caught the train for London the morning of their arrival. She'd never thought to travel such a great distance. The farthest she'd ever been before had been an occasional trip to Dublin, a thirty-minute ride in the Porter's motorcar. But this was a grand adventure and everything she saw was made more exciting because it was brand new.

She and Edward had stood on the stern of the ship and watched as Ireland faded into the misty evening horizon. Then, after a night in a comfortable cabin, they had breakfast as they watched England appear in the east, growing greener with each mile of water that the ship consumed.

A quick trip from the docks to the train station and they were soon onboard the London Midland Scotland line bound for London. Another comfortable compartment was waiting along with a light luncheon and a tea. Everything tasted so much better because she was eating on a boat or a train. The air seemed to vibrate with excitement and all the people she saw were wildly sophisticated. Grace knew, from that moment on, that she would always want to travel.

There was only one dark cloud hanging over the trip. She had left without apologizing to her mother. They'd barely spoken over the ten days between the invitation and her departure. Rose had waited for Grace to bend to her wishes and refuse the invitation, but Grace had been just as stubborn as her mother and was determined to go.

Grace hadn't wanted to hurt her mother. And she knew her mother's fears were not all imagined. But what harm would the trip do? And there was so much to be gained from it. Who was to care if it put grand ideas in her head or made her want more than she could ever have in life? Wasn't it a greater sin to let such a wonderful opportunity pass by?

They took a small suite at the Savoy, a luxurious hotel with electric lights, gilt-adorned lifts and uniformed porters. Their room had a view of the Thames and the Waterloo Bridge. They took some time to get settled and after they'd unpacked, Edward invited Grace to take a stroll through the Embankment Gardens. Geneva begged off, deciding instead to have a cup of tea, then a short nap. They would have supper at five in the hotel dining room and would take an evening boat trip on the Thames.

The moment Grace and Edward walked outside, it was as if the whole world were lying before them. Though she was in a strange city, she felt safe with Edward. He'd been to London before and he was watchful of all the dangers, the busy traffic, the uneven walkways, and even the pickpockets who roamed the streets searching for unsuspecting visitors.

"I can't believe I'm here," Grace murmured as she strolled beside him, her arm linked in his. "I wish Mama could see all this. She would love it so."

"Perhaps the next time, you'll bring her. And you'll know all the very best places to take her."

Grace appreciated Edward's optimism. But they both knew that there would be no trips to London in Rose Byrne's future. As of late, she never even left Porter Hall, not even for church. A stroll in the garden every few days was all she could manage. "Perhaps," Grace said.

They stopped first at Cleopatra's Needle and then everywhere she looked there was something important to see—theaters and historic buildings, statues of famous people, things that she'd only read about in books. "I wonder what it must be like to live in this city," Grace said. "Do you think the people who do consider all of this quite ordinary? Or is it always exciting?" Grace laughed. "I always thought the gardens at Porter Hall were wonderful, but after a time, I stopped looking with such awe. They just became…"

"Landscape?" Edward asked.

Grace nodded. "Yes. But I don't think I could ever consider this ordinary."

"You probably would if you lived here. The trick is to keep moving about the world, always leaving a city just before it becomes a crashing bore and move on to the next location."

"Wouldn't that be fun?" Grace said. "I must remember to marry a man who loves to travel."

"I'll be jealous, you know. For he will have the very best companion."

Grace smiled. "Well then, you could always marry me, Edward Porter." She'd meant the words as a joke, a playful tease. But Edward's expression turned serious.

"I doubt that my father would allow it," he said soberly. "I'm expected to marry someone with wealth and position, just as Malcolm is."

She gave his shoulder a slap. "Then it would be your loss. For you will have your wealth and position and I will be traveling the world, having wonderful adventures." She held her arms out, then spun around, her skirts flying out as she moved. "I'll be certain to send you a postcard, though. You can read it while you and your very dull English wife are having tea. If I remember you, that is."

"I would never forget you," Edward said.

They walked along in silence, stopping at each statue and flower bed, lost in their own thoughts. Grace couldn't help but wonder how it would be between them, years from now. They were like siblings, not joined by blood, but by a deep affection for each other. Would that affection fade as they grew older and found their own lives?

"I have a difficult time imagining it," Grace said.

"What's that?"

"Us. Grown up. We won't live in the same house. How will it be? Will we just forget each other and never speak?"

Edward frowned. "I don't know," he murmured. "It's hard to say."

"You're going off to school. That will change things. You'll find a new best friend and you'll leave me behind." She forced a smile. "But I'll understand. It wouldn't do for you to be friends with a twelve-year-old girl."

"I never really think about how old you are," Edward said. "Charlotte never really thought about how old I was. We were just friends. You're my adopted sister," he said. "So, it's not that odd, is it?"

Grace shook her head. "No. And if anyone says differently, then you must promise to set them straight, right off."

They wandered for several hours, along the Embankment, then back through Trafalgar Square. By the time they returned to the Savoy, it was well past the time they'd promised to be back, but Geneva was probably grateful for the extra rest.

As they walked through the lobby, the desk captain called out to Edward and motioned him toward a quiet corner. "Master Porter. I'm afraid there's been...an incident."

"What happened?"

"It's your mother. She's had a...I'm not sure what to call it. The doctor is with her now. I'd like to cable your father and—"

"No," Edward said. "He's not at home at present. He's traveling on business and can't be reached. Where is she?"

"In your suite. If you'd like, I can accompany you up there."

Edward shook his head and grabbed Grace's hand. "I can get there on my own."

They hurried through the lobby to the elevators, but in the end, Edward was too impatient and they climbed the four flights to their rooms. The door was slightly ajar and when they walked in, they found an elderly man sitting with Geneva on the sofa. He was holding her hand while she lay with her eyes closed and her head tipped back. Grace held back, standing near the door.

"Is she all right?" Edward asked.

Geneva straightened and looked at Edward with lifeless eyes. "Where have you been? It's been days."

He rushed over to sit next to her. "Mother, it hasn't been days. We were just gone a few hours. You must have fallen asleep and when you woke, you were confused."

"I've given your mother something to calm her. She was quite frantic. She came down to the lobby raving about her daughter being lost. Is your sister with you?"

"My sister is—"

"I'm here," Grace said, stepping forward.

"Oh, my darling," Geneva cried, holding out her arms. "Where have you been?"

"Edward took me to see the sights," Grace replied. She dropped down on her knees in front of Geneva. "I'm fine, Mother. There was no need to get so upset." Grace glanced over at the doctor. "She's always been overly protective of me."

"Well, then. You mustn't worry her needlessly again, young lady. I'll stop by later on this evening to check in, but for now, make sure your mother gets her rest. And if she becomes agitated again, you may give her a spoonful of this in a glass of water." He held out a small bottle.

The moment the doctor left the room, Grace and Edward looked at each other, a mixture of fear and relief passing between them. "Mother, why don't you lie down for a bit. We'll order supper brought up to the room. I'm really too tired to go out and Charlotte has a headache."

A worried look passed over Geneva's face. "You're not

feeling ill, are you, darling? If you do, we ought to summon the doctor. They have one on staff here, you know."

"Yes, I know," Grace murmured. She helped Edward get Geneva to her feet, then walked with her to the bedroom. When they had her settled in bed, she dropped a soft kiss on her cheek. "Sleep now, Mother. Everything will be all right."

Grace sat on the edge of the bed until Geneva drifted off, then returned to the parlor where Edward was waiting. He sat on the sofa, his elbows braced on his knees, his head hanging down. Suddenly, he looked so much older to her eyes. Not like a boy of sixteen, but a man.

"Will you send for your father?" she asked.

He shook his head. "You know what will happen. This will push him over the edge. We'll have to stay in London until she's better." He looked up at her. "I'm due at school in four days. If she's not well by then, I'll have to leave her with you."

Grace nodded. "I can handle it. I'll get her back to Ireland."

"I'm sorry." He cursed softly then stood and began to pace in front of her. "You shouldn't have to play a part in this."

She put her hand out and caught his, pulling him back down beside her. "We're in this together, you and I. I'll do whatever you ask. Whatever she needs." She paused. "I've known for a long time that she sometimes thinks I'm Charlotte. I try not to let her believe that, but it's often easier to let it go by."

Edward laughed softly. "Sometimes, I think you're Charlotte. Does that make me barmy, too?"

Grace shook her head. "No. You just miss her." She sat back and sighed. But what did that make Grace, when she allowed Geneva to continue to believe a lie? Her own motives for pretending to be Charlotte weren't always pure and unselfish. She knew the longer Geneva needed her around, the safer she and her mother would be. For as long as her mother needed a warm place to sleep and good food to eat, Grace would provide it.

And if it meant dressing in Charlotte's clothes and learning to play the piano like Charlotte and listening while Geneva talked on and on about things she and Charlotte had seen or done, then Grace would act the part—and act it well.

But there would come a time, after her mother was gone, when she'd be free of the burden, or perhaps the burden would be free of her. Then, her life would begin all over again and she'd have to find her own way.

CHAPTER SIX

"I'LL RACE YOU TO THE end of the lane!"

Grace jabbed her heels into the flanks of the horse and it reared up slightly, its breath clouding in the chilly air before it took off. Edward groaned, then prodded his own horse into a full-on gallop, chasing after her.

Grace had been riding for barely three years, but she'd taken to it like she'd always known how. He had tried to teach her to ride in the English style, with a sidesaddle for ladies, but she'd refused and insisted that she ride exactly like he did, astride. She'd given up the gentle mare that had been her first mount and had instead preferred a frisky gelding with a penchant for reckless runs. Any thought of riding Violet had been put aside, though she still lavished affection on the filly.

He caught up with her at the curve of the road but the moment Grace sensed him gaining, she kicked the horse into action. "You'll never catch me," she cried, her hair flying out behind her.

"Mary Grace Byrne, stop! You'll kill yourself."

When she reached the end of the lane, she drew the horse up and turned to face him, satisfaction glittering in her eyes. She was breathing hard and her eyes were bright with mischief. Edward joined her, reaching down and patting his horse on its neck. "You've been practicing since I've been gone."

"You've been gone far too long, Edward," she replied.

"True," he murmured, smiling at her. He hadn't spent more than a few days with Grace in the last year. It was no wonder she'd changed so much. He'd been home from Harrow for Christmas, one year ago, after his first term. But his summer holiday had been spent with family friends in Euripe, a trip conveniently arranged by his father, without Edward's consent.

Perhaps Henry Porter did suspect a growing attraction between his youngest son and the pretty Irish daughter of his laundress. But he'd never mentioned it.

"Mama still doesn't like me to ride," Grace said. "But whenever Geneva offers I take her up on it. And I always return the horses to the stables after our ride so Sammy and I might have a wee run."

They both dismounted and pulled the reins forward, then walked further down the lane, their horses following. "Mama still thinks I ride a pony," she said. "You won't tell on me, will you?"

Edward chuckled. "You should know that the secrets between us are kept well."

She nodded. "I guess so."

Grace was growing into a beautiful young lady. Though she was just fourteen, he could already see shades of the woman she'd become—proud, spirited. And beautiful. Edward frowned. Was it wrong to have these thoughts for a girl he considered his sister?

It wasn't the same kind of attraction he'd felt with other girls he'd met. Then, he'd thought about their breasts and their mouths and the way their bodies might look naked. He didn't consider those things when he thought about Grace.

Instead, it was more about truth and honesty and trust. He and Grace had always been so close, but now that he had been gone for nearly a year, he'd begun to see her in a different light, the way other boys might see her. She was special, a girl to be treasured, not lusted after.

That didn't stop him from admiring the way Grace sat her horse or climbed a tree or looked in her sapphire blue riding habit. But he forced himself to remember she was, for all intents, his sister, and still a young girl. And he was nearly a man. His admiration could only go so far.

"I beat you," she teased. "With all that studying you do, your bum is getting soft, Edward Porter. Before long, you'll barely be able to ride at all."

"Don't get cheeky with me," Edward said. "I let you win. I could still beat you every day of the week and twice on Sundays."

"Care to have another go?" Grace asked.

Edward shook his head. "No. Let's just walk for a while. We need to talk."

"Why so sober?" Grace asked. "School has turned you too serious."

"I want to know about Mother," he said. "Tell me everything that's happened since I saw you last. How has she been?"

Grace considered his question for a long moment, toying with a button on her riding glove. "Not so well. Ever since London, things are different. Though the dark times aren't frequent, they seem to be getting much deeper. And when she is well, she seems obsessed with putting things in order. I brought her tea last week and found her sorting through her shoes, lining them all up on the bed, then shuffling them about again."

"Has my father seen this?"

She shook her head. "I don't think so. He seems very preoccupied with business. Since you've left, I've become a companion to her. I read to her and walk with her in the garden.

And I help her with her correspondence. I suppose it's the least I can do for all that she's given me and my mother."

"And how is Rose?"

For a long time, she didn't answer and Edward reached out and touched her shoulder. She looked up into his eyes, hers swimming with tears. "You know it, don't you. You know she's dying. She can barely get out of bed in the morning. And I try to do as much of her work as I can, but I don't think we're fooling anyone."

He nodded. "I heard Mother and Father talking about it last night."

"What did they say? Will they put us out then?"

"Father wants to, but Mother won't have it. She'd like to send Rose to a hospital, but is having trouble convincing Papa to pay for it." He sighed. "Business hasn't been so good lately. He's thinking about shutting down one of the woolen mills. And a couple of the mines have played out."

Grace shook her head. "It doesn't make a difference. She'd never go and leave me here. If she goes to a hospital, I would have to go with her."

"But there might be something they can do for her," Edward insisted. "Perhaps she might have a few more good years."

"There will come a day when I'll stand beside her grave," Grace murmured, her voice soft and shaky. "And that will be the end of my life here."

"No!" Edward held her hand tight. "Mother would never let you go," he said. "She's—well, she couldn't do without you. You keep her…calm. And I think Father understands that and is happy to have her mind occupied."

"And what will happen when she finally realizes I'm not Charlotte?"

"Perhaps she never will," Edward said.

A long silence grew between them. "There is something I've been meaning to give you," she said.

"You don't have to give me anything, Grace," Edward replied.

She reached into the pocket of her riding skirt and pulled out a small gold medallion, strung with a thin piece of leather. "We barely see each other anymore and I want you to have something to remember me by. This belonged to my father," she murmured. She fingered the medallion and then held it up to the light. "It's Gaelic."

"What does it say?"

"Love will find a way," she translated.

"I can't take this, Grace. It's an heirloom."

"I want you to have it." She reached up and tied the leather string around his neck. "I want to know that you think of me every now and then." She took a ragged breath. "The world seems to be spinning so fast now. I just wish it would slow down so we could both take a breath."

"Me, too," he murmured. Edward reached out and cupped her cheek in his hand. Their gazes met and for a moment, he thought he saw something there, a spark, an acknowledgment, an attraction. He bent forward, a sudden urge to kiss her teasing at his brain. Her eyes went wide, then, just as quickly as it came, it was gone.

She smiled hesitantly, then turned back to her horse. Edward gave her a knee up, then stood below her as she adjusted the reins. "Thank you," he said. "I'll wear it always."

"Race you back?"

Edward barely had time to turn for his horse before she kicked hers into a gallop. He fumbled with the reins as he mounted and by the time he settled in the saddle, she'd disappeared beyond the curve in the lane. He chuckled to himself. There was no way he'd ever catch up, so he would let her have her win and the chance to gloat about it for the rest of the day.

But as his horse rounded the curve, he noticed Grace's mount standing nervously at the edge of the road, its reins dragging on the ground. "Grace!" Edward shouted. "Don't play around with me." He expected her to jump out of the bushes at any moment to scare him.

And then he saw her, crumpled in a heap, her body twisted at an odd angle. She wasn't playing. He jammed his heels into the horse's flanks and raced up to her, jumping off before he'd pulled the horse to a stop. Edward fell to his knees and gently brushed the tangled hair from Grace's face. Her skin was deathly pale, her lips bloodless.

"Grace? Talk to me. Grace?" Fear overwhelmed him and he found it difficult to breathe. He gently pulled her into his arms, but her body was limp. "Oh, God, Grace, don't do this. You can't do this. Just wake up. Please, wake up."

Edward gulped in a breath of air and tried to think of what he should do. He couldn't carry her back to the house and she couldn't mount a horse. His only choice was to leave her beside the road while he went for help.

He stripped off his riding jacket and covered her with it, then remounted and kicked his horse into a gallop. This was his fault. He never should have allowed her to race. She'd been his responsibility, she'd always been his to watch over and protect. And he hadn't been watching closely enough. It was so easy to think of her as older, as more than just a child. But he'd made a mistake and now he was going to pay for it.

ROSE SAT IN A CHAIR BESIDE the bed, her fingers clutching the upholstered arms. She drew a deep breath and then another, willing herself to remain calm. But as she watched her daughter, lying so frail and helpless in front of her, she wondered if she had the strength to bear this.

Edward had come to get her a few hours before, dressed in a dirty riding habit, his dark hair disheveled, his eyes wild with worry. She'd known from the moment he'd arrived that there was something terribly wrong. And when she'd walked into the yellow bedroom on the second floor of Porter Hall, she saw it for herself.

She'd told Mary Grace again and again that she disapproved of her riding. But her daughter had become so headstrong as of late, so determined to throw herself into anything that Geneva or Edward suggested. Slowly, she'd been drifting away, until Rose didn't feel as though she had any influence with her at all.

She closed her eyes, exhaustion sweeping over her. Though she wanted to fight it, there was some sense to letting it happen. Her illness had progressed to the point where she knew she didn't have many months left. Perhaps if she gave her daughter to the Porters, they might care for her after Rose was gone.

"Mrs. Byrne?"

Rose opened her eyes to find the doctor standing in front of her. She struggled to her feet, but the doctor gently touched her shoulder and she sat down again. "Your daughter is in a serious state," he said. "Her wrist is broken and I believe her clavicle is as well. She's had a very nasty bump to the head. The evening will tell how serious it is, but I suspect at least a concussion. If she has a fracture of the skull, then the prognosis would be considerably worse."

"How will we know?" Rose asked.

"If she wakes up, we'll know." He took her hand. "Now, what about you? You don't look well at all."

"I'm just tired," Rose said. "That's all."

"I'll ask that someone bring you a pot of tea. And some toast. You have to keep up your strength." He paused. "If there is any change, have someone fetch me."

"Yes, sir."

He smiled, then grabbed his coat and left the room. A moment later, Edward entered. He'd changed out of his riding habit and his hair was damp. "How is she?"

"The same," Rose said.

"Mrs. Byrne, I'm so very sorry. I don't know what happened. But I feel responsible."

"Are you?" Rose asked. "Truly, are you responsible for my daughter? Will you take that on after I am gone? Because, if you promise that you will, then I will forgive you this."

"I promise," Edward said solemnly. "I will always look after her. As long as I'm alive, she will never want for anything."

"You're nearly a man now," Rose said. "I expect that I can trust you with this."

He nodded. "You can." Edward crossed the room to the bed and stood over it, his gaze fixed on Mary Grace's face.

Rose had known him since he was just a little boy. He'd changed so much over the years, grown so tall and so handsome. He was nearly six feet tall now, much taller than both of his parents. And he'd begun to shed the last traces of his boyhood. His voice was deep and he'd begun to shave. And when he moved and spoke, it was with conviction and purpose.

He was the only one she could trust. Though Geneva might claim to love Mary Grace, her love was fickle, dependent upon her emotional state. Henry Porter had never wanted them in the household in the first place and Malcolm was quite obvious with his feelings for Mary Grace. No, it would have to be Edward.

"That medallion you wear. It belonged to my husband.

He gave it to me on our wedding day. I have one just like it that I wear."

Edward reached up and fingered it. "Grace gave it to me earlier today. You don't mind, do you?"

Rose shook her head. "You know what it says, then?"

"Love will find a way," Edward said.

"It's right that you wear it. You'll remember your promise then."

"I've brought some tea." Cook bustled into the room, carrying a tray with some supper. Geneva followed silently behind her. Cook set the tray on a nearby table, poured a cup of tea then crossed the room to hand it to Rose.

"Has there been any change?" she asked.

Rose shook her head.

"You'll let me know if there's anything I can do," she said. "She's in our prayers. All of us love her, we do. It's hard not to."

Rose had always had a prickly relationship with the rest of the staff, so Cook's words came as a bit of a surprise. But then, they'd watched Mary Grace grow up into a kind and compassionate girl, one who treated each one of them with the utmost respect and humility. How could they not all love her as much as Rose did? "Thank you."

Rose took a sip of the tea. Once Cook left the room, she turned to Geneva. Lady Porter stood at the foot of the bed, nervously wringing her hands and looking back and forth between Mary Grace and Edward, who stood silently in the shadows. She seemed to be whispering something to herself. Her lips were moving, but Rose couldn't hear a word.

"Thank you for calling the doctor," Rose said.

Geneva looked at her as if surprised she was in the room. "Of course I'd call the doctor. You don't think I'd let my daughter die, do you?"

Rose looked over at Edward. He stepped out of the shadows and took his mother's arm. "Come, Mother. You've seen her now. Let's leave her to rest."

"Your fault," she said, turning on him and pointing her finger at his chest. "Your fault." Geneva began to repeat the two words over and over again beneath her breath. Then suddenly, she reached out and slapped Edward across the face.

He stepped back, stunned by what she'd done. And then, he reached out and calmly took her hand, his grip firm and unyielding. "Calm yourself, Mother. You know as well as I do that this was an accident. Grace fell while she was riding."

"Charlotte is an excellent rider."

"Grace, Mother. Grace is the one who fell. Charlotte is gone. Grace is here."

"Grace?" Lady Porter frowned. "Who is…" She turned and looked at the bed, then rubbed her temple. "Where is my medicine? I must have my medicine."

"I'll go get it for you, Mother. Why don't you sit down and visit with Grace's mother for a bit. I'm sure she'd appreciate your company."

Rose had learned to read the signs. There were days when Geneva appeared quite normal and other times when she teetered on the edge of complete madness. Edward had managed to pull her back from that edge now and as she stood at the end of the bed, Rose watched her try to compose herself, her gaze darting about, her breath coming in quick, shallow gasps.

"The doctor says she may have a concussion," Rose said. "We must hope that she wakes up soon."

"Yes," Geneva said. "Yes, yes."

"When she does, I'll have her taken back to our rooms in the coach house."

"Oh, no. You must leave her here where she can be looked after properly. Edward will see to that. He helps me when I'm not feeling well. He'll help Grace, too. They're great friends." She took a ragged breath. "I'm sorry. I sometimes get confused. I've been so tired lately."

They sat in silence for a long time, both of them watching Mary Grace, waiting. And then, as if by some miracle, it happened. She moaned softly, then raised her hand to her head. Rose stood and sat down on the edge of the bed, taking her daughter's hand and giving it a gentle squeeze.

"Mary Grace, you wake up now. It's time for you to wake up."

"Mama?"

"I'm here," Rose said.

Her eyes fluttered open and she glanced around the room. "Did I fall asleep? Where am I?"

"You're in the yellow room. You fell from your horse and they brought you here. How do you feel?"

"My head hurts." She tried to sit up and then cried out. Her gaze dropped to her wrist, wrapped in a bandage and splint, and she frowned.

"You broke your wrist," Rose explained. "Do you have any other pain?"

"Just in my head," Grace replied. "Is Edward all right?"

"Of course," Geneva said. "He was there when it happened. He came to get help."

"What have I told you about riding?" Rose scolded. "You were riding too fast. Else how could you have been injured so badly riding a pony?"

"I—I wasn't riding a pony," Mary Grace admitted, a sheepish expression on her face.

"Grace is a fine rider," Geneva said. "I've taught her well. She can handle a full-grown horse, of that I can testify. And if she fell, then I'm certain it wasn't her fault. The horse must have balked or stumbled."

"I'm sorry, Mama. I know I promised, but I love to ride. And Lady Porter is right. I'm a very good rider."

Rose slowly stood. She could fight it no longer. She wouldn't try. She would have to satisfy herself with whatever scraps of respect her daughter might toss her way from now on. "I'm glad you're feeling better, Mary Grace. I'm sure you'll be on the mend soon. I have a bit of work to do, so I'll leave you in the care of Edward and Lady Porter."

"But, Mama, I want you—"

"It's fine, Grace," Lady Porter interrupted. "Your mother looks like she could use a rest. You'll come back tomorrow morning for a visit, won't you, Rose?"

Rose nodded and walked to the door. Edward was in the hallway as she passed and he called her name softly. She turned and smiled. "She's yours now," she murmured. "I can't hold on to her any longer."

As she made her way back to the coach house, Rose slowly realized that this was way it was meant to be. It made leaving so much easier to know her daughter didn't need her anymore. She'd fought through so much heartache and adversity, doing everything she could to provide a home for Mary Grace. And now the fight was over and she could finally rest. It would feel good to rest, good to set aside her work and contemplate what was to come.

Though she didn't want to die, she did want to see Jamie again. She would scold him first, then tell him how much she missed him. And after that, she'd tell him everything about their daughter, how clever and talented and beautiful Mary Grace was.

Yes, it would be good to finally rest.

CHAPTER SEVEN

24 December 1845

Happy Christmas. I send that greeting out into the world
in hopes that my Michael will hear it and smile. He must
be thinking of me on this night as I think of him. I made
him gifts, a new shirt and three embroidered handker-
chiefs that I have wrapped to give him when we see each
other again. Every day I wait for a letter, for news that
he has arrived safely. He must have heard by now of our
troubles. Food is scarce and people are becoming desperate. Some have been put out of their homes already
and come begging at the door. Mrs. Grant still employs
me, so there is money to buy what is needed. But she
and her husband talk of returning to England, so frightened are they of what is happening throughout the countryside. No one knows what has brought this on. Some
say it is the smoke from the locomotives. Others say it
comes from lightning. For now, I am well and the baby
continues to grow inside me. I pray that the new year
will bring better tidings.

"You read so well," Rose said.

Grace glanced up from the handwritten pages of the diary

and smiled at her mother. Though it was only an hour gone since supper, her mother had already taken to her bed, exhaustion deepening the lines in her pale face. After Grace's accident, Rose had seemed to take a turn for the worse.

Grace had tried to ease her mother's worries with promises that she wouldn't ride again, but her broken wrist, now splinted, bandaged and held in a sling, was a constant reminder. Grace reached out and took Rose's hand, giving it a squeeze.

"You taught me well, Mama."

"There wasn't much left to teach after Geneva's tutor was done with you, Mary Grace. And you always were a bright girl." A fit of coughing overwhelmed her mother and Grace ran to fetch water from the pitcher on the table. She helped her mother to sit, then let her sip from the chipped mug. "Geneva has dismissed the tutor, hasn't she."

Grace had wondered when her mother would notice. But there had been no time for studies after the laundry and the ironing. "Professor said that I learned everything he had to teach me," she lied. "And I wanted to have the time to help you with your work. Geneva still encourages my drawing. And we play duets on the piano and converse in French so I won't forget."

Rose shook her head. "There will be time enough for work when you're older. When I've regained a bit of my strength, I will be able to help more."

Grace had turned fourteen last month and with each year in her life, she became aware of the realities of who she was and what would become of her when she grew up. She lived in a strange world—two worlds, actually. For hours every day, she she sat a Geneva's side, the prim-and-proper lady with the fine English manners and the careful education. And then, she'd return to the coach house where she worked her fingers to the bone, washing and ironing and mending, so that her mother might not have to exhaust herself.

Though she appreciated Geneva's generosity, Grace was less and less certain of what Lady Porter hoped to accomplish by turning her into a lady. Though an educated Irish girl might be able to make her way in the world with a bit more ease, Geneva spoke of a future in service to the Porter family, taking over her mother's duties as she grew older.

Grace picked up the diary and slowly closed it, marking the spot where they'd left off with a bit of silk ribbon. "We'll continue tomorrow," she said. "Perhaps I should bring something a bit more lighthearted. Something to cheer you. The diary is so awfully tragic."

"It gives me strength," Rose said. "I know her so well, though we've never met. She is like a friend to me. I imagine that some day we might meet in heaven and I will get to hear the whole story."

"Why don't you close your eyes and rest." Grace watched her for a long moment, noticing the sheen of perspiration across her brow. The fevers had come and gone over the past few months and each time, they'd sapped more of her mother's energy.

The cough plagued her waking hours and disturbed her sleep. They'd both done their best to keep the truth of Rose's condition from the Porters, Grace becoming her mother's protector when she had a bad day. But the bad days were now strung together, one after the other, with no good ones in between. Sooner or later the secret would be out.

Grace picked up a damp rag and dabbed at her mother's forehead, then softly hummed an old folk tune that she'd heard many times as a child. "His hair was black, his eyes were blue," she sang in a soft voice. "His face was fair, his heart was true. I wish in my heart, I was with you. *Is go dté tú mo mhúirnín slán.*"

Rose reached up and brushed a dark lock of hair from Grace's forehead. "That song reminds me of your father," she murmured. "I wish you had known him, Mary Grace. He was a fine and handsome man."

"Tell me about him, Mama. Tell me how you met."

"It was on the road into the village. I was sent by my grandmother to sell the eggs at the market and he was just standing there, beneath an apple tree, as if he'd been waiting the day away just to meet me. And when he asked if he could walk me into town, I said no. But then he smiled and there was naught I could do. I fell in love with him that very instant."

"And he was handsome?" Grace asked.

"Oh, yes, very handsome." Rose softly continued the song, this time in Gaelic, her voice thin and breathy. *"Siúil, siúil, siúil a ruin. Siúil go sochair agus siúil go ciúin. Siúil go doras agus éalaigh liom. Is go dté tú mo mhuirnín slán."*

"What does it mean, Mama?"

"Let me see if I remember," she said. "Walk, my darling, Go quietly and carefully, go to the door and return to me, and may you go, darling, safe." She sighed softly. "I used to imagine my great-grandmother sang that song after her Michael sailed away. And I sang it after my Jamie died." She drew a deep breath. "Perhaps you will sing it after I'm gone?"

"You're not leaving, Mama," Grace said, a desperate edge to her voice. "You'll get better. I'll work harder so that you might rest a bit more. And when the weather is better, you'll sit in the garden, in the sunshine, and it will warm that cough right out of you."

Her mother clutched at Grace's hand, her fingers cold as

ice. "We must not fool ourselves, Mary Grace. We must face the future with a brave heart."

"What will I do when you're gone?"

"You will carry on, like all the women before you. And when you struggle, you will read the diary and find strength there."

Grace swallowed back her tears, determined not let her emotions consume her. "I'm going to go to the kitchen and get a bit of bread and ham," she said. "You barely touched your supper, Mama. You should try to eat more."

"Perhaps a cup of tea?" she said. "It might help me sleep."

"I'll go make a pot and bring it right back." Grace set the diary on the table beside the bed, then grabbed the tray that held the empty pot and cups from their afternoon tea. As she walked down the stairs, balancing the tray on her forearm, Grace allowed the tears to trickle from the corners of her eyes.

How was it possible that she'd lose both her father and mother before she was fully grown? What was she to do? As an orphan, she'd have no family to look out for her. Though Edward and Geneva seemed like family, even she knew better than to trust that they'd stand up for her.

She only had one choice. She'd have to make a permanent place for herself here, at Porter Hall. Then they might not put her out on the street. A shiver ran through her and she hurried along, anxious to get back to her mother. But when Edward walked past, she stopped, brushing her tears from her cheeks.

They'd been meeting in the stables after supper nearly every night since he'd come home from Harrow for the holidays. Sometimes, they'd just sit silently, both lost in their own thoughts. Other times, they'd read stories and poems to each other or look through picture books of exotic animals and faraway places.

To most, it might be seen as an odd friendship. Edward was

now eighteen and more a man than a boy. She'd always expected that he might find better things to do with his time, that he'd finally take a fancy to one of the pretty girls that his mother threw in his path. But he seemed quite content to sit with Grace for a few hours each night.

"What's wrong?" he asked, taking the tray from her arms.

Grace shook her head. "Nothing. I can't come tonight. Mama isn't feeling well and I want to stay with her."

"Come later. After she's asleep. I'll wait for you."

"I'll try," Grace said.

"I have something I want to give you."

She sighed. "You give me too much already."

He reached in his jacket pocket and produced an envelope. Grace took it and opened it, surprised to see an invitation for the Porter's Christmas party. The servants had been talking about it for weeks, making preparations. They'd said it was meant to welcome Malcolm's new fiancée and her family on a holiday visit. But Geneva had also made a point to invite a group of young people, boys and girls Edward's age.

Grace handed the envelope back to him. "I can't."

"Why not? I asked Mother and she said it would be all right. She wants you to come. And so do I."

"And how will you introduce me? This is our laundress's daughter. She's Irish and she's Catholic, but we pretend she isn't."

His lips pressed into a tight line and his eyes flickered with anger. "You know that makes no difference to me."

"It does to your mother. I'm good enough to pretend to be Charlotte when needs be. But I'm not good enough to join the family, am I? Are there any other Irish Catholic girls invited to this party, Edward? I think not."

"Why are you saying these things to me?" he shouted.

"I've never treated you any differently because of who you are. You're my oldest friend, Grace."

"Mary Grace," she corrected.

She tried to walk past him, but he grabbed her arm. She yanked away and the tea tray slipped from his grasp and crashed down onto the gravel walk. Grace dropped to her knees and began to pick up the pieces of shattered pottery.

"Leave it," Edward ordered, drawing her back up to her feet.

She twisted away as tears pressed at the corners of her eyes. Her lower lip quivered with the effort to keep them in. Suddenly, it seemed like a huge chasm had opened up between them, their worlds shifting until they were no longer one and the same. And every time she looked, he was getting farther and farther away. Soon, he'd be just a tiny dot on the horizon.

"Just leave me alone," she said. "I don't have time to spend sitting around and reading poetry. I have work to do."

As she walked away, she heard him call her name softly. But Grace didn't turn around. She'd come to depend on Edward Porter far too much. For her own good, she'd need to learn to face the world alone. Like Jane McClary had. She'd find the strength and the will to make a life for herself. And she'd stop dreaming that Edward Porter would be a part of that life.

"WHAT IS IT?" GRACE HELD THE package in her lap, running her finger over the pretty bow.

"I'm not going to tell you," Edward teased, holding a larger gift behind his back. "You have to open it."

"But Christmas isn't until the day after tomorrow." Grace smiled. "You look very handsome in your tails and white tie. Are you looking forward to the party?"

"Never mind the damn party," he said, drawing her along to a nearby garden bench. All he wished was for the silly party to be over. All the noise and confusion in the manor house had driven him outside, to the only place—the only person—who could give him a bit of peace.

He and Grace had gradually repaired the rift in their friendship over the past few days. Though she'd been cool and distant, Edward was certain that by the time he left for school again, all would be back as it was.

"I'm sure you'll get all kinds of gifts. I brought one that I'm supposed to give you from Mother. But I wanted mine to be the first."

Edward loved to see Grace smile. There was so much in her life of late that was sad. He knew she hadn't been sleeping, her night occupied with caring for her mother. Dark smudges beneath her eyes told the tale. And she hadn't been eating properly either. She was far too thin.

Grace carefully untied the ribbon with one hand, then picked at the wrapping. Impatient, Edward grabbed the package from her and tore off the paper, then set the velvet box on her lap. "Sorry," he murmured.

Grace stared at the box and then glanced up at him. "May I open it now? Or would you like to do that for me as well?"

"Open it," he said with a nod.

She undid the tiny clasp then pushed the top up. Inside, she found a beautiful garnet ring of gold filigree and deep red stones. He'd taken care to chose something that he knew she would like. This was a gift meant not for a girl, but for a young lady.

"It's lovely," she said.

"Will you try it on?" Edward asked.

She nodded and he took it out of the box, then grabbed her hand. He slipped it on her ring finger and to his satisfaction, it fit perfectly. Maybe that was a good omen. For with the ring would come something else, something he'd been thinking about for days, weeks actually.

Grace held out her hand. "It's too pretty to wear," she murmured. "It must have cost a fortune."

"I get an allowance," he said. "What better way to spend it?"

"I feel so glamorous wearing this. Like a movie star."

"You're as pretty as a movie star," Edward said.

"You shouldn't say things like that to me," Grace scolded. "It's not proper."

"I hope that someday it will be, Grace. Someday when you're older and I'm older and we can make our own choices."

"What do you mean?" Grace asked.

He took her hand. "I plan to marry you, Grace Byrne. And you might as well know of it right now so that you can get used to the idea. In Medieval times, girls were often engaged by the time they were twelve, so it's not that odd for me to ask now."

"Edward, stop teasing. This isn't a very funny joke. And it's ruining the pretty gift you gave me."

"I'm not joking, Grace. But if you'd rather think it is for now, that's fine with me. But when the time comes and you're all grown up, I'm going to remind you of this conversation. And then you'll have to give me an answer."

She stared at him for a long moment. "I will," she said softly. "I will give you an answer. When the time comes."

Edward grinned. "Agreed. And now, I'll present Mother's gift." He reached down and grabbed the box, then set it on her lap. It was tied with a big red ribbon, but the name of the dressmaker's shop was stamped in foil on the top. "You can guess what it is."

Grace brushed aside the ribbon and opened the box, then sighed. "It's lovely." She ran her fingers over the deep emerald velvet and the lacy bodice, then plucked at the pearl buttons that adorned the front.

"You're to wear it to the party," Edward said. "I expect you to come and so does Mother."

"Edward, I don't think it would be—"

He removed the dress from the box and draped it over her free arm. "We both insist. Now, go get changed. I'll see you inside, all right?"

She reluctantly nodded. "All right."

He watched as she ran back to the coach house, pleased at how his proposal had gone. It had seemed like the most logical thing in the world to him. Edward was certain he knew what he wanted. He'd made a promise to Rose after Grace's accident and he fully intended to keep it.

When he got back inside the house, Geneva was waiting, her fingers fluttering over the beautiful satin gown she wore. Her hair had been swept up and clipped with a diamond swan that Edward had seen only once before. His father was dressed as he was, in formal attire. The entire house had been decorated and presented the picture of a very wealthy family.

Edward wondered if Malcolm's future in-laws knew the truth about the Porter fortunes or whether Malcolm had kept that to himself. His father's business interests had suffered some major losses over the past few years and though they'd continued to live well, Edward knew that borrowed money and mortgaged properties had paid for many of the luxuries they now enjoyed.

He glanced over at Henry Porter and saw the glass of whiskey that had become a permanent resident in his father's hand as of late. His father had tried to convince Malcolm to return to Ireland and help him with the businesses, but Malcolm was still undecided. His fiancée's family owned cotton mills in Yorkshire and Lincolnshire and Malcolm had been promised a position there. If he took it, then Edward was resigned to joining his father's business when the time came.

He stood with his family in the entry hall, greeting each guest as they arrived. His parents had invited all the best English families living in Dublin and many had brought their young daughters, knowing that there was at least one more Porter son looking for a wife. Edward was polite to them all, but he relished the knowledge that he'd already made his choice.

He'd wanted Grace to be there at the party, so he might stand by her and fetch her a glass of punch, so that all the pretty girls might see that they paled in comparison to her. Every time someone walked into the room, he looked up, hoping that she'd finally arrived, anxious to share a smile. Minutes passed, then hours. Finally, Edward realized that she wasn't going to appear.

A light supper was served and he thought he might slip away for a moment, but his father called him to meet one of his friends, a man with a very round wife and a very dull daughter. Edward did his best to make polite conversation, his gaze darting about the room, searching for any reason to leave.

And then he caught a glimpse of her. She was standing at the doorway into the butler's pantry, her hands clasped in front of her, her expression troubled. She wore the same dress she had on earlier. Edward excused himself and hurried over to her.

"Why aren't you dressed?" he asked.

"I need you to ask your mother if we can fetch the doctor. My mother has taken a turn. She can't breathe and she's shivering so. I've tried all the remedies, but nothing seems to give her relief."

"I'll let my mother know. She'll call for the doctor right away."

Grace nodded. "I have to get back. I can't leave her alone."

"I'll come as soon as I can," Edward said. He gave her hand a squeeze, then turned to search the room for his mother. He saw her standing near his father and strode across the room. When he reached her side, he leaned close and whispered into her ear.

A frown wrinkled her brown. "I'll call for him right away," she said.

"Call for who?" his father asked.

"The doctor. Rose is ill."

"Send one of the servants to do it. You are the hostess of this party. We can't do without you."

"I'm going to go and wait with Grace until the doctor gets there," Edward said.

"You'll do no such thing," his father countered. "You'll stay here, where you belong.

He thought about arguing, then realized it would only cause a scene. The party would be over soon enough and then he'd go to Grace and do what he could for her and her mother. He rejoined his father and tried to make clever conversation with the very dull daughter of the very round woman and her very wealthy husband.

He caught Malcolm's eye once or twice and his brother sent him a cynical grin. He could go months, even years, without missing his brother's company. Yet he couldn't seem to go a day without missing Grace. He hoped that Malcolm did take a position in England. Since he'd been home, his behavior to the servants, in particular Grace, had been intolerable.

Malcolm hadn't forgiven Grace for intruding into his family, for trying to take the place of their dead sister. He refused to acknowledge that it hadn't been Grace's fault, but their mother's need that put Grace in the position she was in.

The childhood wounds ran so deep in his brother that Edward wondered if he'd ever put them aside.

When the guests began to play the gramophone in the parlor, Edward joined in the dancing, doing his duties by dancing with each single girl at the party. Once he'd completed the task, he intended to make his apologies and leave. But just as he'd searched out his very last partner, he noticed the doctor standing in the entry hall speaking with his mother.

He smiled at Cecily Fairfax. "Would you excuse me for just a moment, Miss Fairfax? There's someone I must speak to. I'll return for the next dance." He wove through the small group gathered in the parlor and reached his mother just as the doctor was putting on his coat.

"How is she?" he asked.

"Edward, go back to the party. There's nothing you can do," his mother said, her voice trembling.

"Then she's doing better?"

The doctor's expression remained somber. "I'm afraid Mrs. Byrne has passed."

"Passed?"

His mother placed her hand on his arm. "She died, Edward. About a half hour ago."

A wave of nausea surged up inside of him and he gasped softly. "That can't be. Was there nothing you could do to help her?"

The doctor shook his head. "She went peacefully. It was pneumonia, I suspect. More serious than she let on. I think she was prepared to go. She didn't seem to want to fight it."

"I have to go to her. I have to go to Grace," Edward said.

"She asked to be left alone," the doctor replied. "And you must respect her wishes. Give her the time to grieve."

Edward watched as the doctor walked to the door, his mind

numbed by the news. He'd made a promise to Rose and she was barely gone before he'd broken it. He ought to have been there with Grace, to soften the blow, to take away some of the pain. But instead, he'd spent his evening in idle chatter with a gaggle of brainless ninnies intent on finding a suitable husband for themselves.

"I'm going anyway," he said.

"Edward, don't."

He turned and faced his mother. "She needs me. I know she does, Mother. And I intend to be there for her. She's all alone in this world and I belong at her side."

CHAPTER EIGHT
GRACE

23 January 1846

> I write this day with fear in my heart. I had a dream last
> night that my Michael was calling to me. We were caught
> in a thick fog that had rolled in off the sea and we couldn't
> see each other. I would walk in one direction and he
> would call from another. We did not find each other and
> I awoke to an ache in my heart. The constant worry makes
> rest impossible. Has something happened? Has he left me
> and I have yet to find out? Life here grows more difficult.
> It is said that over half the potato crop failed. I can only
> hope that God will provide and watch over us both.

GRACE BURIED HER MOTHER on the day before Christmas,
December 24, 1935. Rose Byrne was laid to rest in conse-
crated ground in the churchyard of a small parish in the
village. Though she hadn't attended mass there, a generous
donation from Geneva Porter bought a pretty spot near the
edge of the cemetery, beneath a chestnut tree.

Though the weather was damp and bitter, Grace stood at the
gravesite without a hat or coat, her body numb to the cold. She
wanted to feel the wind bite into her skin, feel the drizzle chill

her, but nothing seemed to penetrate the haze that she'd existed in since the moment her mother had drawn her last breath.

The night of the party had promised such excitement and she'd decided to attend, if only for Edward's sake. She'd returned to the coach house to find her mother crumpled on the floor beside the bed, a bloody handkerchief clutched in her fingers, her lips blue. Even now, the memory sent a shiver down her spine.

She'd felt helpless to do anything, as if Rose's fate had been decided long ago and Grace was only there to watch it play out. Death had been quick, but not peaceful. And when it had finally come, Grace had been relieved that the agony was over, for both of them.

Only three other mourners attended the funeral—Edward, his mother, and Cook, who'd come to represent the rest of the staff. There were no tears, only silence as the priest hurried through his readings and prayers before rushing back into the warmth of the rectory and his preparations for the Christmas service.

Grace stood over the simple wooden coffin, her hand clutching a small bouquet of violets that Geneva had given her. This was the total sum of her mother's life. She'd worked so hard for so long and this was her reward. Anger surged up inside of Grace and she wanted to lash out at those around her.

It wasn't fair. Rose Catherine Doyle Byrne deserved more than this. She should have had pretty dresses and soft pillows and a handsome husband to take care of her. Instead, she got endless work and failing health and a death that came far too soon…. Grace swallowed hard. And a daughter who had never truly appreciated the sacrifices that her mother had made.

Grace felt ashamed for her part in her mother's unhappiness. It was so simple to allow herself the luxuries that Geneva provided. But now she could see how selfish she had been.

Every time she'd come home with another gift, it had been like a slap in her mother's face, evidence that no matter what Rose did, she could never give her daughter the important things in life. Grace now realized it was far too late to make amends.

She reached up and rubbed the small gold medallion between her fingers. She'd slipped the leather string from around her mother's neck just before the undertakers had come to fetch her. It was all she had left of her family, this medallion and the famine diary. There were a few photos and her mother's clothes, but nothing more.

Would this be how Mary Grace Byrne ended her life? Would she leave the world with so little to remember her by? Or would she fight for everything she wanted? It wasn't enough to just be satisfied with what life offered up, Grace realized. A person had to want more.

She felt a hand touch her elbow and she looked back to find Edward standing behind her. She wanted to fall to the ground and weep for all she'd lost, she wanted to scream and kick and rail at the injustice of her mother's life. But in the end, she held fast to his arm as he led her back to the Porter's car.

At the last moment, Grace pulled away from him and returned to the open grave. She kissed the bouquet of violets and then dropped them atop the coffin. "I'll make you proud, Mama," she murmured. "I'll be strong, just like Jane was. Just like you were. You'll see."

She ran back to the car and Edward wrapped his coat around her shoulders and helped her inside. Geneva glanced over at the two of them, her gaze coming to rest on their hands, clasped tightly together, but Grace didn't pull away. She needed this much, at least for today.

"You'll stay with us," Geneva said. "You can have the yellow room."

Grace offered her a weak smile. "I'd rather stay in the coach house, if you don't mind. It's my home and I want to be at home tonight."

"But you'd be so much more—"

"Mother, Grace has made her choice," Edward interrupted, giving Grace's hand a squeeze. "I think it's best if we allow her that much, considering what she's been through."

Geneva relented. "I just don't want you closing yourself up in that awful little room," she said. "Your life will go on, Grace. Life always goes on."

"It can go on tomorrow, or next week," Grace replied. "For today, I don't want it to go on." She snuggled down into the folds of Edward's coat, leaning up against him for warmth. She hadn't slept in two days, but exhaustion had hung over her like a dark cloud. Perhaps, once she was alone, she might close her eyes and let sleep take her away.

When they reached the house, Edward helped them both from the car. Geneva gave her a hug. "Your mother was a good woman," she murmured.

Edward walked Grace back to the coach house. After he'd settled her in Rose's rocking chair, he started a fire in the coal grate. When it was burning strong, he turned to Grace, sitting down next to her on the window seat. "I'm not sure what I can say that will make you feel better."

She swallowed back the tears she'd been fighting for so long. "You don't have to say anything."

"Would you like me to sit with you for a bit?"

Grace shook her head. "No. I'd prefer to be alone."

"Perhaps tomorrow we might go out for a drive?"

"Perhaps."

He bent close and gave her a quick kiss on the cheek. "I love you, Grace."

She heard the words, but she didn't know how to respond. She'd loved her mother, but had that made any difference at all? Love had absolutely no power over the unpredictability of life. All of them were just swept here and there by the tides of fate. She pressed her hand to her heart, trying to breathe through the ache.

His fingers lingered on her cheek for a long moment before he got up and walked to the door. "If you need anything, you know where to find me."

She nodded. When he closed the door behind him, Grace crawled onto the bed and curled her body into a tight ball, wrapping herself in Edward's coat as if it were his warm embrace. She closed her eyes and tried to sleep, but strange thoughts plagued her mind.

She felt as if she were standing on a precipice, the rocks crumbling beneath her feet. There was no one there to catch her if she slipped, no one to pull her back from the edge. One false step and she'd be gone, tumbling into the air with no hope of rescue.

A sharp rap on the door startled her out of her thoughts and Grace stumbled across the room to answer it. She'd expected Cook with a pot of tea or a bite to eat, but instead found herself face to face with Lord Henry Porter.

"May I come in?"

She smelled the whiskey on his breath and Grace nearly refused, but then realized she had no choice. Stepping back, she opened the door for him.

"I've come to discuss your position here in the household. Now that your mother is gone, there are going to be some changes made."

"Yes, sir." She swallowed hard, trying to keep calm. Would he put her out tonight or would he give her a few days reprieve?

Where would she go? Who would take her in? Her mind scrambled to make a plan. If she had enough money, she might search out her aunts and uncles in America. Perhaps they would welcome her. But she had no idea where they were.

"You've enjoyed privileges because of your mother's failing health and my wife's affection for you both. But from now on, you'll be expected to take on a full share of work."

"I understand," Rose said, a small measure of relief coursing through her.

"You'll continue to do the tasks your mother did as well as provide companionship for my wife when required. And when you're not doing that, you'll help in the kitchens. You'll give up these quarters by week's end and take a room on the third floor with the rest of the servants. Your mother took a small salary, and you will be paid the same. You'll have every other Monday off, like the rest of the staff. And if you don't perform your duties as required, you will be dismissed."

"Thank you, sir," Grace murmured. "I appreciate your allowing me to stay. And I promise to work hard."

"As a member of the staff, you'll report directly to me," he said. "I expect to know of any changes in my wife's condition, do you understand? Your loyalty is to me, not her."

"Yes, sir."

He reached for the door, then turned around again. "And one last thing. You will stay away from my son. There will be no more friendship between the two of you. It is improper and unseemly and I won't have it. If I see you two together while he is home, you will be dismissed immediately and neither my wife nor my son will have a say in the matter. Is that clear?"

Grace nodded. How quickly the lines had been drawn. Henry Porter had never approved of her close relationship to Geneva and it was clear now that Rose was gone, he felt he could assert more control over her daughter. But Grace wasn't afraid of him. He was rarely home, and when he was, he kept himself good and drunk. From what she could tell, he and his wife led separate lives and though he liked to think of himself as head of the household, he knew nothing of what really went on in Porter Hall.

As for his son, Grace would never stop caring for Edward. He was the other half of her heart. But neither one of them controlled their own destinies yet. She would have to protect herself until she was of an age to survive on her own. If she was put out, then she'd end up in some home for orphans. But if she could last just a bit longer, then perhaps she might carve out a future for herself on her own.

EDWARD HELD HIS BREATH as he opened the back door, wincing when the old hinges squeaked. It was nearly 2:00 a.m. and he'd been pacing his room, waiting for everyone to go to sleep. Dennick, his father's butler, had finally turned in at midnight, but Edward knew the man to be a light sleeper and waited until he was certain he wouldn't be heard.

It had been two days since Rose's funeral, two days since he'd seen or talked to Grace. She'd shut herself up in the coach house, refusing food and visitors. His father had wasted no time in exerting his own wishes over her.

Just a few hours after the funeral, he'd called Edward into the library. Edward had looked forward to the chance to discuss Grace's situation, but it seemed that Henry Porter had already made some decisions. Grace would remain in the household as a servant under one condition. She was to have no contact with Edward when he was home from school.

At first, Edward thought to argue the point with his father. But from the way Henry moved and spoke, it was clear he had already had a good amount to drink. And when his father was drunk, he often became foul-tempered and unreasonable. If an argument ensued, Grace just might be tossed out on the street that very night.

Instead, Edward agreed that a friendship with the girl was highly improper. Although his mother could maintain a closer relationship, Edward had to look elsewhere for companionship. He was eighteen and it was time for him to begin looking for a suitable wife.

Edward had sat silent as if in agreement. He would play whatever game was needed with his father, but he had no intention of deserting Grace. He'd made a promise to her mother and he'd keep it.

They had discussed business for a short while before Henry grew irritable and impatient. His father had grabbed the whiskey decanter and headed upstairs to his bed chamber. As was his habit, he drank himself to sleep and was snoring before midnight.

The night air was chilly and damp as Edward ran across the courtyard to the coach house. He glanced up at the windows to Grace's room and found them dark. She'd be asleep as well, but that didn't matter. They had to talk and this was the only chance he could find.

He slipped inside, then climbed the stairs to the second floor. When he reached the door, he knocked softly, but there was no answer. He tried the knob and it opened. The coach house hadn't been wired for electricity yet, but an oil lamp burned low on the bedside table. The room was chilly and no fire burned in the grate.

Edward walked over to the bed. As he approached he was surprised to see Grace with her eyes wide open, staring at the ceiling. He called her name, but she didn't respond, and for a brief moment, he panicked, thinking that death had come and taken her, as well.

He fell to his knees next to the bed and touched her face and to his relief, it was warm. She slowly turned to him, her gaze uncomprehending at first. "I keep waiting for her to come to me," she murmured. "But there's nothing."

Edward gathered her into his arms, holding her close. "She's here," he murmured, pressing a kiss to her silken hair.

"I waited for her to come. I couldn't sleep until she did."

He rocked back on his heels and met her eyes. "We don't have much time," he said. "I have to get back."

Grace pushed up on her elbow. "Your father says we can't see each other anymore. If we do, he will put me out."

Edward shook his head. "That won't happen. We will see each other but it will have to be a secret."

"How?"

"Like this," he said. "Late at night. And when I'm not with you, I'll have to know you're all right. So we need a plan. Some way for you to contact me when I'm at school."

"I'll write letters," Grace said. "I have Mondays off, now. I can walk to town to post them."

"I won't be able to write to you," Edward said. "At least not here, at Porter Hall. All the mail that comes to the house goes through my father."

"You could send letters to me at the post. I'll tell the clerk to hold them for me. Don't write your name on the return and no one will know who they're from."

"All right," Edward said. "But there's something else." He reached in his pocket and withdrew a piece of paper, then handed it to her. "If things get truly intolerable, then you must have this."

She stared down at the paper. "What is it?"

"It's a map. To a spot in the stone fence behind the stable. There's a loose stone near the base and a tobacco tin tucked behind the stone."

"I remember," Grace said. "You used to hide your treasures there."

"I can't show you where it is, but you can find it with this map. I'll take part of my allowance every month and send it to you. I want you to put it there, where no one can find it. And if you ever have to leave, you'll have money until you can contact me."

Grace drew a deep breath and let it out slowly. "Perhaps I should leave. I could go to America and try to find my aunts and uncles. You could come later."

The thought of sending Grace so far away was hard to accept. But she would be safe and watched after. "Do you know where they are?"

Grace shook her head. "No," she replied in a tiny voice. "They left so long ago. I never even knew them. But they must know of me."

"There will come a day when we can make our own decisions," he said, "when we don't have to be afraid of anything. We'll just have to be patient." He sat down beside her on the bed, taking her hand and holding it tightly. "I'm going to try to convince my father to let me work in the business with him after I leave Harrow at the end of the term. I won't go to university. I'll be here to look after you."

"No," Grace said. "You can't."

"I can," Edward insisted. "That way, I can watch over Mother as well."

"I'll watch over your mother," Grace said. "While you go to university. And when you're finished, then it will be time for both of us to leave."

Edward flopped back on the bed and stared up at the ceiling. "It seems like that time will never come, Grace."

Grace laid back beside him. "What will we do when we leave? Where will we go?"

He laughed softly. "We'll have an adventure. Our whole lives will be an adventure, I promise."

"We'll travel," Grace said. "To Spain and Morocco."

"To Australia and India."

"I'll write books about our travels."

"And I'll take photographs," Edward said.

"Do you even know how to operate a camera?" she asked.

Edward shrugged. "Not really. But I'm sure I could learn. And we'll come back to Ireland every year and lecture on all the strange and unusual things we've seen. Like kangaroos and elephants and sea turtles and giant lizards."

"It does sound wonderful."

"And when we get old, we'll retire to a beautiful tropical isle in the South Pacific and you'll sew funny hats for the tourists and I'll carve coconuts into ashtrays."

Grace giggled and the sound of her laughter was like music to Edward's ears. There would be happy times for them again. He pushed up on his elbow and turned back to look down into her pretty face. "Promise me that we'll make it happen?"

"We will," Grace said with a winsome smile. "I know we will."

"I have to go. When can I come again?"

"Your father said I'm to move into the house before the week's end. To the third floor."

"We can't meet there. We'll have to find a spot," he murmured. "The window in the upper hall. I'll leave a note for you there, tucked into the underside of the curtain on the right. No one will know."

"You're a very clever boy, Edward Porter."

He jumped to his feet. "I am. And you'd do well to remember that." He walked to the door and Grace waved goodbye as he slipped out.

When he returned to the kitchen, he was surprised to find Dennick there, sipping at a cup of tea and reading the newspaper. The butler looked up at him and nodded. "How is she then?" he asked.

Edward hesitated before he answered. He was never certain whom to trust in the household, who reported to his father and who maintained their own loyalties to other members of the family. But it was clear that the servants cared for Grace, so Edward decided to take a chance. "Better," he said. "I got her to laugh a bit."

"I remember the day your mother brought those two home. The kitchens were buzzing with gossip. There were a few of the servants who thought Rose might have been your father's mistress. And there were others who were certain your mother had gone to the poorhouse and paid to bring them home."

"Didn't Farrell tell you? We found them in front of Christ Church cathedral in Dublin."

"Farrell was very discreet. He didn't talk much. Not like this new driver, Grady. That young whelp will talk your bleedin' ear off if you let him."

Edward pulled up a stool and sat down at the old wooden table in the center of the kitchen. "You know I care about her, don't you?"

"I do," Dennick said.

"Then will you help me?"

"That all depends upon what you require, Master Edward."

"Watch over her while I'm at school. And if anything happens, ring me up or send me a cable at Harrow. I can be back home in a day or two." Edward paused. "I know your loyalty is to my father, but he isn't always going to run this house. Malcolm will live in England and I'll manage my father's businesses here. I'll be master of this house some day and your loyalty to me will be rewarded. I promise."

Dennick nodded. "I don't think it would do any harm," he said.

"I know you go home to your family when my father is out of town. If I send letters for Grace to you, will you promise to pass them along?"

"I can be quite discreet as well," Dennick said.

Edward pushed back from the table, then circled around it and held out his hand. "Thank you," he said.

Dennick hesitated and Edward knew that the gesture was unusual, a master offering a servant his hand. But Edward had never really subscribed to the idea that the servants were somehow inferior to his family. They were simply people doing a different job.

Finally, Dennick grasped Edward's hand and shook it. "You've grown into quite an admirable young man," he said.

Edward smiled as he walked out of the kitchen and climbed the stairs to his bed chamber. He'd find a way to protect Grace through this confusing time. And now that he had Dennick as an ally, it would be a much easier task.

CHAPTER NINE

GRACE STARED OUT THE WINDOW at the front drive, watching as Henry Porter stepped into the rear seat of the dark blue sedan. Grady, the family driver, glanced up at her as he circled to the driver's side and gave her a wave. She smiled down at him, then stepped away from the window.

Since her mother had died over a year ago, the servants at Porter Hall had become her family. Dennick had become her father, advising her on her comportment, warning her when trouble loomed. Cook had taken over as her mother, making sure she ate properly and got plenty of sleep. And Grady had become an older brother, teasing her and making her laugh whenever he had the chance, bringing her little gifts of sweets and ribbons from town.

Though the work had been taxing and her life lonely with Edward away, she'd still managed to find a measure of happiness at Porter Hall. Grace pulled aside the heavy drapery and looked in the folds, half hoping to find a note from him that she'd missed.

She'd seen him for a few days at Christmas, stealing some time in the stables to catch up on everything that his letters hadn't conveyed. But then the family had left to visit Malcolm and Isabelle in Lincolnshire. And before that, he'd spent the entire summer away from Porter Hall, traveling to America to visit his aunt and uncle.

Grace felt their bond weakening, but she couldn't seem to stop it. Edward had balked at the offer of a trip to America, but Grace sensed that the only thing holding him back had been his concern for her. She'd insisted that he go and in turn, he'd promised to send her a postcard every day.

He'd begun their grand adventures without her. The postcards had come regularly that first month, photos of tall buildings and bridges of New York. But as the summer passed, the postcards dwindled. It was then that Grace began to realize how far apart they'd drifted—worlds apart. And how silly their dreams had been.

He was seeing exciting new places, meeting new friends. There was no need to maintain a relationship with an orphaned Irish girl. Edward had the entire world in front of him, just waiting for him to step into it. For now, her world was inside the stone walls of Porter Hall.

So she'd put aside her loneliness and focused her attentions on Geneva. Over the past year, Lady Porter's emotional health had swung wildly between perfectly normal and nearly insane. It had become Grace's sole duty to "handle" her when things got difficult.

Often, Grace would sit for hours at her bedside, just talking and talking, mostly about nonsensical things. But her voice seemed to calm Lady Porter and given time, she could usually coax her back from the edge of a complete emotional break. It was a grave responsibility for a girl of fifteen. But then, Grace felt much older than her years.

When she wasn't working or tending to Geneva, she concentrated on furthering her education, spending what free time she had reading. She'd gone through most of the novels in Henry Porter's library and had begun to read the biographies and histories, discussing what she read in long letters to Edward.

"There you are!"

Grace jumped, startled by the sound of Geneva's strident voice. Clothed only in a wrinkled morning gown, Geneva hurried over to stand at the window. She grabbed Grace's arm, her fingers biting into the soft flesh above her elbow. "Come with me," she whispered.

"What is it?"

"Come. We must work quickly. He'll be back soon." Geneva pulled her along behind her, down the stairs and into the library. When they got inside, they closed the door and Geneva produced a key from her pocket and locked it. She sighed deeply. "Now they won't be able to get in."

"Who?"

"They. Them. The people in this house who are trying to catch me." She pressed her finger to her lips, then tiptoed over to the desk. "Open this." She pointed to the center drawer.

"I mustn't. Lord Porter wouldn't like it."

"Lord Porter isn't here," Geneva sneered.

Her tone was like a warning bell and Grace immediately knew she was working herself into another one of her fits. It usually began with an episode or two of paranoia, followed by obsessive behavior, and then a complete break with reality. It had happened so many times over the past few years that Grace had become quite adept at reading the signs.

"What are you looking for?" she whispered.

"Proof," Geneva said.

"Of what?"

"His affair. I know he's seeing another woman. I smell her on him when he comes home. She wears cheap perfume. And she has red hair. She's probably some Irish whore. All Irish girls are whores, you know. Out to take whatever they can get from a man."

Grace pasted a smile on her face. It was never any use arguing with Geneva when she was in this state. She didn't think rationally. "I'm sure Lord Porter would never do such a thing. He loves you."

"He doesn't. He never loved me. Well, he might have tried when Malcolm and Edward were young. But not since then. He thinks I'm weak and silly."

"You're not," Grace said. "You're strong and clever. You're the smartest woman I've ever known. The most beautiful and most refined."

"Then why doesn't he love me?" Geneva asked, her voice suddenly turning childlike. She stared into Grace's eyes as if she could see a lie before it was told.

"He's very preoccupied with his businesses," Grace explained. "He wants to be sure he can provide for his family."

"Preoccupied with his whore, more likely." Geneva reached out and rattled the center drawer of the desk. "It's in here. I know it is." She grabbed a letter opener from the top of the desk and shoved it into the lock, twisting it so hard that Grace was sure it would break.

"Please don't do that," Grace begged, trying to snatch the letter opener from her hands. "You know how angry he'll be. And he'll threaten to send you away again."

Suddenly, Geneva pointed the letter opener at Grace, wielding it like a knife. "Is it you? Are you the one he's keeping? Are you his little Irish whore?"

"No!" Grace cried. "Lady Porter—Geneva, look at me. Look into my eyes. You have to stop this now. Put the letter opener back on the desk and we'll go have tea. You'd like some tea, wouldn't you?"

Geneva's hand trembled slightly. Her fingers loosened and the letter opener dropped to the floor. Grace slowly bent to pick it up, then placed it back on the desk. She took Geneva's hand and led her to the door. The key was still in the lock and Grace opened the door, then dropped the key in her apron pocket.

"You mustn't say anything about this," Grace warned. "You have to keep your suspicions to yourself." She gently drew Geneva toward the stairs. "If this is true, Lord Porter will be very angry if you confront him. He might use it as an excuse."

"An excuse for what?" Geneva asked, glancing furtively over her shoulder.

"To send you away." She turned Geneva to face her and stared into her eyes. "Do you understand? Never say anything. It makes no difference whether he is or he isn't. Everything will go on as it has."

Geneva reached up at patted Grace on the cheek. "You're a clever girl, Charlotte. I'm quite proud of how you've grown up." Her gaze racked along the length of Grace's body. "Go change your clothes. That apron you're wearing is hideous."

"I think I'll go fetch that tea now." When Grace arrived in the kitchen, Cook was there, preparing a roast chicken for lunch. Dennick sat at the table perusing a week-old issue of the London Times. "What's wrong?" he asked, reading Grace's uneasy expression.

"Nothing. She's just a bit off today. She locked us in the library." Grace reached into her pocket and produced the key. "She told me she believes her husband is having an affair."

The room grew silent and Dennick sent Cook an odd look. "Then she knows," he murmured.

"It's true?" Grace asked.

Dennick shrugged. "Every Wednesday afternoon and occasionally on Friday nights. It's been going on for years now. But since he's been drinking, he's been getting a bit sloppy about hiding it."

Grace closed her eyes and drew a deep breath. "If this goes beyond suspicion, it will probably drive her right over the edge," she said. "And then we all might be out of a job."

Dennick nodded. "She's right," he said to Cook. "With Edward and Malcolm both out of the house, there's little enough for us to do. And if Lady Porter leaves, there will be nothing. I'll talk to the rest of the staff. We'll do our best to keep Lady Porter in the dark."

"And I'll see if I can't convince her that her imagination has just run wild," Grace added. She filled a teapot with boiling water from the kettle on the stove and let it warm while she arranged cakes and biscuits on the tray.

Cook helped with the tea and when the tray was ready, she gave Grace a soft pat on the shoulder. "I don't know what we would do without you, girl. You're the only one left to keep this family from tearing itself apart. If you aren't a blood relative, then I'm sure they ought to make you one."

Grace giggled. "And then I could be heir to all of this."

"Ah, then maybe I would get the raise in salary I've been asking for," Dennick said. "Would you be a good mistress, Lady Grace?"

"The very best," Grace said. As she waited for the tea to steep, Grace looked over Dennick's shoulder to read the front page of the paper. "What is going on in the world?"

He shook his head, his smile gradually fading. "This Hitler, it is not a good thing what he's doing in Germany with his Nazi party and his secret police. His troops have occupied the Rhineland. And Mussolini with his Fascists, they rule Italy with an iron fist. Dictators are never satisfied to live in peace."

"But they won't bother us," Grace said.

"I would hope not." Dennick sighed and refolded the paper. "But there are many who believe we must stop these two before they grab more power. If Britain does take military action, then it will be good for the mills and the mines. Soldiers will need uniforms and bandages. And the great warships run on coal. Lord Porter will be happy to see it come."

"But what if his sons have to go to fight?"

Dennick shook his head. "Those with wealth are rarely asked to make that sacrifice. Edward will be safe, not to worry."

But an uneasy anxiety grew inside Grace as she carried the tea tray upstairs. Edward might not be asked to fight, but that wouldn't stop him from volunteering if he believed in the cause. He had a strong sense of duty and though his heart was Irish, the blood running through his veins was English. If England went to war, then Edward would follow.

"I will pray every night that it doesn't come to war," Grace whispered as she walked up the stairs. For though she might be able to live with the fact that Edward had found a new place in the world without her, she couldn't bear to know that he was gone from the world forever.

THE PUB WAS DARK, THE AIR thick with smoke. Edward sat at a small table near the back with several of his mates from school. They'd all been invited to a house party in Kent at the estate of his roommate, David Grantham, and had traveled down from Harrow on the train. It was a wonderful night of freedom, something that was in short supply at school.

"Another round!" David called, his words slurred. "Where are those serving wenches when you need them?"

A few moments later, a young girl arrived with jug of ale. She set it in the center of the table, then hitched her hands on her hips. "Will you just be havin' the ale, or do you intend to eat?"

"Do we intend to eat?" David asked. The two other boys across the table shook their heads and David sent the girl a charming smile. "No, darling, I'm afraid we've just come to get completely pissed." He reached into his pocket and pulled out a wad of money, which he pressed into her hand. "This should cover it. Promise you'll take very good care of us."

"Maybe we should have something to eat," Edward said to the girl. "What do you have?"

"We have a mutton stew, shepherd's pie, and bangers and mash."

"Bring us one of each," Edward said. He glanced around the table at his three friends. They'd left Charing Cross shortly after their school day had ended and arrived in Ashford a few hours later. The Grantham family chauffeur was waiting at the station, but David had insisted on showing his friends a bit of the night life in the village before they headed off to his family's estate.

"So, on to the matter of why I brought you three here this weekend. My younger sister, Leticia, has invited some of her friends for the house party and demanded that I bring the three most handsome boys at Harrow. Thus, the reason for Edward's invitation," David teased. "As for you other two wankers, you'll have to relegate yourself to Edward's leftovers."

Martin Wetherby and Miles Fletcher groaned dramatically, but it was clear that they'd be satisfied with any feminine company. "So this entire weekend is about girls," Edward said. "If you tell me your sister is twelve, I'm getting back on the train for Harrow."

"She's seventeen and I have it on good authority that her friends are very…playful." He grinned lasciviously, then took a long sip of his ale. "Those of us at this table who haven't experienced the pleasures of the flesh ought to prepare themselves."

They all looked at Edward and he rolled his eyes. "I'm saving myself," he teased. "I'm considering the priesthood."

"You're not Catholic," Miles said.

"So why haven't you taken the plunge, Eddie?" David asked. "You've had plenty of chances."

Edward shrugged. "I don't know. I guess I always figured I'd wait until it was right. And there is this girl back in Ireland and…"

"What girl?" Martin asked. "Why haven't we seen her?"

"We've known each other since she was just a child. We grew up together."

"And is she beautiful?" Miles asked.

Edward nodded. "She is. Not just beautiful, but…I don't know. Luminous."

"What the hell does that mean?" David asked.

Edward chuckled. "I don't know. It's the only word I could come up with." He took a sip of his ale, then set the mug down. "I just know we're meant to be together. I've known it for a long time."

"And do her parents approve of you?" David asked. "More importantly, do your parents approve of her?

He wanted to tell them about Grace, about her strength and resiliency, about her determination to survive. But he knew they wouldn't understand. "My mother loves her," he said. Their own families would find suitable girls for them, girls from their same social class, girls with good breeding and large trust funds, girls who'd bring more wealth and power to the family. In the end, their marriages would be more about maintaining their social status than true love. Edward wouldn't have that.

"So, what is this beauty's name?"

"Grace," Edward replied. "Her name is Grace."

David held up his mug. "I propose a toast. To the four of us, the bad boys of Harrow. A few more months and we'll be off, ready to make our marks on this world."

The group grew silent and Edward knew what each of them was thinking. Life had been so simple until now. But they were through being boys and now had to become men. They'd choose their directions in life and never look back.

"Where are you off to during your summer holiday?" Miles asked Edward. "Another trip to America?"

"I'm going home," he said. "I have a lot of work to do to convince my father I should be attending Trinity instead of Oxford."

"And I'm off to Cambridge," David said.

"University," Martin said wistfully. "I'd come with you if I could. It's better than what I have waiting." He paused. "As the third son, my father believes my future lies in the military. I'm going to Sandhurst just as soon as the term at Harrow is finished."

"I never thought of the military," Miles said. "That sounds exciting. My father is sending me to Edinburgh, to St. Andrews."

"I would enjoy the military," David said. "My father fought in the Great War. He commanded a cavalry unit. He and his friends still sit around and tell tales about their adventures."

"What do you think it would be like?" Miles asked.

"You may find out sooner than you think," Edward said. "What's going on in Italy and Germany is troubling a lot of our politicians. Germany has the means to wage a war to end all wars and Hitler has already made the first steps to increase the size of his empire. If he goes further, England may have to stop him."

"We wouldn't do it alone," Miles muttered. "The French would fight. The Belgians, Danes. Even the Americans."

"I don't want to think about this!" David cried. "Or talk about this. There's no good in speculation and I find any discussion of war a total and complete bore. I say we find a few more wenches and have ourselves a real party."

Edward sat back and sipped slowly at his ale, watching his

three best friends get pissed. If there was a war, then they would all have to make difficult choices. They were no longer boys, but men, and with that came expectations—from their families, from their peers, and from their country.

He suddenly wanted to be back home, sitting in the garden at Porter Hall with Grace. His fears wouldn't seem so overwhelming there. He could say anything to her and she would understand. Edward closed his eyes and tipped his head back. But it had been so long since he'd been close to her, since they'd really talked. So much time had passed.

Things had changed. It was inevitable. They were both getting older and what began as a simple friendship had suddenly become much more complicated. At one time, it was enough to just be in each other's company. He'd loved Grace like a sister.

Edward wasn't sure when he'd begun to think of her as something more, when he'd begun to see her as a young woman. She'd be sixteen in the fall, an age when girls began to see boys in a romantic light. Would she fall in love with someone else? Or would their love grow into something more?

He needed to know, yet he was almost afraid to find out. When he imagined his future, it always included Grace. Yet, he'd only imagined them as friends and companions. But lately, he'd begun to think of her in other ways. At first, it had seemed odd. But then, it began to seem so right.

She'd been put in his world for a reason, that day so many years ago. He'd found her and he'd saved her. She'd always been meant for him.

"Sir, I believe it's time for you and your friends to go home. Your mother will be expecting you."

Edward glanced over at David's chauffeur. He stood beside the young man, his hat in hand, a perplexed expression on his face. Edward got to his feet and grabbed David by the arm. "Come on, mate. Pull yourself together. You've got ladies waiting for you." Martin and Miles also stood, leaning heavily on each other as they stumbled out of the pub.

"I'm going to introduce you to my sister," David said, his words slurred. "You know, you're the only guy I know I'd trust with her." David clapped him on the back. "She's going to love you."

Edward handed his friend over to the chauffeur, then walked to the bar in search of their serving girl. He found her pulling a pitcher of ale. "Do we owe you anything?" he asked. "Besides an apology?"

"You're joking, right?"

"No," Edward said. "I'm sorry if my friends were a little hard on you. They didn't mean any harm. They were just letting off a bit of steam."

"Not to worry," she said. "And thank you. Usually boys of your sort don't really care what they say or do."

Edward nodded, then reached in his pocket and pulled out another quid. "Thanks."

As he walked out of the pub and into the damp night air, he smiled to himself. His three friends had spent their whole lives in private schools, attending society functions, and never really noticing the world that existed all around them. They were children of privilege and that made them immune to any of the problems that ordinary people faced.

But if there was a war, and Edward believed that there very well could be, it would serve as a great equalizer. A German bullet or bomb couldn't tell if your family had money or position, if your father was a Lord or a lighthouse keeper. In the end, they would all face the same choices, to fight or to flee. And Edward knew already what his choice would be.

CHAPTER TEN

EDWARD STARED OUT THE WINDOW of the car as it wound through the streets of Dublin. He'd arrived on the express steamer an hour before and Dennick had been waiting for him, ready to fetch his bags and his trunk and load them into the car. Though Dennick had pulled the rear passenger door open for him, Edward had chosen it sit up front.

"I expected Grady," Edward said, shaking Dennick's hand.

"I had to pick up some suits at your father's new tailor here in Dublin so I volunteered to drive in. It's good to see you again, Master Edward. You look fit."

He'd hoped that Grace might also come to Dublin to meet the boat and he tried to hide his disappointment when she wasn't there to greet him. He had finished his last term at Harrow and after three years away, was finally coming home. He'd spent last summer in America with his aunt and uncle, but when the invitation had been extended again this summer, Edward had politely refused.

He was to enter university in the fall and would spend the summer preparing. That was the excuse he'd given his father, one of the many half-truths he'd told. He'd decided against Oxford and Cambridge, choosing instead to go to Trinity College in Dublin, news he hadn't yet broken to Lord Porter.

His father had assumed he'd take courses in preparation for

a career running the Porter family mines and mills. But Edward had a secret plan, to take courses that might prepare him for medical school. When the time was right, he'd convince his father that this was his calling, not the world of commerce. And then, he would make a career for himself that would be independent of his family. Once that was accomplished, they could say nothing about his choice of a wife.

But he'd put all the worries about his future to the back of his mind for now. He simply wanted to see Grace again. He'd purchased a present for her before he'd left London and was anxious to give it to her, anxious to see if her smile was as bright as he'd remembered it.

Though he'd met several very nice young ladies while at Harrow, none had struck his fancy. They'd been pretty and well-educated and sophisticated. But he'd found himself comparing them to Grace, to her wild Irish beauty, her dark hair and her pale skin with just a tiny sprinkling of freckles across the bridge of her nose. And though these other girls were charming, they had nothing to match Grace's wonderful honesty and clever wit. There was something about Grace, a light that shone from deep inside her, that drew him in, that made him want to be close to her.

How would it be between them now? He hadn't seen her since last Christmas and the few stolen moments they'd spent together had been awkward, filled with stilted conversation and long silences. She was growing up and they had both noticed an attraction that hadn't been there before. It was difficult to look at Grace and not think about touching her hair or kissing her mouth.

"Your mother has a grand supper planned for you," Dennick said. "All your favorite dishes. And your brother, Malcolm, and his wife are home for a visit. So the whole family will be together again."

Edward wanted to ask about Grace. Dennick had been a friend and an ally to them both over the past few years, passing along letters. She would certainly be at the dinner—his mother would never think to leave her out. But he held his tongue, keeping his questions to himself. "It's good to be back," he murmured.

"Your father says you'll be off to Oxford in the fall," Dennick commented, glancing over at him.

"I'm not sure," Edward answered. "I'm actually thinking of Trinity. But don't say a word about that yet. I haven't broached the subject with my parents." He paused. "How is Mother doing?"

Dennick smiled tightly. "She has her good days and her bad. Thank the Lord for Grace. She manages to keep her on an even keel."

"And how is Grace?" Edward murmured.

"Fine as can be. I've noticed that you two haven't written much since Christmas. Have you had a falling out?"

Edward shrugged. "No. Things are just different between us. Not quite as easy as they used to be."

"You two aren't children anymore. You're getting older. Things will change."

"Even if I don't want them to?" Edward asked.

"I'm afraid you can't stop time, Master Edward. No one can."

As they drove the short distance to Porter Hall, Edward thought back over all that he and Grace had been through. Perhaps Dennick was right. Maybe they had outgrown each other. They'd become friends out of necessity but as they got older, they were far more able to stand on their own.

Dennick honked the horn as they pulled into the circular drive in front of Porter Hall, and a few moments later, Geneva stepped out of the door. She looked well, her cheeks slightly flushed, her lip paint perfectly applied. No matter how much time passed, Edward was amazed at how his mother never seemed to age. Her pale hair showed not a trace of gray and her figure was still slim.

He held his breath, waiting to see Grace, but she didn't come out. When he stepped from the car, his mother ran up to him and gave him a fierce hug. "I didn't think you'd ever get here. Oh, look how you've grown." She pressed her palm to his cheek. "You're a man now. Come, we're just about to sit down to dinner. I expected you a bit earlier." She looped her arm through his. "You know Malcolm and Isabelle have come. They're both excited to see you."

"Let me just help Dennick with my trunk," Edward said.

"Don't be silly. Dennick, bring Edward's things to his room. If the trunk is too heavy, get Grady to help you."

They walked through the entry hall to the back of the house. When Edward entered the dining room, he was surprised to see everyone sitting at the table. Malcolm and his bride to the right of Henry Porter and Edward's spot vacant to the left.

He held out the chair for his mother, then took his place. "Thank you for waiting," he said. "The ship was a bit late getting in. We had a pretty rough crossing."

"Oh, so did we," Isabelle said in a dramatic voice. "Malcolm couldn't bear to stay in our cabin, I was so ill. He preferred to play cards with an entirely disreputable group of travelers."

"Hello, Edward," Henry said. "Good to have you home." His father took a long sip of whiskey from a crystal tumbler he held in his hand. "Would you care for a drink?"

He'd never offered Edward spirits before and Edward wasn't sure why he'd chosen tonight to do so, but he shook his head. "No, thank you, Father."

"You're a man now," Henry shot back. "You can certainly stand a drink."

"Go ahead," Malcolm chided.

"I would," Edward said firmly. "But I'm already tired and I'm afraid I might fall asleep in the middle of dinner. Perhaps after I eat?"

"Suit yourself," Henry muttered.

It had already begun, Edward mused as he glanced around the table. The tension hung thick in the air and he felt if he said one wrong word, then entire room would explode into a vicious argument. His mother rang the tiny silver bell next to her plate, calling for the first course.

Edward toyed with his napkin and when a serving plate was held in front of him, he glanced up. Edward blinked in surprise when his gaze met Grace's. She was dressed in the plain gray uniform of his mother's kitchen maids. He shoved back his chair and stood, tossing his napkin aside. "Grace," he said, grabbing the plate from her hand.

She sent him an odd look. "Welcome back, Master Edward." She gently drew the plate out of his hands. "These are prawns sautéed in wine and butter. Would you care to try some?"

"What are you doing?" he whispered.

"Your mother has ordered all your favorites," she said. "Do sit down. I'm sure you'll enjoy them all."

She sent him a pleading look and Edward slowly took his place. Grace dropped two prawns onto his plate, then moved around the table. When she finished, she curtseyed, then disappeared into the butler's pantry.

"Really, Edward," Malcolm drawled, "if you must have a dalliance with one of the servants, you could at least pick a pretty one."

Geneva gasped. "Malcolm. You will watch your tongue."

Edward sent his brother a pointed glare, then turned to the first course of his meal. This would never do. He'd never be able to survive the entire summer with Grace waiting him and Malcolm ready to pounce at the first chance he got. "It's all right, Mother. I seem to remember Malcolm having a fondness for a little red-haired kitchen maid when he was a bit younger. What was her name again? Sally?"

Isabelle's eyes went wide and he saw a blush of embarrassment crawl up Malcolm's pale cheeks. Edward lifted his eyebrow, issuing a silent challenge to his older brother. If he wanted a war, Edward had far more ammunition in store than Malcolm did. There was no question who would win and who would lose, especially if Grace was brought into the battle.

GRACE STOOD AT THE SINK IN the kitchen, scrubbing out a pot that Cook had used to prepare the soup. She felt strange, a bit light-headed and unable to focus. She'd had days to prepare to see Edward again, days to gather her thoughts and strengthen her resolve. But the moment he looked at her, Grace knew she couldn't stay away.

It was like a missing part of her had been returned. And now she felt right again, as if her world had shifted and come back into perfect balance. She had her friend back, her confidant, the only person in the world she could truly trust. And he was staying for the summer.

Her mind spun with the possibilities. They could ride again and he could teach her how to drive. They'd sit in the garden and read poetry and—

Grace stared down into the dirty water, then sighed softly. It was so difficult to accept that their relationship was changing. They weren't children anymore, but she, at least, wasn't yet an adult. It would be so simple if she could just snap her fingers and the next three or four years would fly by. Right now she felt as if she were caught in limbo, unable to do anything but bide her time and wait for her life to begin.

"Grace, go clear the table for me," Cook said. "They'll be having their dessert in the parlor." She picked up a tray holding an apple pie and a bowl of clotted cream. "Hurry now. There's work to finish before we can all sit down and take a rest. We haven't had this many to serve in Porter Hall for a very long time."

Grace wiped her hands on a dishrag, then grabbed an empty tray and walked back to the dining room. As she cleared, she could hear the conversation drifting in from the parlor, Geneva's bright laughter, Henry's dour tones. Though she'd only known Isabelle for a few days, Grace had found her condescending and pretentious. She expected to be waited on hand and foot and had even threatened Cook with dismissal when her breakfast had not been served on time and her eggs had not been cooked to her liking. As for Malcolm, Grace had caught him leering at her any number of times and she decided it was best to stay as far away from him as possible.

She gathered the silver first, then began to stack the china. When she'd filled the tray, she turned back to the kitchen. But she stopped short when she saw Edward standing in the hallway looking in at her. He took a step forward and Grace held out her hand to stop him, her gaze darting about the room. "Don't," she murmured.

"Grace, please, I—"

"We can't."

"We can. Meet me tonight. In the stables."

"No," Grace replied, shaking her head.

"Yes," he insisted. "I have to talk to you. If you don't come, then I'll come to you. After everyone is asleep. I'll come to your room."

"All right. I'll meet you in the stables." She hurried into the butler's pantry and dropped the tray onto the counter with a noisy clatter. Her heart slammed in her chest and for a moment she felt as if she was about to suffocate.

What was this? Fear? Excitement? Denial? She'd always felt so comfortable around Edward and suddenly that had all changed. When he looked at her, she felt as if her body was on fire, like every nerve was tingling with electricity. Grace ran her hands over her arms, her fingers trembling.

"Grace?"

Startled, she spun around to find Cook watching her from the other side of the butler's pantry. The woman bustled up to her, then stared into her eyes. "Are you all right?" She reached up and pressed her palm to Grace's forehead. "You look a bit ill."

"I—I'm just tired," Grace said. "It's been a long day and I have a bit of a headache."

"Run along then. I'll finish up here."

Grace smiled. "Thank you." But as she was leaving the butler's pantry, Cook's voice stopped her.

"Be careful," Cook said. "I know you think he belongs to you, but there are those in this household who would not approve. Don't give them cause to put you out."

"What about you?" Grace asked. "Do you approve?"

"I can't say that I do," she finally replied. "And not because I don't love Edward. And Lord knows, I think of you as my own daughter. But I'd never want to see either one of you get hurt." She paused. "You're still so young, Grace. Don't let your heart be fooled into thinking you can't live without that boy. We're not meant to mix and those that think we can are setting themselves up for a rude awakening."

Grace nodded. Since her mother had died, Cook had always been there with a kind word or a sensible bit of advice. And Grace knew she was right about this as well. Yet she couldn't just ignore what her heart had been telling her for a long, long time.

She and Edward Porter weren't at the end of their life together. They were at the very beginning.

CHAPTER ELEVEN

HE HAD WAITED IN THE STABLE for two hours before he realized that Grace didn't plan to appear. Edward paced back and forth, a mixture of emotions coursing through his body. Why did everything have to be so complicated? He almost wished they were children again, so that they might say everything that they felt instead of measuring their words and hiding their feelings.

Anger bubbled up inside him and mixed with his frustration and confusion until he wasn't sure what he felt. He'd never been in love before so he had no experience to draw upon. Was this what love felt like? Edward cursed softly. If so, then perhaps he didn't want to love Grace Byrne after all, for it was torment.

He grabbed his jacket and strode out of the stable into the warm summer night. Grace had made her wishes clear. She didn't want to be with him. The friendship they'd shared was over. How could it be any more apparent? The gravel crunched beneath his feet as he walked through the courtyard. He glanced up at the windows in the attic rooms to find them all dark. Why had he even bothered to come home? Maybe it wasn't too late to take that trip to America.

He'd nearly reached the door when a figure stepped out of the shadows. Edward stopped short then let out a tightly held breath. Her features were just visible by the electric light over the kitchen door. He wasn't sure what to say, but then she stepped forward and wrapped her arms around his waist, and he didn't need words.

They held each other for a long time, Edward gently smoothing his hand over her head, her hair silken beneath his fingers. All the anger dissolved and he felt a wonderful sense of contentment. "I didn't think you were going to come," he murmured. "I was sure you hated me."

Grace stepped back and stared up at his face. "I could never hate you."

"I'm sorry," Edward said. "About tonight. I didn't know what to say when I saw you. I thought you'd be sitting at the table beside me, not serving me prawns."

"It's my job," Grace murmured. "It's not so bad. And I have to have a job so I can have a place to live."

"You live here, at Porter Hall, the same as me."

She shook her head and smiled. "No, Edward. Not the same as you. I'm not the same as you. You have to know that."

"I do," he replied. "But I don't want to believe it."

"We're caught in the middle, in this strange place between your world and mine. We can be together here, but we can't make a life in this world. It doesn't really exist. It's just a fairy tale place that we've made for ourselves."

He cupped her face in his hands and stared down into her eyes. His heart slammed in his chest and he felt as if he couldn't breathe for wanting her. Edward bent forward and touched his lips to hers. The contact startled her and she stepped back, but he kept his gaze fixed on her eyes and waited, letting the import of the kiss slowly sink in.

He'd kissed girls before and he'd even touched them beneath their clothes. And what he'd felt had been confusing and unnerving and exciting all at once. He felt all the same things with Grace. But it also felt…right. "Have you ever kissed a boy before?" he asked.

Grace shook her head, a shy smile curling her lips. "Jack Brady kissed me on the cheek once," she said.

"And who is Jack Brady?"

"His father is the green grocer in the village. We talk when Cook sends me to shop for vegetables. He's a nice boy, but he's a bit fresh." She paused. "And what about you, Edward Porter? How many girls have you kissed?"

"Only one that mattered," he murmured. He leaned forward and kissed her again, this time teasing at her lips with his tongue. Hesitantly, she opened beneath the gentle assault and his tongue touched hers. A current of desire snaked through his body and he pulled her closer until she pressed against him.

He could feel her fears in the way she held her body and Edward softened his embrace, determined to show her how beautiful it could be between them. But she was still young and unaware of the effects a woman's body could have on a man. He reached up to touch her face, drawing his thumb across her damp lips. "Do you love me, Grace?"

Her eyes were wide as she looked at him. "I do."

"How do you love me? Do you love me like a woman loves a man?"

She nodded, then slowly ran her hand over his chest. He felt the heat of her palm through the shirt he wore. "I love you," she murmured, pressing her lips to a spot just beside her fingers. "I've always loved you."

He reached inside the collar of his shirt and pulled out the small medallion she'd given him. "Tell me what it says," he murmured.

She pulled out her own medallion, the one her mother had worn. "Love will find a way."

"Promise me you'll never stop believing that."

Grace smiled, then pushed up on her toes and gave him another kiss. "I'll believe if you believe."

He pulled her back into his embrace and gave her a fierce hug. "When can I see you again? Will you meet me tomorrow night?"

She nodded. "In the stables?"

Edward walked with her to the back door, then kissed her once more, deeply and thoroughly, before she slipped back inside. When she was gone, he smiled to himself. He couldn't remember the last time he'd felt so completely happy. They'd have the summer together and if they were forced to meet in secret and hide their feelings for each other, then that's what they'd do. But there would come a day when he'd be able to take Grace's hand and walk into Porter Hall, to sit beside her at the dinner table, without a second thought to the consequences.

FREEDOM HAD COME SURPRISINGLY easy to them. Malcolm and Isabelle had left after just a week, business matters calling them back to Lincolnshire and Isabelle's family. Their visits would never last long, Grace suspected. Isabelle hated Ireland and considered everything about it rustic and provincial.

Edward's father had decided to spend a couple of weeks in Scotland, examining a new kind of loom for his woolen mills. And to Grace's great surprise, Geneva had decided to accompany him to Edinburgh for a visit with old family friends.

Grace and Edward saw Lord and Lady Porter off at the docks in Dublin and as they watched the steamer pull out into the harbor, Edward reached down and took Grace's hand in his, weaving their fingers together.

She felt a secret thrill race through her, the same reaction

she had every time Edward touched her. He'd been so
careful to treat her with respect, to temper his sexual
desires, but there were times when Grace wanted him to
forget propriety and just allow his hands to wander over her
body at will.

She silently scolded herself before she let her thoughts
go any further. Had she attended mass regularly, then perhaps
she'd finally have to confess something truly naughty and
sinful. But she had a difficult time believing any of her
feelings for Edward were a sin. To her, being with him was
like heaven on earth.

Grace knew exactly what went on between a man and
woman. The kitchen maids were constantly chattering about
it and from an early age, she'd listened carefully. Though it
seemed a bit strange and very awkward, Grace could imagine
how it might be pleasurable, this joining of two bodies.

Kissing Edward was pleasurable. And when he pulled her
against him and held her tight, when he put his tongue in her
mouth, there was pleasure in that. Never mind the fascination
that his naked skin held. Twice now, she'd seen him without
his shirt and he was quite extraordinarily beautiful.

Grace smiled as she stared out at the ship. They'd pre-
tended for nearly a month now, avoiding each other's glances,
never speaking with others present, and always meeting clan-
destinely. No one suspected there was anything between them
beyond a cordial respect. But now, for a few weeks, they
could be themselves again. And she planned to kiss and touch
Edward as much as she pleased.

"So what shall we do with ourselves?" Edward asked.

Grace pushed up on her toes, wrapped her arms around his
neck and kissed him full on the mouth. At first, he was
shocked, drawing back and giving her a stern look. "A lady

does not kiss a man in public." But then, Edward shrugged and kissed her back.

"I want to go riding," Grace replied, her mouth still pressed to his. "And I want you to take me to the moving picture show in Dublin, and I want you to teach me how to drive and I want to go on a picnic and—"

"Let's start with supper," he said. "And then, we'll decide the rest while we eat."

They found the car parked near the docks and Edward helped Grace inside, then hopped in behind the wheel. They drove back into Dublin proper, enjoying the warm summer evening and the bustle of people out on the streets. Edward parked the car near Ha'penny Bridge and he and Grace walked along the River Liffey until they found a small pub that served simple fare.

It felt so good to be free of all the restrictions they'd suffered at Porter Hall, to not worry who might see them together or who might tell. "Trinity is just over there," he said, pointing to the east. "I haven't told anyone yet, but I've been accepted there. I'm not going to Oxford."

Grace stopped. "You'll stay here in Dublin?"

He nodded. "I'm going to study medicine. Father won't approve, but by the time he realizes what I'm doing, he won't be able to stop me."

"And why medicine?"

"Don't you see, Grace? If I have a career that I can build on my own, then we'll never need to depend upon my family. I'll be able to support you. There will always be a need for doctors, we could go anywhere in the world. I could give you the adventure I promised you."

They found a table at the pub and ordered a dinner of boiled ham and cabbage. Grace listened as Edward talked about his plans for his future—for their future—and his enthusiasm was infectious. She could almost see it in front of her. But Grace had learned over the past few years to temper her hopes and dreams with a good dose of reality. So many things could go wrong to spoil this all.

It was easier for Edward to be optimistic. Thinking back, Grace couldn't recall a single instance where he didn't get precisely what he wanted—out of sheer determination or blind luck—or the convenience of having a wealthy and powerful father. Edward had never known disappointment, except for Charlotte's death and he barely spoke of her now.

"You've thought about these plans quite a bit," she said.

Edward shrugged. "Occasionally." He grinned. "All right, a lot. Ever since I made that promise to your mother."

She looked up from her meal. "What promise?"

"Before she died, I promised her I'd always look after you."

She frowned, then glanced down at her plate, picking at her food. "I didn't realize you'd agreed to that." The notion that he was with her simply out of duty didn't set well and she met his gaze again, searching for answers in his eyes. "You made that promise years ago, Edward. When things were very different. I—I don't expect you to keep it."

"I intend to keep it," he said stubbornly.

"Maybe I don't want you to keep it. Maybe it would be best to just forget it." Grace shook her head. "I don't understand your sense of honor. You never think of yourself. You've spent your life taking care of your mother and me and my mother. You've earned the right to be a bit selfish now and again. If you want to go to Oxford, then go. If you want to spend the summer in America, then that's where you should be. I'm not your responsibility, Edward. I can take care of myself."

He tossed his napkin onto the table, then pulled a wad of

pound notes from his pocket and laid those down as well. "Come on. Finish your meal. I want to show you something."

They walked back to the Liffey and when they got to Fishamble Street, turned away from the river. They passed a huge cathedral and Edward pulled her along to one of the entrances. He walked over to a spot near a pillar that rose along the outside of the church.

"Here," he said, pointing to the ground.

Grace slowly approached and looked down at the spot he indicated. "What? There's nothing there."

"You and your mother were here when I found you. You were covered by an old blanket and I nudged it with my foot and you began to cry. And my mother rushed over and the next thing you know, you were both in the back seat of our motorcar and we were on our way to Porter Hall."

Grace bent down and touched the cold stone with her fingertips, imagining the scene. "My mother never told me how we came to be at Porter Hall. I just assumed she'd been given a job there after my father died."

"God put you here, outside this church, so I could find you. Don't you see, Grace? So many things happened that day that shouldn't have. My mother was supposed to go to Dublin the day before, but I had a cold. And we nearly stopped by the church on our way into town rather than on our way out. And we usually didn't use that entrance, but that day, Farrell couldn't find a place to park the car. It was all meant to be, just so."

"You think our whole life is planned out for us already?"

"Perhaps," Edward said. "Or maybe our lives are just a series of coincidences that are so amazing we believe them to be our destiny."

She slowly rose and stood beside him, her gaze still fixed on the spot. The revelation should have given her a sense of her past, something to hold on to. But instead, it only made her more aware of everything that stood between her and Edward. "I don't want you to love me because you feel obliged to or because you want to keep some promise you made to my mother. I want you to love me because… because—"

"I do love you. Beyond the promises and the duty and the honor and everything else," he said. "If all of that were to disappear tomorrow, I would still love you."

"Thank you," she murmured, "for bringing me here. For showing me this place."

He took her hand and placed a warm kiss on the back of it. "Come, we'll go inside and light a candle for your mother. Even though it's not a Catholic church, I'm sure God will hear our prayers just the same."

Grace took the hand he offered and walked with him to the door. Edward always seemed to know exactly how to make her doubts and fears disappear. She would say a prayer for her mother. And then she would say one for herself, praying that Edward's love for her would grow stronger with every day that passed.

CHAPTER TWELVE

EDWARD RESTED HIS ARM ACROSS the back of the driver's seat and leaned over to place his free hand on the wheel. Grace reached out and slapped it away. "I'm driving here," she said. "Not you."

"We're not going anywhere," he said, "until you start the car."

Grady leaned over the passenger side door of the Austin. "Mr. Edward, I'm not sure we ought to be lettin' Grace drive your da's car. I'd sure hate it if something happened to it."

"It's my birthday present," Grace said, drawing her jacket up around her neck to ward off the November chill. "Edward promised he'd teach me to drive."

"She can't drive my car. It's far too complicated. Don't worry. I'll keep one hand on the wheel," Edward said. "And if she wrecks it, I'll take the blame."

"I won't wreck it," Grace muttered. "Now, how do you start this thing?"

Edward grinned at Grady, who stepped away from the car. He went through the steps for starting the small sedan and Grace laughed in delight when the engine roared to life. She clutched the steering wheel in her hands and listened carefully as he told her how to operate the clutch. She gnawed on her lower lip, her brow furrowed in concentration, then did as she was told.

To Edward's surprise, the car slid into gear smoothly and

they took off down the drive toward the road. Grace was even more shocked and she turned to Edward and screamed.

"Mind the road!" he cried, pointing through the windscreen.

She turned her attention forward and carefully slowed as they made the turn onto a narrow lane, lined with tall trees. They bumped along through the ruts and a minute later turned onto the paved road that led into town.

He'd made this same drive every Sunday evening on his way back to university in Dublin, but it was far more fun with Grace behind the wheel. His first year had passed so quickly. Though his father had railed at Edward's choice of Trinity, Geneva had convinced him that it would be better to have Edward close to home so that he might learn a bit more about his father's business interests.

He stayed in Dublin at the dormitories during the week, but on Friday afternoons, he hopped in his car and headed back to Porter Hall. When he wasn't studying, he sat with his father in the library discussing business. And late at night, when the rest of the house was asleep, he'd sneak out to the stables to meet Grace.

"I want to go faster," Grace said.

"Absolutely not," Edward replied. "This is quite fast enough for you to begin with."

She'd nagged at him for months now about learning to drive and had even enlisted Geneva's help. Geneva had convinced him that she'd enjoy a day out every now and again and Grady was often busy driving Lord Porter between the mills and the mines. Grace was old enough to handle such a simple task, she reasoned.

Grace's eyes were bright and her smile wide as they rolled down the road. She seemed to take to driving the same way she'd taken to riding, with a natural ease and confidence.

Edward had to wonder what kind of girl she might have become had she been given the advantages of wealth and social position. She was certainly as clever as any he'd ever met. And she was smart as a whip. He'd never met a woman as well read as she was and as able to converse about such a wide variety of subjects.

He tried to imagine Grace at a society party. No doubt every young man in attendance would be vying for her attentions, for she had the beauty to match her quick wit. When the time came for her to take her place alongside him as his wife, he would be proud to introduce her, proud that she'd chosen him to love.

"Turn in here," he said, pointing to a small lane lined by fuschia bushes. They bumped along until the lane ended in a wide meadow. In the distance, they could see Porter Hall and the surrounding estate. He reached over and switched off the car.

"What are we doing here?" she asked.

"I have something I want to give you," Edward said.

Grace laughed softly. "And I have something I want to give you." She twisted around in the seat, then wrapped her arms around his neck and kissed him. Over the past months, they'd done a lot of kissing and Edward had to admit that she'd become quite an expert at that as well.

Her tongue darted inside his mouth, teasing and tempting him until he groaned softly and returned the kiss. Emboldened, she crawled across the seat and straddled his lap, her skirt riding up on her thighs. Edward rubbed his palms along her silk stockings, his fingers slipping beneath her skirt.

She moaned softly, then took his hand and placed it on her breast. Edward held his breath, then drew it away, but she seemed only more determined to seduce him. "Grace, stop," he warned. "I don't think we should—"

Edward gasped as she slowly unbuttoned his shirt. She bent her head and pressed her lips to his nipple, then bit softly. "I think we should."

"You're going to put us both in a spot of bother," he said. "A girl your age shouldn't—"

"I'm sixteen now. A girl my age can get married," she said. "I could have married when I was twelve if I had wanted to. The church says I can. You could have married when you were fourteen."

"And what would we have done with ourselves then?" Edward asked.

"All the things we aren't doing now?" Grace replied.

Edward laughed and pulled her into his arms. Yes, she was sixteen now and he'd turn twenty before the end of the year. And it had become very difficult to resist the lure of her body. But he intended to protect her virginity for as long as possible. "There will be a right time and a right place," he said.

"And you'll be the one to decide?"

"We'll both agree," Edward said. He reached into his pocket and pulled out a small wrapped package and placed it on the dashboard of the car. It was enough to distract her.

"What is that?"

"Your birthday gift," he said.

Her eyebrow arched as she examined it coolly. "What is it?"

"Open it and find out. Or don't. It's entirely up to you."

Grudgingly, she snatched up the box and tore the paper off. She opened the box and inside found a garnet necklace and earrings to match the ring he'd given her the Christmas her mother had died.

"They aren't diamonds or pearls, but I promise that some-day they will be."

Grace smiled as she ran her fingers over the deep red

stones. "I don't need diamonds," she murmured. "These are perfectly beautiful."

Edward reached out and plucked the necklace from the box, then fastened it around her neck. Grace had never asked for much more than his affection and his company. And Edward wasn't sure whether he'd ever be able to buy her expensive gifts. But he would always do his best to make her happy.

She leaned over and kissed him, her lips lingering against his, her tongue slipping along the crease of his mouth. "Come on," he murmured. "It's about time I teach you how to drive in reverse."

12 March 1846

> Nearly a year has passed since my wedding day and I have wondered at how my world has changed so much. I look back through his diary and I see all that I have had to bear, all that we in Ireland have suffered. The government has brought some relief, offering jobs to the poor. And there is some food, corn that they have brought from America. But it is hard to tolerate and does not satisfy as potatoes do. We all pray that the new crop will bring an end to this terrible time and we may all fill our bellies again. I send my love to Michael as the wind blows west. I hope that his letter arrives before the baby is born and that my child and I will soon call America our home.

Grace lay back on the blanket they'd spread out in the hay mow, then stared up at the ceiling of the stable, clutching the diary to her chest. "Life was so different for her. So difficult. Sometimes it's hard to imagine that I would ever face such uncertainty."

Edward stretched out beside her, his arm resting around her waist. He nuzzled his face into her neck and sighed. "What happens to her? Does she live?"

"Of course. If she hadn't lived then I wouldn't be here."

It was a warm spring day outside and the sun shone through the high windows above the hay mow, the rays illuminating dust motes in the air. It had become their spot, the place where they met when they wanted to be alone. It had become easier as of late to sneak away. Edward's father spent very little time at home during the day and his mother had become more dependent on her medicine to keep her calm. Though it did that, it also made her sleep most of the afternoon away, leaving Grace free to do as she pleased.

She suspected that the servants knew what was going on, but no one had said anything to her. Though Lord Porter paid their salaries, they were fiercely loyal to each other. As long as Grace finished her work by the end of the day, Cook didn't question her occasional absences from the kitchen or the laundry. Besides, there was far less work to do now that the Porter's had purchased a new electric washing machine. It did Grace's work in half the time with little effort on her part.

She rolled over on her stomach and turned to the next entry in the diary. "Would you like to hear more?"

Edward smiled as he drew her closer. "No. I'd rather you kiss me."

Grace was happy to oblige. She set the diary aside and rolled over, stretching out on top of him. They had the whole afternoon and evening together. Lord and Lady Porter had gone to Dublin to attend the wedding of the son of one of Lord Porter's business partners. The moment they'd left, Grace and Edward had raced to the stables, tumbling into the hay and kissing each other until they'd both had their fill.

"I could stay here all night and all day," she murmured. Grace smoothed her palm over Edward's chest, working open the buttons on his shirt as she went along. When they were undone, she brushed aside the fabric then placed a kiss on the tiny patch of hair just below his collarbone. With a playful laugh, she ran her tongue down to his nipple, flicking at it until he moaned softly.

They did as they had done many times before, slowly tugging at clothes, until they could both put their hands on bare skin. His hand cupped her breast and Grace rolled on her back and watched as he pushed her chemise up. His lips trailed kisses over her belly and she sighed as currents of pleasure shot through her body.

Such delightful sin, she mused, wondering how anyone could resist these feelings. She ran her fingers through his hair, guiding him back up to her breasts. They usually stopped after a short time, knowing that there was a line they couldn't afford to cross. Grace knew that girls her age had intimate relations with men. There were plenty of illegitimate Irish babies to prove the point. And she also knew that by giving herself to Edward, she'd risk becoming pregnant. But that didn't stop the wanting and the needing.

Edward rolled on top of her, nestling his hips against hers as he kissed her. He murmured her name softly, running his hands over her body and tearing at her clothes. Grace wasn't sure when she realized that they'd gone past the point of no return. Perhaps it was when he stripped off his shirt or when he rolled down her stockings. But gradually, they rid themselves of their clothes until they lay on the blanket naked.

Grace had expected to be embarrassed, but instead, she found herself fascinated by the details of the naked male form. She'd studied nude sculpture but a living, breathing man was much different. She sat back on her knees and stared down at him.

With a trembling hand, she reached out and touched his shaft, amazed at how smooth and hard it was. This was nothing like Michelangelo's statues, she mused. Was there something wrong with Edward or had modern men somehow evolved to this?

"You've never seen a naked man before," he murmured. "A naked, aroused man?" He took her hand and wrapped her fingers around him.

"Does it hurt?" she said.

"No," he replied. "It doesn't stay like this. It's only this way because I'm…excited." He moved her hand up and down along his length. "If you do that, it feels good."

"Should I do that?" she asked.

He nodded.

"If I do, will I have a baby?"

Edward shook his head. "No. I have to put myself inside you for that to happen."

"I don't think that would fit," she said, growing more confused by the second.

"I would," he said. "Someday, we'll try it and you'll see."

She slowly began to stroke him, watching his face as she did. At first he seemed to enjoy it, a look of rapture settling in his expression. He closed his eyes and tipped his head back, moaning softly. But then, his breathing quickened and Edward pushed up on his elbows and watched what she was doing.

Suddenly, Grace felt nervous, wondering if she was doing something wrong. His breath caught in his throat, once and then again, and he bit his lower lip as a look of pain crossed his face. She stopped and he groaned.

"Don't," he gasped. "Keep going."

"But it's hurting you," she said.

"No, it doesn't hurt."

Grace had to trust him. He was older, he knew what this was all about. Determined to please him, she carried on and when his breathing quickened again, he moved her hand at a quicker pace. She could see she was giving him pleasure but Grace was unsure of how it was happening. And then, suddenly, he cried out. Her hand was wet and she yanked it away, certain that she'd hurt him.

Grace watched as he continued to stroke himself, his body jerking. And then, it was over. He opened his eyes and smiled at her. "You don't have to be afraid. That's supposed to happen. It feels good when it does."

She felt a warm blush creep up her cheeks. "I thought you were dying," she said.

"It feels like it, but then it's the most incredible pleasure, made better because you were doing it to me." He chuckled. "I normally do it to myself."

"Why?"

"Because it feels good. It relaxes me."

Grace considered all the information she'd been given, then nodded. "I liked doing it."

He wrapped his arm around her waist and pulled her down beside him. "Girls can have such pleasures as well. Have you ever touched yourself down there?"

"Oh, no," Grace said, shocked that he would think such a thing. "That would be a sin."

"It's not," Edward assured her. He slid his hand along her belly until it rested between her legs. Then, he slipped his finger deeper, parting the folds of her sex. Grace held her breath as tiny sparks of pleasure shot through her body. This was all so new and so perplexing. But as he continued to touch her, the pleasure intensified.

At first, Grace was afraid to let the feelings go on. She felt dizzy and light-headed, as if she might faint. But at the same time, she didn't want him to stop. Some instinct drove her on. Edward bent over her and took her nipple into his mouth, gently sucking at it.

The pleasure increased and she cried out, raking her hands through his hair. How was this possible, that her body could feel these things and she'd never known? Did every woman learn these secrets? Is this why women couldn't resist men?

Edward slipped his finger inside her and she jumped, the sensation so unusual, so tantalizing. Grace closed her eyes and gave herself over to his touch, pushing aside her fears and insecurities. She trusted Edward. He'd do nothing to hurt her.

Wild new sensations pulsed through her body and Grace arched against his touch, unable to keep herself from wanting more. It was all too wonderful, too overwhelming to resist and as the feelings built inside of her, she understood what Edward had said. It was a bit like dying.

It washed over her like a warm summer rain, her body tensing then dissolving into exquisite spasms. Her eyes flew open and she looked at Edward, stunned by the intensity of the pleasure she was experiencing. And then, the touch that she had craved became too much to bear and she grabbed his hand and pulled it away.

They lay together on the blanket, their arms wrapped around each other, streams of sunshine filtering through the high windows and bathing their bodies in a soft golden light. Grace smiled to herself as she remembered all the strange stories that she'd heard from the kitchen maids and all the conclusions she'd drawn.

Though she hadn't experienced everything with a man, she now understood the fascination. It was better than the feeling she got when she rode her horse over the meadow as fast as he could go. It was better than driving Geneva's car down the road with the accelerator pressed to the floor. It was better than standing in the middle of a summer storm and letting the rain pour down on her body.

"Are you sure what we did won't give me a baby?" she asked.

"Very sure," Edward whispered.

"Then, can we do it again?"

"Right now?"

"Soon," Grace said. "Very soon."

CHAPTER THIRTEEN

GRACE SAT AT THE OLD WOODEN table in the kitchen of Porter Hall, a sack of apples in front of her. They'd picked the first crop from the trees on the west end of the estate and tomorrow, she and Cook were planning to make apple butter. From the parlor, she could hear the sound of the wireless as Edward tuned into the BBC for the Sunday night broadcast.

He'd spent most of the day in his room, his anatomy books spread across his desk as he prepared to enter his third year of university at Trinity. He'd planned to jump ahead on his studies over the summer, but he'd found it difficult between his work at the hospital and the time he spent poring over newspapers for word of the impending war.

Grace had determined to put all the talk of war out of her mind, to worry about it when the worst came to pass. Instead, she chose to focus on the future, on her life with Edward. Lord Porter had finally accepted Edward's choice of schooling, an easier decision after his business prospects had improved considerably since talk of war had begun. Woolen fabric was selling as fast as the Porter Mills could make it and Henry was determined to realize a tidy profit from every bolt that was sold.

She and Edward spent as much time together as they could, still hiding their affection from the rest of the household. But their relationship had become more and more intimate with every day that passed. She was no longer a girl, infatuated with the handsome boy who lived in the manor house. Edward was the man she loved, the man who had touched her heart and her soul. She wanted him to possess her body as well.

Was this what her mother had felt, this undeniable need? She couldn't go a moment without wanting Edward to touch her or to kiss her. There were times when her body felt as if it were on fire and his hands were the only thing that could extinguish it.

"Grace?"

She glanced up and found Edward standing in the doorway, a grim expression on his face.

"What is it?" she asked.

He took a deep breath, then let it out. He slowly crossed the room to stand in front of her. "Chamberlain. He just spoke on the BBC. Britain has declared war against Germany."

Grace felt the blood drain from her face and her ears began to ring. "No," she murmured.

Edward held out his arms and she stood and stepped into his embrace. His fingers found her hair and he wove them through the soft waves as he tipped her face up to his. He kissed her softly and Grace sank against him. Suddenly, there didn't seem to be any need to hide their love for each other. The world had been turned upside down and the only way they could right it was to hold on to each other.

"You won't have to fight," she whispered, her fingers clutching at his shirt. "They won't make you go."

"My country is at war, Grace."

"No!" she said. "Not your country. Ireland isn't at war. Ireland is your country and they'll remain neutral."

He took her face between his hands and kissed her again, his tongue seeking out hers. Even now, with him in her arms, she felt him slipping away. He'd talked about this war for so long, worried over it, wondered when it might happen. And now, it was here and there was nothing she could do to stop it.

"Grace, I—" They both turned to find Cook standing in the kitchen doorway, a stunned expression on her face, her voice dying in her throat.

Grace made to step away, but Edward held tight, his arm wrapped around her waist. He stared at the woman for a long moment, as if exacting a silent promise from her. Cook nodded, then turned and walked away. Edward let out a tightly held breath. "Why am I surprised that she's surprised?" he murmured. "Are we that good at hiding our feelings for each other?"

Grace glanced up at him. "She won't tell."

"I don't care if she does," he said. "I'm not afraid of my father. He can't keep us apart any longer."

"Edward, this is the time we must be the most cautious. We don't know what the future holds."

"It holds you and me, together. This war can't last long. There will be other countries that join us in the fight. Ireland will sooner or later. And once America steps in, there'll be a quick end to all."

"Maybe it will be over before you have to go," she said.

"It won't be over next week," he murmured.

"But you won't leave right away. You'll finish university first."

He shook his head. "They need men now. And I might not be on the front lines. I could end up in a military hospital or working as a medic."

"Yes," she said. "A medic. You could save lives. That's much more important."

"I'll go where they need me."

"Maybe they won't need you. Maybe there will be enough soldiers."

He hugged her hard, then kissed the top of her head. "I should go see if there's more news. Let's keep this between the two of us, all right?"

"You won't tell your parents that you plan to enlist?"

Edward shook his head. "If I go, I'll enlist first and then tell them. Otherwise, they'll try to talk me out of it. It's better they not know for now."

"Why couldn't you have given me the same courtesy?" she murmured.

He reached out and cupped her cheek in his palm. "I love you, Grace. Everything will be all right." He smiled. "Love will find a way."

He walked out of the kitchen, leaving Grace to stand alone and wonder at the speed at which lives could be changed. She hadn't felt so afraid since the night her mother died. She wanted to run and hide, to crawl into her bed and pull the bedcovers up over her head. It was so much easier to pretend that life would never change. But that wasn't the way of the world. Life never stopped changing.

She stared at the bowl of apples on the table, then shoved them away. Suddenly making apple butter didn't seem like the most important thing in the world. Grace walked out of the kitchen toward the parlor. The servants had gathered outside, the sound of the wireless drifting into the hallway. Dennick, Grady, Cook and Sarah, one of the kitchen maids, watched her approach, then made a spot for her.

She could hear Geneva weeping and Lord Porter muttering to himself. Grace fought the urge to walk into the parlor and sit down next to Edward, to take his hand and link her fingers with his. Suddenly, it felt very important to hold on to the one thing in the world she truly loved.

EDWARD DIDN'T BOTHER TO wait until the house was quiet before he snuck up to the third floor. He knocked softly on Grace's door. A moment later, it swung open and she quickly pulled him inside.

"I thought we'd meet in the stable later on," she said.

He shook his head, then grabbed her face between his hands and kissed her. Ever since he'd left her in the kitchen, he'd been thinking about this, about being with her, holding her, kissing her and whispering her name.

He gently pushed her back toward the bed and they fell onto it in a tangle of arms and legs. Grace sighed softly as he rolled her beneath him. "This bed is very small," he murmured.

"We could always go to your room," she replied.

He moved away from her and got to his feet, then held out his hand. "Come. Everyone's gone to bed. We won't be heard."

Grace shook her head. "Let's stay here. I feel safer here." She held out her hand and when he took it, she pulled him back down on top of her. They slowly undressed each other, as they had so many times in the past.

"I've made a decision," he said. "I'm going to finish out one more year of school and then enlist."

Grace drew a deep breath and slowly let it out. "I think that's for the best," she said.

He knew what she was really thinking. That the war would be over in a year and he'd never have to serve. But Edward knew better. "I'm going to spend as much time working at the hospital as I can. And when I come back, I'll only have one year of university left to finish before I can enter medical school."

"Will you fight?"

"I'll go where they need me," he said. "I'm not going to tell my parents, Grace. They would only try to talk me out of it. This is between you and me and no one else."

He reached down and ran his hand over her belly, then cupped her breast in his palm. He'd grown to know her body as well as he knew his own, the sweet curve of her shoulder, the soft skin of her backside, the tantalizing triangle of hair between her legs. It was all perfect and it was his.

As he caressed her, she began to stroke him. But Edward wanted more than just her hands on his sex. He wanted to lose himself inside her body, to push away all thought of what was happening in the world around them and create a world of their own. He reached down to the floor and grabbed his trousers, then took a small packet from the pocket.

"Do you know what this is?" he asked.

Grace shook her head.

He opened the packet, then took the johnny and showed her. He put it on, smoothing it over his penis until he was completely sheathed.

Grace's eyes went wide. "Where did you get that?"

"There's a place that sells them near the university."

"But Jenny, the kitchen maid, said they're against the law."

"You can buy them in London, why not in Dublin?"

She considered his reasoning for a moment. "It's a sin," she said. "The church says it is."

"I want to be close to you tonight. Is that a sin?"

Grace stared down into his eyes and he saw the doubt there. She'd always tried to be a good Catholic and it was very clear how the church felt about these matters. But he also knew how much she wanted to consummate their relationship. They'd come so close so many times and then stopped short. She finally nodded and Edward pulled her down and kissed her.

He'd never made love to a woman before but it all seemed to come so naturally between him and Grace. Settling himself between her legs, he waited until she was ready, then gently pushed inside of her.

Grace held her breath and he withdrew. This time, he moved a bit deeper and when he did, he met resistance. "This may hurt," he whispered. "But only for a moment."

She nodded and he pushed harder, past her virginity, past the remnants of her girlhood. And when he was buried deep inside her, Edward knew that nothing could ever come between them. He and Grace were meant for each other, meant to spend their lives together, meant to live and love and raise a family together.

He began to move again and Grace shifted beneath him. He braced his elbows on either side of her head and stared down at her face. "Tell me how it feels," he murmured.

"Oh," she said as he drove a bit deeper. "Oh, yes. Oh, Edward, it feels so good."

As he began to move faster, she clutched at his shoulders, holding on as tightly as she could. Wrapping her legs around his waist, she moved with him. He felt himself coming close and he slowed his strokes, but Grace would have none of it. She arched beneath him, continuing the rhythm he'd set.

His release came quickly and he drove into her one last time as his body convulsed. They'd waited for so long and it was over so quickly. But Edward couldn't regret that it had happened the way it had. There would be other times to linger, to make her feel the way that he had.

"Are you all right?" he asked.

Grace nodded. "I suppose I understand now why this might be a sin if you're not married." She drew a shaky breath. "Anything that feels that good has to be a sin. Otherwise people would want to do it all the time."

"People do want to do it all the time," Edward said. He rolled over and gathered her in his arms, tucking her backside into his lap and resting his chin on her shoulder. They'd sleep for a short while and then he'd sneak back to his own room before the servants began to stir at dawn.

"I love you," Grace murmured in a sleepy voice.

He ran his hand over her hip, then wrapped it around her waist. "I love you, Grace. I will always love you."

Edward closed his eyes and thought about the days ahead. From this night forward, they would subtract instead of add days together. And then, the night would come when he'd hold her in his arms one last time. He could survive a war knowing that Grace was waiting for him at home. He could walk onto a battlefield and have the courage to fight knowing how much she loved him.

He'd tried to find a reason for his determination to enlist. He'd never been particularly patriotic. Nor did he believe that the British couldn't fight the war without him. But he had a stake in the future of this world, a future that his own children and his children's children would live. He would do what he could to make that future better and safer for them.

He would go to war. And he would return. And in between, Grace's love and devotion and faith would see him through.

CHAPTER FOURTEEN

THE EARLY LIGHT OF DAWN filtered through the tiny window in Grace's attic room and she closed her eyes to block it out. She and Edward hadn't slept at all. They rarely did when they spent the night together. Instead, they'd hold each other for hours, talking about the past and the future, trying to accept that they might be separated for a very long time.

Last night, they'd made love and it had been sweet and slow and gentle. Grace had cried when it was over and Edward had kissed away her tears, promising that he would keep himself safe until it was time to return.

He'd traveled to Belfast by train the previous week and had enlisted in the Royal Army Medical Corps upon the recommendation of his supervising physician at the hospital. A letter had detailed his qualifications and his academic accomplishments and though he'd offered to go where he was needed, he'd immediately been assigned to medic training. His papers had been signed and Edward was told to report for duty in a week's time.

A week had seemed like plenty of time to say goodbye. But their moments together had been stolen, bits and pieces throughout the day when his parents weren't looking, a night in her room and another in the stable.

Grace's growing distress was noticed by both Cook and

Dennick, and they questioned whether she might be coming down with an illness. She wanted to tell them how her heart was breaking, how a part of her soul was about to disappear into the early morning light. But she'd kept her promise to Edward.

Grace had begged him to tell his parents, to give them a chance to say a proper goodbye, but he'd decided to write them a letter and leave it on his father's desk. In truth, she'd hoped they might try to dissuade him or engage in an argument that would make him reconsider leaving. But in the end, she knew nothing could change his mind.

So much had happened since that night last September when war had been declared. Poland had been occupied by both the Germans and the Russians, and the war escalated from there. Civilians began to flee London in anticipation of a German bombing campaign and the British government began a rationing program. By winter's end, the Nazis had invaded Denmark, Norway, France, Belgium, Luxembourg and the Netherlands. And just two days ago, Hitler had arrived in Paris.

Though the British Empire was at war, America continued to maintain its neutrality, as did Ireland. In truth, the politicians in Ireland had been using the war as a means of driving a greater wedge in between the Irish and their former occupiers, the British. Before war had even been declared by England, the Irish government had recognized the Franco regime in Spain and de Valera had met with Mussolini in Italy.

Lord Craigavon, the prime minister of Northern Ireland, had called the government's insistence on neutrality cowardly. Two days later, de Valera announced that all references to the King of England and the government of Great Britain would be erased from Irish passports.

The chaos seemed to feed upon itself, each day new battle lines were drawn. Grace had never paid much attention to the politics of Britain and Ireland, but she'd begun to read the papers in earnest, hoping to make sense of it for Edward's sake.

"I should go," he murmured, pressing his lips to her forehead.

They'd said goodbye twice already and still, she wasn't able to let go. But with the sun quickly rising, he couldn't stay much longer. Grace sat up in bed, pulling the sheet up over her naked body. But Edward gently tugged it down. "I want to remember you just like this," he said.

Grace stretched across the bed and reached into a small drawer in her nightstand. She opened the cover of the diary and withdrew a photograph, then handed it to him. "Cook took it last summer," she murmured. Grace had been working in the garden. She wore a pretty cotton dress and a straw hat and was kneeling in front of a beautiful blooming rose bush. "This is how I want you to remember me."

Edward stared at the picture for a long moment. "You're beautiful, Grace. You are and always will be the most beautiful woman I've ever known."

Grace wrapped her arms around his neck and kissed him, a soft, sweet, lingering kiss that she hoped would last forever. "You have to go," she said, finally resigned to the fact that she couldn't stop him.

Edward nodded, then crawled out of her bed and began to pull on his clothes. She grabbed the simple cotton dress she'd worn the night before and pulled it over her head. And when he walked to the door, she followed, her fingers tangled in his, her free hand holding tight to his arm.

They walked through the silent house and through the kitchens to the courtyard. His car was parked behind the coach house, his bags already in the boot. Edward stood next to the car, then reached into his pocket and handed her an envelope. "Would you put that on my father's desk?" he asked.

Grace nodded.

"And tell my mother that I will come back as soon as I can. I'll probably get a furlough at some point."

Grace wrapped her arms around his neck, unable to stop the tears from falling. "I don't want you to go," she said, her voice tight with emotion.

"I know," he said. "I know."

"You'll keep yourself safe, won't you? You won't try to act the hero."

He chuckled softly, then kissed her mouth. The sound of footsteps on the gravel drive caused them both to turn and they saw Cook and Dennick approaching. Edward sighed softly and looked down at Grace. "I didn't tell them," she murmured. "I swear."

Dennick handed Edward a small envelope. "This arrived late last night," he said. "After you'd retired. I managed to keep it from your father."

Edward opened the envelope and withdrew a telegram. "It's from the surgeon I worked for in the hospital. He's enlisted as well and requests that I serve with his unit as a medical support officer." He glanced up at Dennick. "Thank you."

"Good luck, Master Edward," Dennick said.

Edward held out his hand. "It's just Edward, Dennick."

Dennick shook his hand. "I'll keep forwarding your letters to Miss Grace. And if you'd like, I can drive you to the train and bring your car back."

"I'd like that," Edward said.

Cook held out a paper bag. "For the trip. Cakes and biscuits and some ham and bread. Better than the food you'll find on the train." She brushed a tear from her eye, then turned and hurried back to the house. Dennick climbed into the car and waited while Edward drew Grace aside.

"I'll be back before you know it," he said.

"And I'll be here, waiting for you." She placed her hand on his cheek then pushed up on her toes and kissed him gently. "I love you."

"I love you." Edward took one last long look at Grace, letting her image burn into his brain so that it might stay there for a very long time. Then, he turned and walked to the car. He tried not to look back, knowing that it would be difficult to control his emotions. But in the end, he hung out the car window and waved to her.

She stood in front of the coach house, her arms wrapped tightly around herself, a sad smile curving the corners of her mouth. Just before the car turned out onto the road, she raised her hand and waved.

He'd left her behind many other times, when he'd gone to Harrow, when he'd traveled to Europe and then to America. But he'd always known he'd be coming back. He didn't know that now, but he'd have to believe it with all his heart. He and Grace would have a future together. They'd been destined for each other from the moment he'd first seen her beneath the dirty blanket at Christ Church cathedral. She was his.

EDWARD STARED DOWN AT THE blank piece of military stationery, the fountain pen poised in his hand. He'd just finished a double shift and was ready to fall into his cot and sleep. But he'd been anxious to write to Grace all day and hadn't found a free minute to put pen to paper.

He'd been in the western desert of North Africa for two months now, arriving in early December when the offensive against the Italians began. The field hospital where he worked was nothing more than a collection of canvas tents which could be moved at a moment's notice, progressing forward with each battle won. Bardia and Tobruk had been recaptured from the Italians and the British and Australians had pushed them back to Beda Fomm, where the Italian Tenth Army had tried to make its escape. Fierce fighting had raged for the past three days and the wounded had been arriving hourly in jeeps and truck and ambulances.

He glanced around at the large medical tent, lined with soldiers lying on small canvas cots. Those unable to go back to their units would be evacuated to a hospital ship in the Mediterranean and then returned to England. The others would walk back onto the battlefield. He rubbed his eyes as he thought about going home. He'd been away for eight months, yet it seemed like eight years.

Though he'd taken on a great many jobs at the field hospital, his primary responsibility was to assist the surgeons in the operating theatre. Edward was amazed at what he'd learned over the three months, the types of surgeries he'd watched and participated in, the surgical responsibilities he was given when the other surgeons were too busy.

It was a better education in trauma surgery than any medical school could ever provide. But it was also difficult to bear. Though they managed to save a decent percentage of the patients that came to them, the most seriously wounded died a slow death from internal bleeding or massive infection. In a city hospital, the success rate might have been better. But in the middle of nowhere, they were working under difficult conditions with insufficient supplies and not enough support staff.

He closed his eyes, then took a deep breath. He'd seen so many men die. Though the field medics tried to save everyone, they often were overly optimistic about the capabilities of the hospital surgeons. If Edward had learned anything, it was that surgeons were human, unable to work miracles on demand.

He picked up Grace's latest letter and smoothed his finger over the address she'd printed on the envelope. When the mail found him, he'd tried to catch up on life back in Ireland. But letters arrived only sporadically, so he was never sure what was really happening at home.

He tried to imagine the very moment she'd written his name across the front of the envelope. What had she been wearing? Had her hair been pulled back in a ribbon or was it hanging loose on her shoulders? Did she smell of rosewater perfume or that face cream that she liked to use at night?

There were times when, if he focused very hard, he could almost feel Grace's skin beneath his palms. It was in those moments that he knew he'd be able to go on. She was waiting for him at home.

He pulled the letter from the envelope and reread it, then set it down on the desk in front of him. He'd expected one of her chatty letters, filled with news about day-to-day life at Porter Hall. Grace avoided talk of the war, even though the news had told of terrible horrors on the homefront. Britain had been under siege with bombing raids by the Luftwaffe, the attacks leveling neighborhoods in many large cities. Instead, Grace spoke of the new colt that had been born to Violet and the roses that she'd nursed back to health in his mother's garden.

But the final part of her letter brought disturbing news. Malcolm had returned to Porter Hall with his wife, Isabelle, and their infant son at Christmas. Isabelle had been frightened by the air raids over England and felt neutral Ireland would be a more suitable place to wait out the war. Their father had welcomed his eldest back with open arms, ready to hand him responsibility for the mills and mines that had begun to prosper during war time.

According to Grace, Lord Henry Porter was now far more

interested in drinking the day away than putting in a long day at the office. There had been several occasions when he'd gotten so drunk he'd forgotten where he'd been and what he'd done. He'd been banned from three of the local pubs and many of his friends and business associates had fallen away, unable to deal with his temperamental moods.

The news about Edward's mother wasn't much better. She'd taken his enlistment very badly and spent most of her days sitting in front of the wireless. Every bit of news was discussed over and over again until she'd work herself into a frenzy. Then, Grace would closet Geneva in her room for three or four days and try to draw her back to a rational state.

He didn't have to hear Grace's voice or see her face to know that she was troubled. And he felt powerless to do anything from where he was. He could write to Malcolm and beg his indulgence, but he and his brother hadn't communicated at all since the Christmas party at Porter Hall over five years ago. Edward doubted that his brother's feelings for Grace had changed in that time.

It wasn't Grace he was most worried about. If things got intolerable, she could leave. He'd sent most of his pay to her in care of Dennick and he'd been assured that she had put it all in the bank, along with her own. His mother was the one who was most vulnerable.

Malcolm had always exerted a great deal of influence on their father. And in his drunken state, Lord Porter could be convinced to do almost anything. Malcolm wouldn't think twice about tossing his mother into a hospital and leaving her there, seeing a chance to settle old scores.

Edward had gone over and over it in his mind, but he couldn't think of a way to protect his mother. He'd thought to encourage her to visit her sister in America for the duration of the war, but ocean travel had become risky with all the U-boat activity in the Atlantic. Though military ships were usually the target, civilian ships had also been sunk.

"Lieutenant Porter?"

Edward turned to see Major Farraday standing at the entrance to the tent, dressed in his surgical gown, his mask hanging from around his neck. Edward stood and saluted. "Major."

"I've been meaning to talk to you all day, but haven't had the chance." He glanced down at the desk. "Writing a letter to your girl?"

Edward nodded. "Yes, sir."

"You can drop the sir," the major said. "I'm going home. I'm being rotated back to a military hospital in England. I'm allowed to take three staff members with me and I was wondering if you'd be interested. You're going to be a fine surgeon someday and I'd like to say that I had something to do with that. There are a lot of things I can teach you once we both return to Dublin."

Edward considered the offer for a long moment, then shook his head. "If it's all the same to you, I think I'd prefer to stay here. We've got the Italians on the run and I'd like to see this through to the end. The work I do here makes a difference. I'm not sure anyone could do it any better."

Farraday clapped him on the shoulder. "That's what I like about you, Edward. You have the unflinching confidence of a surgeon. Don't ever lose that. It will make you great."

"Thank you, sir." They shook hands and Edward watched as Farraday walked out of the ward. A sliver of guilt pricked at his heart, but he ignored it. He ought to have accepted the offer. A military hospital in England was a far safer posting than a field hospital just twenty kilometers from the fighting.

But he'd still be miles away from Grace, so what did it

really matter? He was doing some good here and learning more than he'd ever learn in a regular hospital.

He sat back down at the desk and picked up his pen. But he'd barely written a greeting when an orderly rushed in. "Lieutenant Porter, we have wounded arriving. Major Percy had to take a patient back into surgery, so he's asked that you sort them as they come in. Major Farraday will be waiting in the operating theater."

"Thank you, Private."

Edward tucked the letters in his journal, then placed the book in the top drawer of the desk. He glanced once around the tent, then walked out into the chilly night air. The desert was supposed to be hot and dry and it was, during the day. But the nights were chilly, as cold as Ireland in the winter.

A few minutes later, the ambulances rolled up. Medics jumped out and began to unload the stretchers, giving him a quick summary of a soldier's condition before moving on. "We've got an officer here," one of the field medics shouted.

"I'm all right," the officer shouted, pushing up on his elbows. "Take care of my men first."

Edward recognized the voice immediately and he hurried over to the spot beside the lead ambulance. "Miles? Is that you?"

"Jesus, Edward." Miles sat up and held out his hand. "Edward Porter. What the bloody hell are you doing here?"

"Taking care of your men," he said as he lifted the dressing from Miles's leg. "This doesn't look too bad. The bleeding is minimal." He touched Miles's toes and found them warm.

"A bit of shrapnel in the leg, that's all. Tend to the others. I'll be here when you're finished."

Edward grabbed the medic and asked if he'd move Miles inside a nearby tent. "He'll be fine. Ask one of the orderlies to fetch him a dram of whiskey and tell him there will be no serving wenches to bring him more." The medic frowned. "He'll know what I mean."

For the next three hours, Edward sorted and prioritized the wounded soldiers. Those given Priority 1 were moved immediately to surgery. Priority 2 and 3 were less urgent. Priority 4 were taken to a quiet tent where they could die in peace for they were already too far gone to be helped.

Only two of the twenty-seven soldiers that had arrived with Miles were given Priority 4 status and left to die. By the time dawn broke, all of the most seriously injured were in surgery. Edward walked back to the tent and found Miles where the medic had left him. He'd managed to locate an entire bottle of whiskey and he was sipping at it.

"Remind me to have all my wounds treated here," he said, waving the bottle at Edward. "I prefer your medicine to that nasty sulfa powder they keep pushing at the other field hospital."

"How are you doing?" Edward squatted down and pulled the dressing away. He waved to an orderly, who hurried up with a bowl of warm water and some dressings. Edward tore the leg of Miles's uniform up to the knee and began to wash the dried blood from his calf.

"How are my men?"

"You lost two," Edward said. "Another two are in critical condition but it looks like they'll pull through. The rest were just minor or superficial wounds."

Miles laid back on the stretcher and sighed. "This thing is almost over," he said. "We've got the Italians surrounded. They'll surrender soon."

"Then what?" Edward asked.

"I don't know," Miles said. "I'm an officer in the British Seventh Armoured Division. I go where they tell me to go."

Edward examined the wound on Miles's leg. "And if they tell you to go home?"

"This is were I belong," Miles replied. "I'm a soldier. I guess my father knew what he was doing when he sent me to Sandhurst." He chuckled softly. "Besides, I don't have anyone waiting at home for me. What about you? Are you married?"

"No," Edward murmured. "But there is someone who's waiting." He sighed. "Earlier tonight, I had an offer to go back to England, to work in a military hospital there."

"You're going, right?"

Edward shook his head. "No. I'm like you. I'm going to stay until the job is finished. She'll be there when I get home."

"What's her name?"

"Her name is Grace," Edward said. He loved to hear the sound of her name on his lips. "Grace," he repeated.

"Ah, yes," Miles said. "The luminous one."

Edward frowned, then remembered the conversation they'd had in the pub four years ago. He chuckled softly. "That's the one."

CHAPTER FIFTEEN

GRACE STARED DOWN AT THE copy of the *Irish Times* she'd spread on the kitchen table. She rubbed at her eyes, then tried to focus on the story she was reading. Though Ireland had maintained its neutrality, the war had managed to come to Ireland. The papers were filled with news of Irish citizens being killed in Europe, in England, in the north, and on the Atlantic.

Neutrality had come at a price. German bombers and fighter planes had been crossing the Irish Sea regularly to land on neutral soil when they weren't able to make it back to the continent. Yet these very same planes were killing Irishmen who served with the Royal Army in North Africa. Grace couldn't reconcile the two, couldn't understand why her country wouldn't come to the aid of the man she loved.

In April, the Belfast Blitz had nearly destroyed the northern capital. Two hundred German bombers attacked and more than one thousand people died. Of those left, a quarter were homeless. The bombing of Belfast had scared them all. Isabelle had insisted on blackout curtains, certain that an errant German bomber would drop a bomb on Porter Hall. Malcolm had derided her for her fears and then, on the night of the thirtieth of May, 1941, the Germans bombed Dublin.

The Germans later claimed it was a mistake, but there were those in Ireland who believed it had been retribution for Irish help in putting out the fires from the Belfast Blitz. One of the German ambassadors even claimed that the bombing was carried out by British pilots in captured German aircraft.

That night, the Porters and their servants had listened to the distant sound of explosions and watched as the night sky was illuminated by the fires. Thirty-four people had been killed and the realities of the war had been brought home.

Day-to-day life at Porter Hall hadn't changed a great deal. Isabelle now ran the household as Geneva retreated further and further into a world of her own. Lord Porter was drunk for most of his waking hours, but Malcolm had stepped in and taken over the family's business interests.

Malcolm Porter hadn't changed much over the years except to become crueler. When he wasn't railing over the Irish and their lazy, good-for-nothing work ethic, he was berating his wife or his mother or scolding his small son. Grace had managed to stay out of his way for the most part, but it had only been with the help of Cook and Dennick.

"Lady Porter is calling for her tea," Cook said as she walked into the kitchen. "Perhaps you can convince her to have a bath. Since Malcolm sacked her maid, she hasn't been keeping herself very tidy."

Geneva's maid had been the third servant girl sacked at Porter Hall since the beginning of the year. The most recent, Margaret Flynn, had been fired after she had accused Malcolm of raping her in her room late one night. Isabelle immediately leveled accusations of her own, that the girl was trying to extort money from the family with her lies. No one knew whether money had been paid, but the authorities had never been called and Margaret did not return to her position.

Grace had thought seriously about leaving. It was only a matter of time before Malcolm turned his attentions to her.

Every time she entered a room, she felt his eyes following her. And several times, he'd stood behind her, his body just barely touching hers, as if challenging her to resist him. He was like a cat toying with a mouse and Grace was afraid that he would soon grow tired of the game and pounce.

She refolded the newspaper and stood. "I'll see what I can do," Grace said. "If she won't get in the tub, perhaps she will, at least, let me wash her hair."

"We have to do more to keep Lady Porter well," Cook said. "I overheard Malcolm talking about sending her back to the hospital. He was telling Lord Porter about a new doctor in Dublin who administers electric shocks to moderate the moods."

Grace shivered. She was the only one standing between Geneva and that horrible treatment. How could she possibly consider leaving Porter Hall now? "I'll talk to her," Grace said.

Cook smiled, then reached in her apron pocket. "And here is a bit of good news for you." She held out an envelope and Grace recognized the familiar military stationery that Edward used. "Dennick slipped it to me before he left with Lord Porter."

Grace snatched it from Cook's fingers, then tucked it in her own apron pocket.

"Look at the postmark," Cook urged.

She pulled it out again. "London? This is from London." Tears flooded Grace's eyes and she bit her bottom lip, trying to control the emotion. "He's not in Africa anymore."

"That is good news," Cook said, giving Grace a hug.

Grace quickly prepared the tea tray. A letter would no doubt arrive soon for the Porters and once Geneva heard the news, her spirits would be lifted. Edward was safe, and he was home. Surely he'd be returning to Ireland soon.

She climbed one flight of the servant's stairs and turned down the hallway to Geneva's room. But she was stopped by

Malcolm, who stood in front of Geneva's door, his shoulder braced on the doorjamb.

He chuckled softly, yet Grace could detect no humor in the sound. "It is beyond me why you continue to treat her like a lady," he muttered. "You'd be better off pouring that tea over her head than down her throat. She hasn't bathed in days."

"I was just about to draw a bath for her," Grace murmured.

"You were, were you?" Malcolm leaned forward until his face was just inches from hers. She could smell the whiskey on his breath and she turned away. "Tell me, when do you bathe, Grace? And do you take all your clothes off? I'd like to be informed so that I might watch on occasion."

"Step aside," Grace murmured. "Your mother is expecting her tea."

He reached out and ran a finger along her cheek. "I could never understand why my brother found you so fascinating. But I must admit I'm coming to appreciate your…special qualities." He dragged his finger across her bottom lip. "And your spirit."

"If you touch me again, I'll tell Isabelle," Grace threatened, meeting his gaze directly.

"Do that and you'll be out on the street, right back where you came from." He grinned, then stepped aside. "And then where would my poor, poor mother be without her darling Charlotte? Perhaps a psychiatric hospital? Or maybe an insane asylum might be a better choice? But then, I've always prescribed to the notion that when an animal is sick, you put it down."

Grace balanced the tea tray on her arm and opened Geneva's door, then stepped inside. When she closed the door behind her, she leaned back against it, breathing deeply to still the pounding of her heart. Would Malcolm really try to do his mother harm? She believed he was evil, but Grace couldn't believe he'd actually commit murder.

She drew another breath and waited until her hands stopped trembling before she crossed the room to the bed. Geneva lay on her side, curled into a tight ball, the bedcovers pulled up to her nose. "I've brought you tea," Grace said softly.

She set the tray on the table, then gently drew the covers back. Geneva's once-beautiful hair was tangled in a mass of knots and she'd bitten her fingernails down to the quick. Her skin looked sallow and wrinkled, making her appear much older than she actually was.

Grace reached out and smoothed her hand over Geneva's hair. "Wouldn't it be nice to have a bath?" she said. "You can soak in a hot tub and then I'll get you all powdered and perfumed and we'll go downstairs for dinner." Geneva didn't react. "Wouldn't you like that, Mother? Would you do that for your Charlotte?"

Lady Porter slowly turned and looked at Grace. "You're not Charlotte," she muttered.

"Of course not," Grace replied. "But Charlotte is watching you from heaven and I'm sure she would like to see you clean and pretty again. She wouldn't want her mother to be so unhappy. Would you like a bath, Lady Porter?"

She shook her head. "I just want to sleep."

"There is another reason to get out of bed. I have a feeling that Master Edward might be coming home soon."

"How do you know?"

"I don't. Not for certain. It's just a feeling."

This seemed to stir Geneva, and she slowly sat up and brushed her hair out of her eyes. "I haven't seen Edward in such a very long time."

"Then we must make you beautiful again, so that when he

comes home he will know that you've been well." Grace stood beside the bed and helped Geneva to her feet. "There," she cooed. "You look better already."

She walked with Lady Porter to the adjoining bath and turned on the faucets to fill the tub. Then she stripped off Geneva's night gown and helped her into the tub. "See," she murmured. "Doesn't that feel better?

Had Geneva been well, then perhaps Grace could have thought of herself first. But she had always cared for Lady Porter. Geneva had done so much for her over the years. And she owed it to Edward to watch after his mother for as along as he was gone. For if she didn't, who else would?

EDWARD STOOD ON THE DECK of the military transport ship, watching as the crew secured the vessel to the Belfast dock. He'd spent the last two hours on deck, watching as Ireland grew larger and larger on the horizon, his anticipation growing.

He'd been in England for nearly a month now, stationed at a military hospital just outside London. Though he hadn't expected to return, he'd been chosen to accompany a British Major General who had been wounded at El Alamein, fighting Rommel and his Afrika Korps. The officer needed 24-hour-a-day care on the hospital ship and Edward had accepted the assignment, knowing it might give him a chance to see Grace again.

He'd thought about writing to his parents and letting them know he'd be back in England. But he didn't want anything to interfere with seeing Grace. He'd managed a three-day furlough and had cabled Dennick and asked that he make arrangements for Grace to get to Belfast. With a day of travel each way, he'd have twenty-four hours, which after two years apart, seemed like an eternity.

Edward wasn't even sure she'd be there. He'd had to leave England before a return cable could be sent. But he was willing to take the chance for just one night with the woman he loved. He reached into his shirt pocket and pulled out the photograph she'd given him the morning he'd left. It was tattered and faded, but he didn't care. They would take another photo in Belfast, the two of them together, and he'd carry that for the remainder of the war.

When the British and Australians had routed the Italian army out of North Africa, everyone had thought it would be the end of the campaign. But Hitler had decided that North Africa was far too strategic to give up without a decent fight. He sent Rommel and his panzer tanks to back up the Italians and the battle had begun again in earnest.

He'd seen Miles a few times in the months before he'd returned, relieved that his friend was still alive. Miles had been promoted to Major and now commanded a forward squadron of the Seventh Armoured Division. And when Miles had asked if Edward would be interested in training field medics in his battalion, Edward hadn't thought twice.

He'd grown frustrated, sitting at the field hospital, waiting for the wounded to come to him. With some simple changes in battlefield care, Edward was certain he could increase the rate of survival for wounded soldiers. Miles had introduced him to the Lieutenant Colonel who commanded the battalion and a transfer had been arranged. When he returned to North Africa, he would no longer be kilometers behind the battles, he'd be with the soldiers who were fighting and the medics who cared for them.

A long, low whistle sounded and Edward grabbed his kit bag and hoisted it over his shoulder. He'd managed to find a small hotel that hadn't been damaged in the Blitz and reserved a room for Grace. As he walked down the gangplank, Edward said a silent prayer that she'd be there waiting.

He hopped a bus into the center of Belfast and was stunned at the devastation the Germans had wreaked on the city. All around him, buildings had been turned to a mass of rubble. Some streets were still just barely passable and some were untouched. The Blitz had finally ended over a year ago with the Luftwaffe incapable of penetrating airborne British radar and antiaircraft guns.

He found the hotel after hopping a second bus. When he arrived, it was nearly two in the afternoon, two hours later than he'd intended. Edward strode across the street, avoiding a lorry carrying a load of rubble, then walked into the small lobby.

He saw her almost immediately and for a long moment, they stared at each other, unable to move. Then she slowly stood and walked toward him. Edward removed his cap and dropped his kit bag, then covered the distance between them in three long strides. He pulled Grace into his arms and kissed her, his mouth finding hers as if by instinct.

Running his fingers through her hair, he dislodged the hairpins that held the strands in place and when he finally stepped back to look at her, she looked as if she'd just rolled out of bed. All the feelings came back full force and he couldn't help but smile. "You're beautiful," he murmured.

"I can't believe you're here." Grace's hands smoothed over the front of his jacket, her fingers toying with the brass buttons. "You look wonderful. Older." She touched his face. "But just as handsome."

He kissed her again, this time lingering over her mouth with his tongue. He'd dreamed of this moment for months and now that she was in his arms again, he wondered how he'd ever been able to get by without her. "Have you registered?"

Grace nodded. "I told them I was Mrs. Porter. I wasn't certain they'd let me in the room if they thought we were unmarried."

"It wouldn't have made a difference," Edward said.

"I suppose they get a lot of soldiers and their—"

"No," he interrupted. "It wouldn't have made a difference because we're going to get married. Right now. There's a registry office just down the street." He dropped to one knee and held tight to her hand, then looked up into Grace's eyes. "Mary Grace Byrne, I've loved you for as long as I can remember. And I'd be honored if you'd agree to be my wife."

Tears swam in her eyes and she nodded, pulling him back up to his feet. "Of course I will."

"Then let's do it. Let's spend what little time we have together as husband and wife."

"How long do we have?" she asked.

He kissed her softly. "Not long," he murmured. "Not very long at all."

"After this war is over, we'll have the rest of our lives," Grace said.

Edward left his kit bag with the desk attendant and he and Grace ventured out into the city. He'd wanted to buy her a wedding band, but Grace had insisted that they use the garnet ring he'd given her as a gift so many years before. They did stop at a jeweler to buy a plain gold band for Edward, before making their way to the registry office.

As they walked in the door, Grace stopped and turned to him. "We can't marry. We haven't posted the banns," she said.

"I arranged for a special license," Edward said. "It was posted three weeks ago."

"How did you do that?" Grace asked.

"Dr. Farraday helped. He called a Major General, an old friend of his, and he was able to smooth the way. They've had to make some exceptions to the rules for soldiers on leave. We will be legally married, so there will be no backing out, Grace. You don't mind that it's a civil ceremony, do you?"

Grace shook her head. "I just want to be your wife. I don't care how it happens."

An hour later, they walked out of the registry office as husband and wife. Edward had tucked the marriage certificate into his jacket pocket and when they returned to the hotel and asked for the room key, he was prepared to show proof that they were indeed married. The desk attendant simply slid the key across the counter and nodded, then went back to reading his newspaper.

The moment he closed the door behind them, they came together, tearing at each other's clothes until they stood naked. As he buried his face in the curve of her neck, Grace wrapped her fingers around his shaft and began to stroke him, knowing exactly what would please him. Until that moment, he hadn't realized how much he craved her touch.

Edward reached down and gently pulled her hand away. "I think we'd better go slow," he said. "It's been a long time and I don't want to finish too quickly." He pulled her along to the bed and they stretched out on top of the coverlet, their legs tangling together, their hands skimming over naked skin.

"I've thought about this so many times," Edward murmured, trailing kisses across her breasts. "I'd close my eyes at night and you'd be there, above me, around me."

Grace crawled on top of him. "Above you," she repeated, straddling his waist. She grabbed him and guided him to her entrance, then slowly sank down on top of him, taking in each inch with exquisite leisure. "Around you," she murmured.

The simple act of slipping inside her again nearly drove him over the edge. Edward knew they ought to stop, to get the condoms from his kitbag. But the feeling of their bodies in such intimate contact put all rational thought from his mind. Grace began to move, drawing him in and out of her in a delicious rhythm.

He reached between them both to touch her and her breath caught in surprise. A tiny moan slipped from her lips and she moved faster. Wild sensations raced through his body and Edward fought to maintain control. When Grace shuddered above him, he waited, urging her on to completion. And then he yanked her down on top of him, kissing her deeply as he lost himself inside her.

They lay together for a long time, gasping for breath. Edward slowly ran his hands through her hair, trying to memorize the feel of her skin against his. He would want to keep this memory for later, so he might bring it to mind and savor it all over again. It had been different than the last time they made love, not because of what they'd done, but because the bond between them had been strengthened.

He dropped a soft kiss on her lips, then ran his tongue along the crease of her mouth. She laughed softly, then did the same to him. "I don't think we should leave this room," she said. "We can send for our dinner and spend the rest of the night naked."

"This is our honeymoon, Mrs. Porter, and whatever you want, I'd be more than happy to provide."

CHAPTER SIXTEEN

GRACE STARED OUT THE WINDOW of the train as the Irish countryside passed by. She closed her eyes and thought about the last few moments she'd spent with her husband, trying to recall each detail, the words spoken, the kisses shared.

A fresh round of tears threatened and she swallowed them back. They'd spent the entire night together making love, losing themselves in the pleasures of the flesh. Edward had almost managed to make her forget that their time together was limited. It was only in the morning that she found out how quickly it had gone.

They'd enjoyed a single day together. He was scheduled to catch another troop transport from Belfast that evening and rather than leave her alone in the city for another night, he'd accompanied her to the train station to catch the late train back to Dublin.

They'd stood on the platform, holding each other, for a very long time. Grace had wept, unable to put her feelings into words. Her heart ached and her soul felt as if it were being torn from her body. And in the end, he kissed her once, a sweet, deep kiss, then turned and walked away.

Grace glanced down at the handbag resting in her lap. She opened the clasp and withdrew the marriage certificate. She was his wife now and she would learn to bear the separation like thousands of other wives had. She must focus on the future, on the life they'd share after the war, on the family they'd have and the home they'd build together.

Grace tucked the certificate back into her purse. She and Edward had talked about how she'd break the news to his parents. Edward had wanted to ring them up from Belfast and tell them personally, but Grace had thought it best to keep the news to themselves for a time.

There would no doubt be accusations and anger. Lord Porter would probably do his best to have the marriage annulled, though Edward would testify that it had been legal and consummated. Grace had been afraid that Malcolm might see fit to put her out entirely. He had no loyalty to Edward and therefore, no responsibility to Edward's wife. And with Geneva in such a vulnerable state, neither Grace nor Edward was willing to risk leaving her without an ally at Porter Hall.

In the end, they'd agreed that Grace would break the news when the time was right. Before they had left for the station, Edward had written a letter to his father that Grace would pass along at that time, explaining their decision and his wishes for Grace's treatment in the household.

He'd also given her a banknote, making her promise that she would open an account at a Dublin bank and send him the account number. Edward would forward his pay to the account for the duration of his service and if she ever needed to leave Porter Hall, she'd have the means to do it. Along with the money that Edward had sent her through Dennick, Grace finally felt as though she had options if life at Porter Hall became to difficult to bear.

Her thoughts skipped to Malcolm and she shivered as she thought of how he might react once he knew the Irish servant girl he hated was now part of his family. If he touched her again, then she would have the right to rebuff him. After all, he would be lusting after his brother's wife, a married woman, a far more serious offense than lusting after a family servant.

The three-hour trip from Belfast to Dublin was over before Grace knew it and when she stepped from the train, she saw Grady standing on the platform. He walked up to her and gave her a hug, then took her bag and led her back through the station. "Edward rang and asked that I come to pick you up," he said. "It was good to hear his voice again."

Grace gave him a weak smile. "Thank you for coming."

They rode back to Porter Hall in silence. When he pulled the car into the driveway, he parked it behind the coach house. "They think you've been tending to a sick neighbor," Grady said. "No one has asked any questions, but if you return with such a sad expression, they might."

She nodded, then pasted a smile on her face. "I'll just be sad on the inside."

"How is Master Edward?" Grady asked.

"He's fine," Grace said. "A bit thin, but healthy."

"And will he spend the rest of the war in England?"

"No," she replied. "He's going back to North Africa soon. He feels he can be of more use there. And he says he's safe behind the lines, so I shouldn't worry."

"I'm sure if Master Edward says that is so, then it is. You'll see, Miss Grace, he'll be home before you know it and this war will become a distant memory in all of our minds."

When she reached the kitchens, Grace kissed Cook on the cheek, then quietly made her way up the servants' stairs to her room on the third floor. She sat down on the bed and closed her eyes, trying to fight the flood of emotion she felt. In the end, she pulled the diary from her beside table and opened it to a familiar page.

22 March 1846

My baby has found her way into this world, a little girl
that I have named Elizabeth after Michael's mother.
She was born beneath a roof, with food in the pantry and
a peat fire burning in the hearth. But I cannot know for
sure whether this will be the way of her life. Though
food is still scarce, it will soon be time to plant a new
garden. I will plant potatoes, but will try other crops as
well. I have heard news that the blight was worse in the
west but I can't imagine how this could be as it was
terrible here in Wexford. Landlords have already put the
poorest of the tenants off the land and they are left to
wander in search of work and the necessities in life. I
am thankful for what I have.

Grace reached down and put her hand on her belly. Was
there a baby growing inside of her? She closed her eyes and
said a silent prayer that there was, that Edward had left her
with a bit of himself. She smiled and thought about how he
might take the news. Though he might be far away, they
would have something wonderful that would connect them,
something that belonged to both of them.

If she was pregnant, then she would know soon. Jane had
given birth to her child in the midst of a famine. If Grace had
to give birth to hers while the world was at war, then she knew
she could survive as well.

"THE DOCTOR IS DUE WITHIN the hour," Cook whispered.
"Malcolm and Lord Porter have been shut inside the library
all day discussing Lady Porter's condition. I fear that they are
going to take her away and we'll never see her again."

Grace reached across the table and placed her hand over Cook's. "We have to do something," she said. "There has to be some way to stop them from doing this."

While the war raged on in Europe, a smaller war had descended on Porter Hall, with secret maneuvers and clandestine battles. Geneva had been "ill" for nearly three months now and Malcolm was impatient with his father's reluctance to institutionalize her. Isabelle had set herself up as the lady of the manor and as such, she felt the family's social status was being undermined by Geneva's condition.

No one called, invitations to parties and receptions had all but dried up, and Isabelle had found herself excluded from polite English society in Dublin. No one had bothered to tell her that with a war going on in the home country, the family's English friends had severely curtailed their social engagements. And Isabelle's haughty ways had not endeared her to a population of Anglo-Irish who had learned that their future wealth depended upon dealing with the Irish instead of simply demeaning them.

"When will they take her?" Grace asked.

"Malcolm wants her gone by week's end," Dennick replied. "We must contact Master Edward. Is he still in England? Can we send a cable?"

"I don't know," Grace said. They'd been married six weeks now and Grace had received just one letter from Edward, posted from the hospital near London. Dennick had brought it last week and in it, Edward had told her he would be leaving for North Africa soon. "Perhaps he's still there." She grabbed a scrap of paper and a pencil and wrote down the address of the hospital. "Send a cable. Tell him there is an emergency at home and he needs to return immediately."

"What if he's left already?" Cook said.

"Then we will have to take more drastic action," Grace said.

Dennick frowned. "And what would that be?"

She cleared her throat. "I'll take Lady Porter and we'll go to Dublin or Belfast. We'll find a place to hide until she gets better again. I have a small amount of money saved. It should last five or six months. By then, we will have heard from Edward. He can tell us what to do."

Grace had already made the decision to leave Porter Hall. Three nights ago, a drunken Malcolm had come to her room and tried to get inside. Dennick had installed a lock just a few days before and Grace had been safe. But the next evening, when she'd returned to her rooms, the lock was gone. That night, she'd moved her dresser in front of the door. It was only a matter of time before he tried again and Grace didn't intend to be there when he did.

She reached beneath the kitchen table and touched her stomach. She had more than her own safety to consider now. The time for her monthly flow had come and gone and Grace suspected she was pregnant. A pregnancy complicated her position in the household even more and it just seemed prudent to leave. She'd sent a letter off to Edward just yesterday, telling him of her plans and of her hopes that she might be carrying his child. And though she hadn't thought of taking Geneva with her, it was the best way to protect them both.

"We'll wait and see what the doctor says," Grace suggested. "Meanwhile, we need to pack some things for Geneva and hide them in the coach house. If we leave, we'll have to sneak out in the middle of the night. Malcolm and Lord Henry sleep more soundly when they are drunk so I don't think they'll notice, but Isabelle is always prowling about the house."

"It's a good plan," Dennick said, nodding. He held out the scrap of paper. "I'll drive into town and send the cable."

A loud knock echoed through the house and Grace slowly stood. "That will be the doctor."

Dennick walked out of the kitchen to do his duties at the front door. Grace and Cook stood silently, waiting for him to return. A few moments later he did. In his hand, he clutched a small envelope. His gaze darted back and forth between the envelope and Grace. Grace heard Cook gasp and with a trembling hand, Dennick held out the envelope. His hand shook. "It's a cable from the War Department," he murmured.

Grace felt the breath slowly leave her body. Her legs buckled beneath her and Cook quickly moved to grab her and help her to a chair. "Is it for me?"

"It says Mrs. Edward Porter," Dennick replied. "I'd assume that's you?"

Grace drew a ragged breath, then nodded. "Take it away. I don't want to see it." She stumbled to her feet and snatched it from Dennick's hand, then tossed it toward the hearth.

"There was another delivered for Lord Porter at the same time. I took it to him in the library."

Grace felt the scream build inside of her before she heard the sound. And then it came, a cry so wretched that she didn't recognize it as her own. She collapsed onto the stone floor of the kitchen and wailed, the pain so overwhelming that she was sure it would smother her.

Cook knelt down beside her and held her tight, but Grace fought against her embrace. This couldn't be happening. She'd just seen him and touched him and kissed him. They'd made love and he'd been warm and alive and wonderful.

Dennick picked up the crumpled cable and removed it from the envelope. "Her Majesty's War Department regrets to inform you that Lieutenant Edward Porter is missing and presumed dead. His transport ship, HMS Wildemoor, was sunk by a

German torpedo in the North Atlantic on October third 1942. Survivors were rescued the next day. Lieutenant Porter was not among them. Our deepest sympathies go with you."

Grace moaned and rocked back and forth, the tears flowing in unceasing streams, the stone floor growing damp with them. He had been so careful to stay safe. She'd never considered he might be killed going to or from a battle rather than in it. Vivid images swirled in her head and she pressed her hands to her temples to try to push them away.

Raging fire and icy water. Deep, dark depths and then blackness. Which had claimed her husband's life? Had he thought of her at the very end? Another sob wracked her body as she realized he wouldn't have known he was to be a father. Her letter was probably still somewhere in Ireland.

"Come," Cook said, gently pulling her to her feet. "Dennick will take you up to your room and I'll bring up a pot of tea."

Grace tried to climb the stairs, but her legs felt boneless. In the end, Dennick picked her up and carried her. When he reached her room, he set her gently on the bed, then sat down beside her, stroking her forehead. "I can't know the loss you feel," he murmured. "But I know how much Edward loved you. And that love just doesn't die because one of you is gone. You must call on that love now to get you through this."

"How am I supposed to go on?" Grace said. "We were meant to love each other forever, to grow old together."

"He will never grow old," Dennick said with a quiet smile. "In your mind and in your heart, he will always be that handsome young man who taught you to ride a horse and to drive a car. Who carved those little animals for you."

Tears welled in her eyes again and Dennick bent down and kissed her forehead. "Cook will be up with the tea in just a minute. I'm going to go down and see how Lord Porter and Malcolm are doing."

"Geneva," Grace said, clutching at Dennick's hand. "They can't tell her. Not now. She'd never recover."

"I don't think they'll be sending her away anytime soon. It would look bad and Isabelle is far too concerned with how things look."

She watched as Dennick walked to the door. When she was alone, she rolled over on her side and stared at little shelf full of carved animals that Edward had made for her. Grace stood and grabbed the rabbit with broken ears and clutched it tightly in her hand.

She wanted to go back to that time, when they were so young and life was so simple. If she just wished it hard enough, it would happen. And then, she would do everything in her power to save him from this fate. She closed her eyes tightly and concentrated her thoughts. But when she opened them again, she was still in the dingy attic rooms.

Grace sat down on the edge of the bed, then opened the drawer of her nightstand. She withdrew the diary, then turned to a page she'd read a hundred times over.

7 August 1846

Michael is dead. I write these words but I still cannot believe them. A letter has arrived today from John Cleary. He had first sent a letter to his parents to give to me, but with the famine, they had made their way to America as well. And so he sent another and in it he tells me that my husband has been gone for nearly a year. Michael died onboard ship of a terrible fever three weeks into the voyage and was buried at sea. All along

I have imagined him in America, working for the day
that he might send for me and Elizabeth. But instead,
he has been watching us from heaven. Could he not have
given me a sign? I have waited for word and now it is
come and I cannot bear to hear it. May the Lord have
mercy on us all.

CHAPTER SEVENTEEN

GRACE EXHAUSTED HERSELF WITH weeping, unable to shed any more tears. She lay on her bed until the house around her went silent, the little carved rabbit clutched in her hand. She didn't care how the others were grieving. What difference did it make? She was the only one who loved Edward as deeply and completely as he deserved.

She closed her eyes and tried to sleep, but strange sounds and unbidden images swirled in her head. Once, she thought he was there, beside her, and she bolted up in bed and searched the darkness for him. Cook came in before she went to bed and sat with Grace for a time, but Grace heard nothing she had said. No words could take away the sorrow she felt.

She focused on breathing, taking air in and letting it out, again and again. She'd sent up prayer after prayer, trying to convince God that he'd made a mistake, that he'd meant to take another woman's husband instead of hers. Perhaps Edward was alive and he just hadn't been found, floating on a piece of wreckage or washed up on some distant shore. Perhaps he'd never gotten on the ship. Any moment, he'd open the door and walk inside and everything would be right again.

The hinges of her bedroom door creaked and Grace slowly sat up, brushing the tangled hair from her eyes. "Edward?" A tall, lanky figure stood in the doorway, outlined by the glow from the lights in the hall. Grace rubbed her bleary eyes. "Is it you?"

"Expecting Edward is a bit optimistic, don't you think?"

The sound of Malcolm's voice sent a current of fear crackling through her. He closed the door behind him and Grace scrambled to her feet, stumbling back against the dresser. "Get out," she said. "Get out or I'll scream."

At first, she thought he'd heed the threat, but then he came across the room and grabbed her. Before she could take a breath, he'd spun her around and clapped his hand over her mouth. "I think we need to come to an understanding," he whispered, his breath hot against her ear. "You do what I say or I'll put you back out where you came from. This doesn't have to go badly for you. We could have a lovely little arrangement here that would benefit us both." He moved her toward the bed. "If you're willing to consider my offer, nod your head. If not, we'll simply have to do this another way."

Grace tried to remain calm. Malcolm was drunk. She had that advantage over him. And he was unfamiliar with her room. And he had always underestimated her intelligence and resolve. It wouldn't do to provoke him further. She'd have to make him believe that she was willing and then wait for her chance to escape. Grace slowly nodded.

"Then you won't scream?"

Grace shook her head.

Malcolm took his hand off her mouth, but he didn't let go of her waist. He held her body against his, slowly running his free hand over her belly and breasts, pushing against her backside with his hips. "I'm glad you understand who is in control here."

"You said we could come to an understanding," Grace murmured. "What did you have in mind?"

He chuckled and the sound made Grace's blood run cold. "I always knew you were just a greedy little slut waiting for your chance. Now that Edward is gone, I suppose I'm the next best target. Money is what you want?"

"What else?" Grace said.

He turned her around to face him. "I think we can reach an accord. You give me what I want and I'll give you what you want."

"Perhaps we should come to terms first," Grace said. She took a step back as soon as he loosened his grip, but she kept his attention focused on her hand as she ran it over his chest. If she could just put some distance between them, she could run for the door. Once she was in the hall, she could scream and Cook or Dennick would be there in a matter of seconds.

She reached for the top button on her blouse and toyed with it for a moment, then gently pushed him down to sit on the bed. He'd relaxed and she knew she'd have to take the chance. Drawing a deep breath, she lunged for the door. But Malcolm anticipated her move and he jumped up and grabbed her again.

This time he wasn't gentle. His hand covered her mouth and her nose as he picked her up off her feet and pulled her down on the bed. Grace scratched at his arms, trying to get a breath of air, but he seemed immune to pain. And then she saw the dinner tray on the nightstand next to her bed. Sitting atop the folded linen napkin was a knife. She twisted in his arms, reaching out for it, the lack of air causing her head to spin. And then it was in her hand.

Without hesitating, she reached back and plunged the knife into his side, once and then again. A low grunt burst from his throat and Malcolm immediately released his grip on her waist. He dropped back onto her bed and Grace scrambled away from him, gasping for air.

He touched the handle of the knife, still embedded in his side, a stunned expression on his face. Blood oozed from the wound and Malcolm tried to get to his feet but his legs wouldn't support him. Grace frantically glanced around the room, panic setting in.

She ought to call for help, but she knew what would happen. Malcolm would find a way to blame this on her and she'd end up in prison. Instead, she quickly gathered what belongings she could grab and wrapped them in her apron. The diary with her passport, her marriage certificate tucked inside the front cover, her bank account book, the tiny silk bag that held her garnet jewelry that Edward had given her, and the collection of carved animals from the shelf.

When she'd taken what was truly important to her, she glanced back at the bed. Malcolm's eyes were closed and his breathing had become labored. Blood soaked the side of his shirt and had begun to drip onto the bed.

Grace backed toward the door, watching him, waiting for him to pounce once again. But he wasn't moving and she slipped into the hall. She considered waking Cook or Dennick, but in the end she hurried by their rooms to the stairs. She had done what she had to do. If that had been murder, then so be it. She'd only been protecting herself and Edward's baby.

She hurried through the house, clutching her apron in front of her. When she got outside, she wasn't sure what to do. If she began walking to the village, she'd be easy to catch. There was a bus that came through on the way to Dublin every few hours, but not this late at night. Could she afford to wait until dawn?

She untied her apron and gathered it into a small bundle, securing it with the ties. It was then she realized she didn't even have a few shillings for the bus. Closing her eyes, she took a deep breath. She'd have to go back inside and steal some cash.

Then she remembered the stone fence. Edward had once put money there for her, until he'd begun to send it to Dennick. Perhaps there was some in the little tin box, enough to get her to Dublin. He'd hidden the map in the hay mow of the stables. Grace drew a deep breath, then ran across the courtyard.

When she reached the stables, she found a small lantern and lit the wick. The light cast eerie shadows on the old stone walls. She hurried past Violet's stall, turning away when the horse hung its head over the door looking for its usual lump of sugar. She couldn't afford to be sentimental. Violet was the least of what she was leaving behind.

Grace found the map exactly where Edward had left it. She unrolled the paper and scanned the directions. "Three stones down, six stones over," she murmured. Sitting back on her heels, she drew a ragged breath. He'd always promised to protect her. But how could he do that now, especially after what she had done to Malcolm?

Grace reached for the medallion she wore, pulling it out from beneath her blouse. "Love will find a way," she murmured. With an angry sob, she yanked the medallion off her neck, the thin leather string breaking easily. Love hadn't found a way and it never would. She was a silly girl to have believed in the sentiment.

Now, she would leave her girlhood behind, along with all of the dreams she'd imagined for herself and Edward. Grace wrapped the medallion around the map and set it back in its hiding place. She could love just one man in her life and that man was now gone. It was time to think about herself.

She made her way to the fence by the light of the lantern. The stones all looked the same in the dark, but she found the red stone immediately, then counted down and across. Setting the lantern at her feet, she clawed desperately at the stone, trying to pull it from its spot.

At first, it didn't move, then suddenly, it slid easily out. Grace reached inside the hole and her fingers found the tin box. She pulled it out and opened the top. A tiny sigh of relief slipped from her lips. It was full of money, at least a hundred pounds or more. She closed the box and tucked it into her bundle.

She had enough to get her to Dublin now and then perhaps on to Belfast. She'd find a way to lose herself, to start a new life in a new place. Grace gathered her things then hurried back to the courtyard. Edward's car was still parked in the coach house. She'd take it to Dublin and then leave it there. After all, she was his wife. What was his was now hers.

Once she steered the car out onto the road, Grace allowed herself to breathe again. It was only then that she realized what she had done. The moment she'd stabbed Malcolm had not only been the end of his life, but the end of her life as she'd known it.

Tears flooded her eyes and she brushed them away, willing herself to remain calm. Everything she'd known was at Porter Hall, every memory she'd ever held dear. Her mother, Edward, Cook and Dennick, Geneva, all the people who had been hers to love. And now, they were all gone. Grace's breath caught in her throat. Except one...

She reached down and placed her hand on her belly. She still had her baby—Edward's baby. They would build a new life together, only this time, Grace wouldn't let fate determine their future. She would do whatever it took to keep them safe and secure.

THE CATHEDRAL WAS QUIET AND peaceful, the occasional sounds of footsteps the only thing to break the silence. Grace knelt in a pew near the front, her head down, her hands clasped together. She'd been in Dublin just two days and already she'd realized that facing life all alone would be nearly impossible.

With the money from her bank account, she'd be able to survive six or seven months at best without work. It would have been enough time, had Edward been alive. He would have sent more of his pay and she would have told his family about the marriage. They'd had options back then, but now she had none. No one would hire her without references.

So she'd come to Christ Church cathedral to pray, believing that the spirits of her mother and her husband would look for her here and give her guidance. "Hail Mary, full of grace," she whispered. "Blessed art though amongst—"

She swallowed back tears, the effort causing a lump in her throat. She did feel closer to Edward here, in the place where they'd first come together. But it did nothing to quell her grief. A sob tore from her throat as the memories came flooding back and she began to weep again. Grace remembered the last time she'd seen him, remembered kissing him on the train platform in Belfast and then watching him walk away.

Why hadn't she taken more care to look at him, to realize that it might be the last time she saw him? They'd both been so foolish, ignoring the realities of war in favor of a fairy-tale ending. There were so many things she still needed to say to him, so many words that would remain forever unspoken.

Grace felt a hand on her shoulder, startled by the contact. She slowly turned to find a soldier sitting behind her. "I—I'm sorry," she said, her voice wavering. "Was I disturbing you?"

"Are you all right?" he asked. "Is there anything I can do for you?"

He was American. Grace could tell by his accent. She shook her head. "I'll be fine."

"Would you like me to sit with you for a while?"

She'd felt so alone over the past few days. It might be nice to have someone to talk to. He circled around the pew and slid in beside her. They sat next to each other for a long time without speaking, their gazes fixed on the altar.

"My name is Adam," he finally said. "Adam Callahan."

"I'm Grace. Grace Byrne." She paused. Not Byrne, but Porter. She'd never introduced herself using her married name. Had she really been married at all? Was a quick ceremony in a Belfast registry office and one night in a hotel enough to call a marriage?

"Why are you so sad, Grace Byrne? Maybe there's something I can do to help."

She wanted to tell him about Edward, about the man she'd loved with all her heart, about their life together. But her emotions were still so raw. Weeping and wailing in front of a complete stranger would be humiliating, and uncomfortable for him. "I—I lost my job," she said. "I've been looking for a new one, but no one wants to hire me."

"What do you do?"

"I worked in a grand house outside the city. I was a maid and a seamstress and a companion to the lady of the household. I also worked in the kitchen." She smiled. "I see you're a soldier."

"I'm an engineer. I build bridges and roads. I'm stationed in Belfast but I'll be going to Europe soon. I came to Dublin to do a little sightseeing. My grandparents were born here. Not in Dublin, but in Ireland."

"So you aren't mourning anyone either?"

He shrugged. "Naw. My girlfriend broke up with me before I left. She thought I was going to ask her to marry me when I graduated college. Instead, I told her I'd enlisted."

Grace glanced over at him, taking a good look at his face. He had dark hair, like Edward's, and blue eyes. But while

Edward's features were more sharply drawn and aristocratic, Adam Callahan's were boyish and friendly. "I'm sorry," she said. "About the girl."

"She wasn't the one," Adam murmured. "I guess the one is still out there somewhere. Though I'm not going to find her in a barracks with fifty other soldiers."

"You'll find her," Grace replied.

He glanced around. "This is a beautiful church. We have churches like this back home, in Boston. Not as old, though. My mother will be glad to hear that I at least set foot in a church once while I was over here."

"You know this isn't a Catholic Church," Grace said.

"It isn't?"

She shook her head and laughed softly. The sound seemed so foreign to her ears. Still, it felt good, like a balm for all her pain. "It's an Anglican church. The Church of England."

"Hmm. I guess that won't do. Do you know if there's a Catholic church nearby?"

"There's St. Audoen's. You should see the tower there. It's the oldest in Ireland. It was built in the twelfth century. And there's a gateway to the old city and some of the city walls left standing. It's truly quite historic."

"You know a lot about Dublin then?"

Grace shook her head. "No. I went there yesterday to pray. I read the pamphlet they give out to tourists."

Adam laughed, a deep, rich sound that echoed through the church. He quickly clapped his hand over his mouth. "I have a few more days here in Dublin," he whispered. "And I don't know a soul here. Would you like to see the city with me? Maybe we could search out a few more Catholic churches. I wouldn't want to go to war without God on my side."

Grace hesitated at first, but then nodded. It would be nice to have something to take her mind off of her sorrow. "I was thinking of going to Belfast," she said. "There might be a job there for me. The English are always looking for domestics."

As they walked out of the church together, Grace considered the man standing next to her. He was kind and intelligent, and handsome enough. He had no attachments, nothing to prevent him from falling in love. She, on the other hand, had no home, very little money, and a baby growing in her belly.

Adam Callahan could offer her security. He could offer her safety and perhaps a way out of Ireland before the Gardai caught up with her. She would not give birth to her child in an Irish prison. No, she would do everything in her power to keep them both out of harm's way.

"Tell me about Boston," Grace said as they walked out into the sunshine of a Dublin afternoon. "I understand there are many Irish there."

CHAPTER EIGHTEEN
EMMA

6 November 1846

I am alone in this strange and terrible place I once called home. I look around me and see nothing familiar, nothing that might bring a smile or a pleasant thought to mind. I see only heartache and despair, and hunger, always hunger. People walk the roads, aimlessly searching for something to eat or a place to die. The crop has failed again. All our hopes for a bright future have been dashed and the famine that began a year ago continues. The blight has spread throughout the country and there is not one potato that hasn't been touched. The government provides no help. The British say the Irish must form their own relief committees so we might help ourselves. But there is no one to contribute a spare shilling. I fear that help will never come and we will all die. Surely God must have mercy on us soon.

"WELL, I DON'T KNOW WHAT he expects us to do with her. She can't just move in with us. He married her, he's supposed to provide a home for her." Theresa Callahan lowered her voice to a whisper, but it was still loud enough for Grace to hear in the parlor. "I have my doubts about that baby. How does he even know it's his?"

Grace glanced down at her belly, now seven months along in size and entirely obvious beneath the maternity dress she wore. She'd expected a rather uneasy welcome from Adam's family, but she'd never anticipated they'd be blatantly hostile toward her.

She and Adam had married just a week after they'd met, repeating their vows in a registry office in Belfast, not far from where she married Edward. Adam had called it a whirlwind affair, love at first sight. But Grace knew better. From the first day she'd met him, her choices had become clear. Adam Callahan would provide a way out of her dilemma. He'd give her a home, a new name, and a father for her baby, all at once.

She'd expected to stay in Belfast for the duration of the war. Adam would ship out and like Edward, send his pay to her so she might find a comfortable room in a boardinghouse. All had gone as planned until Grace had sent him the inevitable letter. Three months after their marriage, she'd informed him she was pregnant…with his child.

She hadn't heard a word from him for nearly two months after that and then, he'd arrived at her door, armed with a week-long furlough, his face beaming with pride. Grace had played her part well, telling him how excited she was that they were going to be parents, how nothing could have pleased her more.

The happy news had soon disintegrated into a bitter argument, though. Adam had insisted they find a way to get her back to the States as soon as possible, so their child might be born in America. But Grace had grown comfortable in Belfast, certain that she was now safe from the authorities in Dublin.

Her argument was bolstered by common knowledge that it was nearly impossible to make a journey across the Atlantic without special dispensation. There were commercial planes, but Grace refused to consider that option. And any military ships that made the crossing were always in peril of being sunk by the German U-boat patrols.

So Adam had left Belfast without any resolution to their disagreement and Grace had been relieved she would give birth to Edward's baby on Irish soil. But a month later, she received another letter from her husband, this one full of details of the transport he had arranged for her.

It was only then she learned Adam Callahan's father was Congressman Jack Callahan of Marlborough, Massachusetts, a powerful Irish-American politician with close ties to the military. According to Adam's letter, his father had pulled strings to find her a spot on a hospital ship returning to the States with wounded soldiers.

Grace had nearly run again, ready to take what possessions and money she had and go to Scotland or England. But her baby had begun to move inside her and she'd been forced to admit that running would put them both at risk. So she'd waited and in early March, she'd boarded a ship in Belfast, bound for New York and her new home.

As she'd stood on the deck in frigid weather, watching as the Statue of Liberty passed by, her thoughts were not on her husband and the home they'd make in America, but on Edward. He had made this very same trip, had seen this same view, marveled at the skyline filled with tall buildings gleaming in the morning light. They'd always imagined the adventures they'd share, but Grace could never think of this time as an adventure. In truth, she felt nothing but fear and apprehension, a stranger in a strange land.

"Don't you think it a little odd that he never wrote to us about this girl?"

Grace closed her eyes and leaned back against the door of the parlor. She was supposed to be napping, but she'd come downstairs to get something to settle her stomach. It was so odd not to hear the familiar lilt of Irish English. Americans spoke in such flat tones that made it seem as if they were supremely bored by everything they discussed.

Grace already recognized the voice of Adam's older sister, Theresa, a thin, whining tone that already grated on her nerves. From the moment they'd met, Grace had seen a look of utter contempt on the young woman's face, as if she thought Adam's marriage to an Irish girl was the worst mistake he could have made.

Adam's mother, Verna, wasn't much more welcoming. From the time they'd picked her up at the docks in New York, Verna had watched her with suspicious eyes, staring down her long, narrow nose at Grace as she silently evaluated every word she said.

"You wouldn't be happy with any girl your brother married," Verna said as she set the dining room table. "What's done is done. We'll just have to make the best of it. As long as she doesn't embarrass the family, then I have no complaints."

"But he was supposed to marry Francine," Theresa said. "Then she and I would have been sisters. Besides, Francine is one of us. She's from our social class."

"You forget that Francine broke off with Adam before he left and not the other way around."

"But she still loves him. She told me so. She was just angry that he'd enlisted without telling her first. She's written him six letters and he hasn't answered a single one."

"That's because your brother is married now. I would expect him to honor that vow, no matter who he's made it to."

"Did you hear her say she was a servant before she met

Adam? A kitchen maid? Daddy is thrilled, of course, though I can't imagine why."

"Your father's district is mostly Irish," Verna explained. "Grace could be a political asset, especially when Adam runs for office himself. She's a working-class girl made good."

Theresa laughed dismissively. "Much better than she deserves." She groaned. "I don't know how we'll even be able to take her to the parties in Washington. She'll never fit in. She's so…common. And those clothes. It's obvious the Irish have no fashion sense at all. I think she actually sewed them herself."

The pair walked into the kitchen, their voices growing inaudible behind the swinging door. Grace slowly wandered around the parlor, perusing the pictures on the wall. The house was not as large as Porter Hall, but it was much more finely decorated. The furnishings and draperies were new and fresh, unlike the faded and tattered fabrics in her former home. It was clear that the Callahan's were wealthy and they weren't afraid to show it.

She walked over to the baby grand piano and sat down at the keyboard, running her fingers over the keys. A tiny smile twitched at her lips and she launched into a complex Bach invention she'd played many times for Geneva. Grace's fingers danced over the keys and she was surprised that she remembered the piece.

A few moments later, Verna and Theresa appeared in the doorway to the parlor. Grace stopped playing midphrase, then placed her hands on her lap. "I hope you don't mind," she said. "It's a beautiful piano." She looked at Theresa. "Do you play? Perhaps we could play some duets?"

"No," Theresa said in a flat voice. "I don't play. I thought you were napping."

Grace stood. "I couldn't sleep. It seems I'm hungry all the time now."

"Theresa, go ask Livvy to make us a pot of coffee," Verna said to her daughter. "And have her bring us some cookies and some of that banana bread she made. We don't eat dinner until seven, so I hope that will tide you over," she added, turning to Grace.

"I'm afraid I don't drink coffee," Grace said. "But tea would be nice."

"Tea," Theresa muttered. "I'll see if we have any."

When Theresa stepped out of the room, Verna crossed to the piano. "You play quite well," she said.

"Thank you," Grace replied. She knew Verna was curious to know to how an Irish servant girl might have learned the piano, but Grace wasn't about to tell her. "Do you play?"

Verna shook her head. "We have the piano for parties. We often hold little receptions and cocktail gatherings here for some of my husband's important constituents."

Grace walked around her and picked up a framed photo from atop the piano. She recognized a teenaged Adam and Theresa. But there was another, older boy in the photo. "I didn't know that Adam had an older brother," she said.

"I suppose there are a lot of things you don't know about Adam," Verna said. "Considering what a short courtship and engagement you had." She took the photo from Grace's hand and set it back in its place. "Patrick lives in Upstate New York with his wife. She comes from a very prominent Saratoga family. He'll be making a run for the New York State Senate next fall. We have high hopes for his political career, as we do for Adam's."

"But Adam is an engineer. He told me he wanted to build bridges and skyscrapers."

"Of course he'll have a profession. But then he'll follow his father into politics, I'm sure. There's no future in building bridges," Verna said. "As his wife, I'd expect you to support him in this."

Grace shrugged. "Support him? I'll support *him* in whatever he chooses to do."

"Yes," Verna said.

They both sat down, an uneasy silence descending over the parlor. Five minutes later, Theresa wandered back in, followed by the family's maid, Livvy, a young Negro girl. The girl set the heavy tray down on a side table, then picked up a tea strainer and began to fill it with dry tea. Grace walked over to her and gently took it from her hand. "Let me show you," she murmured, giving the young woman a smile.

She spooned a measure of the dry tea into the pot and gave it a stir, then set the strainer over the cup. "I'll make sure to do it right next time, miss," Livvy said.

"That's all right," Grace replied. "I'm not so high and mighty that I can't make my own cup of tea." When she finished, Grace stacked a plate with biscuits and tea bread, then took her cup of tea and sat down on the sofa. She silently munched on the treat that Verna had called a "cookie" and found it quite satisfying.

"Tell us about your family," Verna said. Theresa perched on the arm of Verna's chair.

Grace took a sip of tea. "I don't have one. I never knew my father. And my mother died when I was fourteen."

Theresa gasped. "You never knew your father? Then are you…"

"Illegitimate?" Grace asked. "No. At least I don't think I am. My father was murdered before I was born. He belonged to the IRA and he was killed in an ambush. My mother died of consumption." Grace paused. "But I do have aunts and uncles who live here in America. I've never met them before. I'm sure they don't know I even exist. But I believe I'd like to try to find them all someday."

"Yes, well, that's all very interesting, dear. But I would keep your father's political activities to yourself. My husband has had to step very carefully around the issue of a unified Ireland." Verna motioned to Theresa and they both stood. "We'll let you enjoy your tea. I have some letters to write and Theresa has to get ready for a party she is attending this evening."

Grace nodded. "I'm sure I'll find something to occupy myself. Livvy could probably use some help in the kitchen."

"You'll not work in the kitchen," Verna said sternly. "I wouldn't hear of it. If you make friends of the help, then they get lazy and take advantage. Read a book or a newspaper. It would do you well to educate yourself a bit more about this country. Theresa could suggest some reading for you."

"Oh, I'm sure I could find something in your library," Grace said. "I'm particularly fond of your writer Nathaniel Hawthorne. And I've read a great deal of Mark Twain as well. As for the poets, Walt Whitman is a favorite of mine. But no one will ever replace Yeats and Joyce in my heart, as they are Irish, you know."

Verna forced a smile, then walked out of the room without another word. Theresa dutifully trailed after her, glancing back at Grace with a perplexed expression. When they were gone, Grace grabbed another cookie and gobbled it down.

She'd been through far too much turmoil and sorrow in her twenty-one years of life to allow Verna and Theresa Callahan to get the better of her. After all, she'd battled Malcolm Porter and won. The two women were pathetic little weaklings compared to him.

Grace sat back and nibbled on another cookie. She couldn't help but wonder what Senator Callahan and his snobbish wife would think of her if they knew she'd committed murder. Her father's IRA activities might not look so very objectionable next to that little bit of history.

GRACE STOOD ON THE PLATFORM of the train station, her daughter, Emma, in her arms. Adam's parents had insisted that the entire family, including his older brother, be there to welcome him home. She glanced over at them and wished that their first meeting could have been accomplished in a more private setting, without curious eyes taking in her every reaction.

She was greeting a stranger. Though she had been dutifully writing to Adam every week for almost three years, it hadn't served to strengthen their relationship. She barely remembered what he looked like and the photos he'd sent home seemed to spark no sense of attachment at all. He had become a man in a soldier's uniform, an acquaintance at best, a lover who had passed in and out of her life long ago.

The war in Europe ended on a warm sunny day in late spring, May 8, 1945. Grace had been playing in the backyard with Emma when she'd heard the church bells begin to peal. A few minutes later, Verna had rushed outside with the news that victory had been declared in Europe. Adam would be coming home. But then he'd been immediately sent to the South Pacific and they'd waited another three months for the Japanese to admit defeat in August.

Grace had wondered how she'd feel at the very moment she saw him again. Her husband would be returning home from the war, but not the husband she'd wanted. The end had come far too late to save Edward.

She'd given birth to her daughter, Emma, two and a half years before and named her after a heroine in the Jane Austen novel she was reading when she went into labor. Verna had argued that the baby ought to be named for a family member, her own mother being the top candidate, with her husband's mother coming in second. But Grace had steadfastly refused to name her daughter Alice or Susan, names she found entirely too plain for the child of Edward Porter.

Her labor had been long and difficult and though the doctor had offered her some relief for the pain, Grace had refused. She had wanted to remember every moment of Emma's birth, as if the pain might bring her closer to Edward again.

She'd returned to the Callahan house with her baby in her arms and the wait had begun anew. But raising Emma had occupied her every waking hour and it had been wonderful to find a task that suited her so perfectly. Of course, Verna had hovered, offering parenting advice whenever she felt it necessary. Grace had learned to ignore her, using her own common sense and her mother's example as a guide.

She disciplined quietly and made her expectations simple to understand. Yet she offered her daughter the freedom to explore her small little world, to taste and touch and see life for what it was—a grand adventure.

She looked at her daughter and smiled. Emma wore a pretty summer dress that Grace had designed herself and sewed from fabric she'd purchased on sale at Woolworth's. Verna had insisted that Emma wear a frilly little dress she'd found at Filenes in Boston, but Grace had politely refused to consider the ridiculous tulle and organza confection, instead dressing her daughter in a more practical and understated manner.

"Who is coming home today?" Grace asked.

Emma looked at her with wide blue eyes, eyes that reminded Grace of Edward. "Papa," Emma replied.

"Yes," she said. "Papa is coming home."

"Daddy?"

Verna had insisted on referring to her son as Daddy around Emma and she'd thoroughly confused the poor child. "Daddy is Papa," Grace said. "And what are you going to do when you see Papa?"

The little girl slapped her palm to her mouth and threw a kiss. "Good girl," Grace said. "Mama will have to give him a kiss, too." She tried to sound enthusiastic about the prospect. Though she could freely admit to herself that she didn't love him, she owed Adam Callahan a great deal. And in return, she would try to be a good wife to him.

A distant whistle sounded and Grace felt the butterflies in her stomach begin to flutter in earnest. She pasted a bright smile on her face and drew a deep breath. As the train neared the station, she tried to remind herself of what was at stake. She couldn't afford to let this marriage fail.

Adam stepped off the train before it had even come to a complete stop, swinging down to the platform with athletic ease. Though she recognized his face, his mannerisms were completely unfamiliar to her. He saw his parents first and rushed over to them, pulling his mother and father into a long hug. Theresa kissed him on the cheek and his brother, Patrick, grabbed Edward's hand and shook it.

Grace watched as he slowly drew away and scanned the platform. Their eyes met and his grin widened. He didn't hesitate, just strode over and gathered her and Emma into his arms, his mouth coming down on Grace's in a deep and intimate kiss. Grace tried to relax, but it was impossible with so many people watching.

When he finished, Adam turned to Emma. "Do you know who I am?"

Emma stared at him warily, nuzzling closer to Grace.

"This is Papa," Grace said.

"Papa," Emma repeated.

He grinned. "That's right. Your papa has missed you very, very much. And he's wanted to meet you for a very long time." Adam held out his hand and Emma reached out and took it. "I do believe that you are the prettiest little girl in this whole train station."

Though she didn't understand the compliment, his soft voice and warm smile pleased Emma and she looked at her mother for approval. Grace nodded and Emma leaned forward and wrapped her arms around Adam's neck, giving him a hug. A few moments later he held her in his arms.

Grace swallowed hard, then forced another smile. If only her reaction to Adam had been so simple. But she was married to a stranger and they were about to begin their life together. Nothing had ever seemed quite so daunting.

CHAPTER NINETEEN

"I DON'T UNDERSTAND WHY I have to be there," Grace said. "Once we arrive, you go off and talk politics while I'm forced to make conversation with people I hardly know and don't even like."

Adam stood in the doorway of the kitchen of their small house in a working class neighborhood of Marlborough. He and Grace and Emma had moved out of his parents' home a year after he'd returned from the war. To a casual observer, their life might appear perfect—a happy couple, a beautiful child, a nice home. But beneath the surface, the marriage had been unraveling since his arrival back home three years before.

Adam knew the adjustment would be difficult. He and Grace had barely known each other before they married and under other circumstances, he might have considered more carefully such a hasty wedding. But the war had made every feeling and emotion so much more intense that he'd ignored common sense and let his heart rule the day.

"This is part of the job," he said. "As a city councilman I have to attend these events. And it's for a good cause."

Grace shook her head. "Don't you understand how difficult it is for me? These women, they see me as a foreigner, with my funny accent and my strange ways. I've tried to fit in, but they don't accept me."

"You don't try, Grace. You hold yourself back from them and they see it, not as shyness, but as arrogance or pride."

"They don't like me."

"They don't know you," Adam corrected.

Grace laughed dryly. "They think they do. Your mother and your sister certainly never hesitate to tell them all the little details of my life. How I was a poor orphan in Ireland, taken in by a wealthy English family and raised to be a lady. They have no idea what my life was like."

"They're just trying to help."

"Who? You or me? I know what they're about. They think if they spread these stories that it will get you more votes. They're using me and I don't like it one bit."

Adam groaned. "I'm a politician, Grace. I have to grab every advantage I can. And I'm not going to deny that your past is an advantage."

"Oh, yes," Grace said. "All the working-class Irish just love me. I've become their patron saint, a girl from the old country. But I'm not allowed to socialize with the working class. Instead, I'm forced to chat on and on with snobby wives of self-important businessmen."

Adam studied his wife for a long time. She was so beautiful, so spirited, and so very stubborn. But he'd never been able to capture that spirit and hold on to it. Whenever he tried, she just seemed to slip through his fingers, like water in a rushing stream.

How much longer could they go on like this? Divorce just wasn't an option, not if he wanted a future in politics. But if they didn't divorce, then they'd have to come to some type of agreement. Suddenly, he felt so exhausted by it all. His life had almost been easier when he was fighting a war. In Europe, everything had been black and white, the choices so simple. But here, he couldn't seem to see things straight.

"I'm going to ask you a question and I want you to answer me truthfully," he said.

Grace glanced over at him, then nodded.

"Did you ever love me?"

She opened her mouth to reply, but at that moment, five-year old Emma bounced into the room, still dressed in the plaid skirt and white blouse of her school uniform.

"Daddy," she cried, throwing herself into Adam's arms. "You're home." She grabbed his hand and pulled him along to the refrigerator. "Look what I made in school today." She pointed to a painting of three stick figures. "Me, Mommy, and Daddy. One, two, three."

Adam bent down and slipped his arm around her waist, giving her a hug. "Very nice. And what is this?" he asked, pointing to an odd blob of paint next to Grace.

"Oh, that's the baby," Emma said.

"The baby?"

She nodded her head, her dark curls bouncing. "Kevin Flannery said that when his daddy brought the baby carriage down from the attic, the very next day, there was a baby in it. I think we ought to buy a baby carriage. Else how are we ever going to get a baby?"

Adam glanced up at Grace. Her cheeks were flushed pink and she had an uneasy smile pasted on her face. "How indeed," he murmured.

"That's what I want for my birthday," Emma said. "A new baby."

"Your birthday is next week. I don't think there's time," Adam replied. He gave her a kiss on the forehead, then patted her backside. "Run along and change out of your school clothes. Then you can go outside and play for a bit before supper."

When Emma had left the room, Adam crossed the kitchen

to Grace. He boosted himself up on the counter and watched her as she worked at the sink. "She makes a interesting point," he said. "Maybe I ought to go out and buy a baby carriage. It might work better than what we've been doing." He chuckled softly. "Oh, that's right. We haven't been doing anything."

"That's not entirely true," Grace said.

"You know what I mean," he said. "I thought when I got back from the war that we'd have more children. Emma would like a little brother or sister. And my parents are beginning to wonder if there's—"

"Your parents?" Grace snapped. "Whatever would they have to do with this?" She held up her hand. "Forgive me. I forgot that they have a say in everything that happens in our marriage. From where you work, to what church we attend, to the school that Emma is enrolled at. Maybe we should send them out to find this baby you're so keen to have."

Adam felt his temper flare. "What the hell do you want, Grace? What would make you happy? I've been trying to figure out what it might be, but I'm at a loss here."

She grabbed a dish towel and began to wipe her hands, her gaze cast downward. "I don't know," she murmured. "I just don't want to fight with you."

"That's not good enough," he said.

"I want us to leave here, to go someplace new, where we can have our own life. Where we don't have to live the life your parents have planned out for you."

"What is so damn bad about that life?" He cursed softly. "Don't answer that. We've been going around and around with this for far too long. I don't need to hear it all again."

He walked across the kitchen, a feeling of utter defeat overwhelming him. The realization had hit him long ago that he really didn't know his wife at all. When he'd met her,

she'd been a fragile, vulnerable girl, someone he could protect. But since then, she'd built a wall around her that he
couldn't seem to penetrate.

He paused before he walked through the doorway into the
dining room and turned back to her. "Is she mine?"

Grace's head snapped around and her gaze met his. "What?"

"Emma? Is she mine?"

A cynical smile twisted at Grace's lips. "Have you been listening to your sister?"

"No," he said. "I just need to know. It won't change the way
I feel about her. I'll still be her father. But I need to know if
she's mine."

"Of course she is," Grace said, turning her back on him.

Adam wasn't sure whether he ought to believe her. But
then, what difference did it really make? In his heart, Emma
was his daughter and nothing would change that. And if she
was the only child he ever had, he could never be sorry.

GRACE PICKED UP THE MAP, then squinted up at the street signs
as they passed. Emma sat next to the window, her nose pressed
against the glass. They'd hopped on the bus in Marlborough
at nine that morning. The route took them through some of
the outlying towns before heading into downtown Boston.

"Are we almost there?" Emma asked.

"Just a little longer," Grace said.

"Where are we going?"

"To the library," Grace said. They had the entire day, so
even if they made a mistake and took the wrong city bus, she'd
still get home in time to cook Adam's supper

She closed her eyes for a moment, fighting exhaustion. For
the past few months, strange nightmares had plagued her
sleep. She'd first had the dreams when she'd been living alone

in Belfast, a few weeks after Adam had shipped out to Europe. And then again after she'd given birth to Emma, and again, right before Adam came home.

Grace wasn't sure what had brought them on this time, but now, she had to find a way to stop them once and for all. She'd been afraid to close her eyes at night, afraid she might say something in her sleep while Adam was lying next her.

The images were always the same. Malcolm. His face, his hands, his voice. He'd cover her mouth and she'd begin to suffocate. She'd become frantic for oxygen, clawing at his arms until her fingers were bloody, but he'd never let her go. And then, just as she was about to lose consciousness, she'd awaken, gasping for breath, a cold sweat covering her body.

Grace had taken to lying awake until Adam dozed off, then sneaking off to the guest bedroom so she might close her eyes without fear. Adam had found her there in the morning twice now and she'd made up a feeble excuse about his snoring. But sooner or later, he'd realize there was something else going on.

Her fears had only served to push them further apart. How could she possibly trust him with her secrets? No man could ever accept that his wife was a murderer, especially not a man with grand political ambitions. But she couldn't forget what she'd done. Every time someone knocked at the door, she convinced herself that she was about to be revealed. Grace looked around at the passengers on the bus and wondered what secrets they hid. What fears kept them awake at night?

Perhaps she just needed something worthwhile to occupy her mind. Now that Emma was in school full-time, Grace had thought about finding work or perhaps taking some classes at the local community college. Keeping house for Adam just wasn't enough.

She remembered the promises she and Edward had made,

to live their life together as an adventure, to travel to exotic places and see strange and beautiful things. Grace still had dreams like that, but it seemed as if she were trapped in a life that was stealing the very last shreds of the person she really was.

She and Emma got off the bus a block after it had passed the public library, then walked back to the imposing building. Grace stared up at the inscription on the facade. "The commonwealth requires the education of the people as the safeguard of order and liberty," she read out loud.

"What does that mean?" Emma asked.

A tiny smile twitched at the corners of her mouth. "It means that you must study hard and get a good education or someone will steal your freedom away from you." She grabbed Emma's hand and led her to the front door. "That's what happened in Ireland, you know. The British took our freedom and we had to fight very hard to get it back. It took a long time, much longer than it took the Americans to get rid of the British. But now, Ireland is free."

Just three months ago, at midnight on April seventeenth, 1949, the twenty-six counties of Eire officially withdrew from the British Commonwealth. The event drew little notice on the radio news broadcasts, but there were celebrations in Irish neighborhoods throughout the Boston area. Still, the die-hard IRA supporters saw the event as a failure in their campaign for a unified Ireland.

She thought about her father, about what he might have to say about it all had he lived. He wouldn't have been any older than Adam's father was now. Her life would have been so different—she would have grown up with two parents, perhaps in a cozy little cottage, with brothers and sisters. She never would have met Edward Porter, never would have had Emma.

But then, maybe her family might have emigrated to America and maybe they would have settled in Boston or even in Marlborough. And maybe she would have gone to college and met the son of a U.S. Congressman and fallen in love with him.

Grace frowned. What had Edward said about destiny? Life was nothing more than a series of coincidences so amazing that we believe it's destiny, she recalled. Perhaps this had been her destiny all along. Or maybe she'd found it with Edward and then lost it forever.

They walked through the front door of the library and into the grand entry hall. A vaulted ceiling arched overhead and she turned slowly to take in the architecture. She and Emma wandered through the beautiful rooms, enjoying the silence and the echo of their footsteps on the stone floors.

When they reached the reference desk, Grace nodded at the librarian. "Hello," she said. "I'm wondering if you might have back issues of any Irish newspapers."

"Published here or in Ireland?" the librarian asked.

"In Ireland. In Dublin. The *Irish Times,* perhaps?"

"Lonely for home?" the librarian asked.

Grace nodded.

"We have current issues on the rack, although they're usually at least a week or two old. Back issues are on microfilm, some are bound into books. Do you have a specific date you'd like to see?"

"Yes," Grace said. The date was burned into her brain, so deeply that she'd never forget it. "The tenth of October, 1942. And the month following that."

"Just fill out this request," the librarian said. "Do you have a library card?"

"No," Grace said. "But I'd like one."

The librarian bent over the desk and smiled at Emma. "I think you need a library card as well."

Emma nodded. "Yes, ma'am."

"Go back down to the circulation desk and they'll help you out. I'll put in your request and by the time you come back with the card, it will be up from storage."

Fifteen minutes later, Grace and Emma returned. They'd made a stop in the children's library to pick up some picture books for Emma. The librarian handed Grace two large books and she carried them over to a table and sat down.

"Are you going to read those books?" Emma asked, her eyes wide.

"I'm just going to look at the pictures like you do."

Grace flipped through the newspapers until she found it— the date she'd run away from Porter Hall. She drew a deep breath and moved forward, scanning the headlines for each article and looking for news of the murder of Malcolm Porter. When she didn't find anything in the first few days, she went back and looked again, then forward a few more days. But there had been nothing reported. Surely, it would have been newsworthy, the son of a prominent Englishman stabbed in his own home.

And then she saw it—a picture of Lieutenant Edward Porter. Her breath caught in her throat. It was a photo of Edward in his uniform, the same photo she'd kept tucked in the pages of the famine diary. She'd looked at the very image so many times and here it was again, printed above an obituary of Edward. Grace's eyes blurred with tears as she ran her fingers over the type.

"Mommy, are you all right?"

Grace looked up at Emma and smiled. "Of course, love, I just got a little dust in my eyes."

Emma got up and circled the table, then peered down at the page. "There aren't many pictures," she said.

"Look at this one," Grace said, pointing to the photo of Edward. "Isn't he handsome?"

Emma studied the photo, then cocked her head. "I like his hat."

"He looks like a very brave man," Grace said. She drew a ragged breath. "And I like his hat, too."

"What's his name?"

"Edward. Edward Porter." Grace began to read the obituary below. And when she got to the survivors, she stopped breathing entirely. "Survived by his parents Lord and Lady Henry Porter, and one brother, Malcolm," she murmured. "Survived by Malcolm." Grace drew in a shaky breath. "Oh, my God. He's alive."

She sat back in her chair and closed her eyes. Her life could begin again. Grace reread the obituary two more times. There was no mention of her, no mention of the wife that Edward Porter had. No one knew, except for Cook and Dennick, and even after what had happened to Malcolm, they hadn't said anything. It was as if her marriage had never existed.

Maybe it hadn't, Grace mused. She'd been the only one holding on to it, refusing to let it go. If she finally did, there might be a chance to build a life with Adam. But could she ever truly forget Edward?

She slowly closed the book and turned to her daughter. "Are you ready to go?"

Emma nodded. "May I take the books with me?"

"You may. I think we should come to the library every week while you're on your summer school holiday. We'll take the bus in and we'll have lunch in the city and do a bit of shopping. Then will visit the library and go home. Would you like that?"

"I'm hungry now," Emma said.

Grace stood and took her daughter's hand. They walked back through the library and out the front doors. When they got outside, she paused and took a deep breath. Tonight, she could sleep. Malcolm Porter would no longer plague her dreams. But there was still Edward. Until she banished him from her heart, she could never make her marriage to Adam work.

CHAPTER TWENTY

EMMA SAT AT THE KITCHEN TABLE, her homework spread out in front of her. Since she'd entered high school, it seemed all she did was homework, every evening, on weekends, even on vacation. Though she had attended a Catholic grade school, where the nuns had stressed diligent study habits and proper behavior, her parents had finally relented and allowed her to enroll in Marlborough High.

She'd found her class work there surprisingly simple and she did what was necessary in order to make the honor roll. But her main focus, from the very first moment she'd walked through the doors, was her social life—namely, boys.

Emma Callahan had thrown herself into high school life with an enthusiasm that her friends found exhausting. She never missed a sporting event, a school dance, a club meeting or a house party. As a sophomore, she'd been elected class secretary, was president of the Pep Club, was a varsity cheerleader, and already had gone through three steady boyfriends.

She smiled to herself as she read the directions for her history homework. If she could just finish this bloody report, then she could join her friends down at the park. Tommy McDonald had promised to meet there and he would no doubt want to sneak away for a bit of necking behind the bushes.

Emma reviewed the directions for the history project. She

was supposed to compose a family genealogy, interviewing both of her parents and her grandparents if possible. But her mother had been strangely uncooperative. "We're supposed to go back three generations," she read from the direction sheet.

Emma found the chart she'd made, then handed it to her father. He looked it over and nodded. "The Callahan side is right," he said.

"Now, where were you and Mom married?" Emma asked as she grabbed her pencil.

"In Belfast, Ireland," her father announced. "I was stationed there during the war. We were married on October 23, 1942."

"I thought husbands were supposed to forget their anniversary date," Emma teased.

"How could I forget that?" he said. He glanced over at her mother and his smile faded slightly. There were times when her mother could be such an old poop, Emma mused. Grace Callahan had absolutely no sense of humor.

Emma wrote the date down, then stared at it, counting ahead to her birthday. It was only eight months. Wasn't it supposed to be nine?

"You were born a month early," her mother murmured from her place at the sink. "If that's what you were thinking."

Emma smiled. "So, who were my maternal grandparents?"

Her mother turned and grabbed a dish towel, then dried her hands. "Is it really necessary to provide details of our private life for your school teachers to enjoy?"

"Mom, everyone has to turn a history paper in. We're studying our immigrant ancestors. They said we should be proud of our heritage. Besides, half the kids in school are Irish, so what's the big deal."

"I'm your immigrant ancestor," Grace said. "That's all you need to know."

Adam cleared his throat, putting an end to their argument. "Grace, I think you could provide a bit more information. It's nothing to be ashamed of. And it certainly won't be of interest to anyone now that I'm out of politics for good."

Emma sent her dad a grateful smile and he reached out and tweaked her nose. After her Grandfather Callahan's mistakes, her father's career in politics had come to a very quick end. Even her uncle Patrick had decided not to run for reelection. She hadn't really known what had happened with Grandpa Jack, but everyone had called it a scandal. "Come on, Mom. Just give me some names and dates, at least. I have to finish this. I promised Ellen I'd meet her down at the park. We're working up a new routine for cheerleading."

"All right. But if you really want to know about your ancestors, then I have something to show you." Her mother walked out of the kitchen and up the stairs. Emma glanced over at her father and he gave her a shrug. When Grace reappeared, she was carrying a small leather-bound book. She held it out to Emma, open to a page that was marked by a ribbon.

"What is this?" Emma asked.

"It's a piece of your family history. Your great-great-great grandmother wrote that diary in the late 1840s during the Irish famine. Read it."

23 April 1847

A family came to my door this morning, dressed in rags and begging for food, their bodies no more than skeletons. I didn't answer but instead took my daughter and hid in the shadows, waiting for them to move on. They are the living dead, those who can still walk. There is no hope for them and soon, they will succumb to fever or hunger and wherever they fall, they will die. For a time, there was a desperation in their eyes, but now I see only acceptance. They know the end is near and there is no way to avoid it. Landlords continue to evict tenants throughout the county. Sometimes they throw the husband in jail and put the family out to fend for themselves. Others buy passage for their tenants on ships to Canada, but many die on the way. I will put my faith in God and stay for one more summer. And when the earth is warm enough to turn, I will plant a new crop of potatoes. If it fails again, I will board one of those ships with my daughter and pray that we might find a new life across the ocean.

Emma set the diary down. "Is that really true?"

Her mother nodded. "It is. That's your legacy, Emma Callahan. You come from a long line of very courageous women. My mother, Rose Catherine Doyle, was one of them. She married Jamie Byrne and he became involved with the IRA, fighting for Irish freedom. He was shot dead in an ambush right after the government signed the treaty with the British. My mother gave birth to me a month later. And when I was three, we lost our home and we lived on the street. For months, we slept in parks and beneath bridges and my mother picked through the rubbish for food to feed me."

Suddenly Emma didn't want to hear more. The family history on her mother's side was tragic. Yet she was curious to know how the story came out. "Were you scared?"

"I don't remember being scared because my mother always made me feel safe. Then, one day, a nice lady took us home with her and we worked in her house. My mother did the laundry and the ironing and the mending. And in my spare time, I learned how to be a lady. And when I was fourteen, my mother died and I became an orphan."

"What did you do then?" Emma asked.

"I did the laundry and the ironing and the mending. And when I was older still, I decided to leave and make my own way in the world. And that's when I met your father. I had just come to the city to look for work and we met in a big church in Dublin."

"Your mother was crying because she couldn't find a job," Adam said. "And I asked her if there was anything I could do for her. I thought she was just about the prettiest thing I'd ever seen."

"Really?" Emma asked. She glanced over at her mother and saw a tiny smile twitching at the corners of her mouth. "Was it love at first sight?"

"I think it was," Adam said. "We got married after just a week. But things were different back then, with the war going on. Soldiers wanted to hold on to a bit of home, to know that there would be someone there, waiting for them. It was scary knowing you might be going off to battle and never come back again."

"Were you scared, Daddy?" Emma asked.

Her father nodded. "I was."

"It was just as bad waiting," her mother added. "I was afraid I might end up like my own mother, all alone, without a husband, raising a child."

"But then, I sent your mom to live with Grandma and Grandpa Callahan and I came home at the end of the war. And that's when I met you. And it was love at first sight all over again."

Grace crossed to the table and sat down on the other side of Emma. "Why don't we finish this up now. It's getting late and you have other homework to do."

Emma listened carefully as her mother filled in the rest of

the family history, giving her the family tree back to Jane McClary, the woman who wrote the diary. Emma decided to copy several of the diary entries into her report, knowing that she'd get extra credit for the effort. And when she was finished, she ran her hand over the cover of the diary.

"Can I read it?" she asked.

"Someday," her mother said, picking it up and holding it close to her heart. "Someday it will be yours. It's your legacy."

THE CLOCK ON THE MANTEL struck twelve and Adam closed the book he'd been reading and took off his glasses. He looked over at Grace who had been standing at the window for the past hour. "Standing there is not going to bring her home any sooner," he said.

"We should call the police," Grace murmured.

"She's an hour late for her curfew. Maybe the basketball game went into overtime. Let's give her a chance."

"What if she's hurt? What if there's been an accident?" Grace demanded. "It's snowing out and the roads are slippery. I don't know why you allowed her to drive."

"She's seventeen years old. She's old enough to drive and as a teenager, she's going to break curfew occasionally. Next fall, she's going away to college. What are you going to do when you can't watch over her every minute of every day?"

Grace turned back to the window, continuing her silent vigil. They didn't agree on much and raising Emma had been no different. Throughout Emma's childhood, Grace had hovered over her, as if some invisible force was waiting around the next corner, ready to snatch Emma away at any moment. She saw danger where there was none, trouble before it had even happened. She'd tried to control Emma's life from the minute she woke to the minute she went to bed.

In return, Emma had first resisted her mother's interference, and then rebelled.

Perhaps if they'd had another child, Grace might not have been quite so focused on her only daughter. But they hadn't been blessed, though not for lack of trying. There had been a short time in their relationship when Adam thought they might be able to work through their problems. It had come shortly after Emma had started school. Grace had seemed more open to the idea of adding to their family and they'd developed an understanding between the two of them that alleviated some of the tension in the house.

But after three years of trying, Grace was ready to give up on the idea of more children. Adam insisted that they visit a doctor and find out what was wrong, but she had refused. And gradually, the affection that they had discovered for each other had disappeared. They went back to the way things had been before.

He'd thought so many times about divorce. Now that his political career was over, there was really nothing to stop him. He could find happiness with another woman and Grace could finally be free of him. But if he gave up Grace, then he'd also give up Emma, and Adam wasn't willing to let his daughter go.

Perhaps when Emma was older, after she'd left the house, he might reconsider. But for now, he intended to respect his marriage vows, even if there was very little resembling a marriage left.

"Grace, please. Sit down. She'll get home when she gets home. And we'll deal with it then."

She turned and faced him. "We'll deal with it? Adam, you never deal with it. If you had your way, you'd let her run wild."

"She's a smart, sensible girl. She knows her limits and I happen to trust her. I think you might do the same."

"Don't tell me how to raise my own daughter!" Grace shouted. She stormed out of the room and a few moments later, Adam heard pots and pans clanging in the kitchen.

There it was again. It always seemed to come up when they had a disagreement about Emma. *My daughter.* Not once had Grace ever referred to Emma as *their* daughter. Every decision regarding Emma had been made by Grace—where she'd go to school, who she'd be allowed to date, what colleges she should apply to. Never once had he been consulted.

The suspicions had always been there. Yes, Emma had been born "early," but she'd also been a small baby, only five pounds, two ounces. And though she had her mother's dark hair and blue eyes, Adam did see a bit of himself in her smile and in the way her eyes lit up when she laughed.

He'd thought about submitting to a paternity test but then realized that if he did challenge her paternity and he wasn't her father, he'd have absolutely no legal claim to her. Grace could divorce him the very next day and take Emma away and he couldn't stop her. So they both continued with the charade, the secrets between them standing in the way of any chance they had at a real marriage.

He walked over to the liquor cabinet and poured himself a whiskey and another for Grace, then wandered back to the kitchen. He found her pacing in front of the stove, her hands twisting a dish towel into knots. He held the tumblers in one hand as he gently unwound the towel from her fingers.

"We're both going to have to let her go soon," he murmured, handing her a glass.

Grace took a sip of the whiskey, then nodded. "I know."

"And once she's gone, we're not going to have anything keeping us together."

Grace met his gaze. "What are you saying?"

"If you want out of this marriage, I'll give you a divorce, Grace. Emma will be gone, she's old enough to understand why we can't live together. You can keep the house and I'll continue to support you. But we're both still young. We can at least try to find some happiness for ourselves."

"Is that what you want?"

Adam reached out and touched her cheek and for the first time in a long time, she didn't flinch from his touch. "I loved you from the first moment I saw you. And maybe I did take advantage. I knew you needed someone to take care of you. And I was certainly willing to do the job. I don't blame you for not loving me."

"I took advantage of you," she said. She closed her eyes and drew a deep breath, as if she were carefully considering her next words.

Adam knew what was coming, but he didn't want to hear it. It didn't make a different. He pressed his finger to her lips before she had a chance to speak. "I know. I think maybe I've always known. But it doesn't change anything. At least not for me. She's my daughter and I'll always love her."

Tears swam in Grace's eyes and for a long time, she couldn't meet his gaze. "I'm so sorry," she murmured. "I've treated you so badly and it's nothing you've ever deserved." She drew a ragged breath and cursed softly. "I've made you miserable, made you pay for a secret I've kept for far too long. I punished you for wanting to love me. But I don't want to do that anymore. I'm just so tired of feeling this way."

"So what do you want to do, Grace? I'll do whatever you want."

She reached out and grabbed his hand and held on to it so tightly that Adam thought his fingers might go numb. "I—I'm not sure."

"I have a suggestion," he said.

She smiled ruefully. "I'd be willing to entertain a suggestion at this point."

"We could start again. Start over. Forget about the past and get to know each other again. I'd be willing to try that, Grace, if you would. Just leave everything behind, with no regrets."

"You could forgive me?" she asked.

"We'd forgive each other," he countered.

She gnawed on her bottom lip as she considered his offer. It was their last hope. If she didn't agree, then he wouldn't stay with her. He'd cut his losses and let the marriage go.

"I think I'd like to try," she said. "But I'm not sure where to start."

He took her hand and drew it up to his lips, then pressed a kiss just below her wrist. "My name is Adam Callahan," he said.

"I'm Mary Grace Byrne," she replied. "Mary Grace Byrne Porter Callahan."

"Porter?"

She nodded, her gaze cast downward. "My first husband. He was killed in the war. We were married for just a month."

Adam hooked his thumb beneath her chin and forced her to look at him. "I'm sorry for your loss. He must have been a good man."

Grace nodded. "He was. And I loved him very much. But that was a long time ago."

Adam leaned forward and brushed his lips against hers. Grace pressed her forehead to his, her eyes closed. "It's been so long," she murmured. "I'm not sure I remember what to do anymore."

"Why don't we just take our time, then."

She slowly wrapped her arms around his neck and tipped her face up to his. And then, she kissed him, her lips soft and inviting. Adam skimmed his hands over her hips, leaning in and enjoying the feel of her mouth on his. They were like two strangers, meeting for the very first time. So much had changed in the eighteen years since they'd married, but his attraction to her hadn't.

The sound of the front door interrupted their kiss and Grace drew back, as if they were a couple of teenagers caught necking. Adam grabbed her hand and pulled her along with him to the back hallway. He pressed his finger to his lips and they both listened as Emma tiptoed upstairs.

"I'm going to go talk to her," Grace said.

Adam shook his head. "It can wait until the morning. Then we'll both talk to her."

Grace nodded and Adam took her hand and walked with her to the stairs. When they reached their bedroom, Adam wasn't quite sure what he should do. Though they'd slept in the same bed since he'd returned from the war, they hadn't touched each other in years.

In the end, they lay down together and slept, his arms wrapped around her, her face pressed against his chest. The rest would come, Adam thought as he felt her relax in his embrace. They had the rest of their lives now.

CHAPTER TWENTY-ONE

"YOU HAVE TO COME. NICK is bringing a date for you."

Emma shook her head and looked up from the novel she was reading. "I'm really not up to going out tonight." She held up *Valley of the Dolls*. "I've got a good book, a six-pack of Tab and a frozen pizza. What more could I need?"

Diane sat down on the sofa and gently took the book from Emma's hands. "I know how much you miss your father. But I think he'd want you to live your life and have fun."

Emma pulled her feet up on the sofa and wrapped her arms around her knees. Her father had died suddenly, six months ago. One day, he had been there, laughing and teasing her, instructing her on the kind of car she ought to buy and helping her move a new sofa into her apartment, and the next day he was gone, dead of a heart attack.

It had been such a shock that for a long time, Emma hadn't been able to grieve. She'd always assumed he would be there, to walk her down the aisle, to play with his grandchildren, to tell her all the things she needed to know about life but had never asked.

And he'd seemed so happy lately, thinking about starting his own consulting business. Emma knew her father and her mother had had a troubled marriage, but over the past few years, they'd seemed to grow much more attached to each other. Perhaps it wasn't a passion to end all passions, but they'd been happier.

"How is your mother doing?" Diane asked.

Emma shrugged. "It's difficult to tell. You know her, stiff upper lip and all. She never really let my father in, so why would she reveal her feelings to me? I have to wonder if she even cares that he's gone." Emma groaned softly. "Oh, I shouldn't have said that. I think she misses him."

"You know, you probably shouldn't attach your own ideals about relationships to your parents' relationship. They're from a different generation, when men didn't communicate as openly and women were more complacent. And everyone kept their feelings to themselves. Maybe they had a great marriage and you just couldn't see it."

"Maybe," Emma said. Diane was a graduate student in psychology at Boston College and often provided a differing viewpoint.

Even if her parents' marriage hadn't been a disappointment, then her father's professional life had certainly been. When Jack Callahan had been indicted for taking a series of bribes, the scandal had sullied the family name, enough to affect her father's bid for a seat in the state senate. The campaign ended in the primary a few days before her grandfather had resigned.

Verna Callahan, her social status now in tatters, had demanded that they sell their home in Marlborough and move to California, where memories were short and the weather was warm. Her aunt Theresa, still unmarried, had gone with them and had found an exciting new life working as a secretary for the head of a Hollywood movie studio. And Adam Callahan went back to work as a civil engineer for the state of Massachusetts.

"My mother wanted me to move back home after the funeral," Emma said, staring at her toes. "In some ways, I wanted to be there, where I could feel closer to my father. But then I thought, if I go back, I'll be there the rest of my life."

"I'm glad you moved in with me," Diane said. "I'm not sure I could have found another roommate I like as much as you, Emma Callahan."

She and Diana had been matched as roommates their very first year in college and had lived together ever since. She'd been accepted at Wellesley and Mt. Holyoke, but the family finances could provide only enough for a state school, so Emma had chosen the University of Massachusetts in Amherst.

In the end, it had been the perfect place for her. She'd never really been cut out for the more conservative atmosphere at an all-girls college. That had been her mother's dream, Grace Callahan's one last attempt to turn her daughter into a proper lady.

But in Amherst, she'd begun to see the power that women were beginning to have in society, the freedom to make choices about careers and relationships and—sex. Emma became involved politically, in women's issues, in the anti-war movement, in social causes, and by her sophomore year, she'd decided to major in social work. At age twenty-five, she was now a successful, single career woman, running a youth center in South Boston. It was a job she'd come to love, though her salary barely paid the rent.

"Are you sure you won't come out with us?" Diane asked. "We don't have to stay long. We'll just have one drink and then we'll go."

"And this guy won't be disappointed?"

"He's new in town. He'll have to learn to live with it."

Reluctantly, Emma crawled off the sofa and smoothed her hands over the skirt she'd worn to work. "Will I have to change?"

Diane gave her the once-over. "Comb your hair and change out of those ugly shoes into a pair of heels and you'll be fine."

They walked the three blocks to their favorite bar in the Back Bay section of Boston. When they got inside, Emma stood behind Diane. "If he looks like a lunatic, I'm going to turn around and walk out. You can tell him I had to—to stay home and wash my hair."

Diane searched the bar for her boyfriend. "There's Nick," she said, "standing in back by the pool table."

"And the guy with him?"

"His back is to me." Diane paused. "Wait, Nick sees me now. He's turning around and—"

"And?" Emma groaned. "And what?"

"Oh, he's cute," Diane said excitedly.

"Cute?"

"Let me rephrase. Gorgeous. Handsome. Wow, why didn't my blind dates ever look that good?"

"If you're lying to me, I'll—"

"No," Diane said, turning around and grabbing her arm. She dragged Emma forward. "There. See for yourself. Go ahead, give them a little wave and smile. Look like you're happy to be here."

Emma did as she was told. "He is really cute," she said as she slipped out of her jacket. "What's his name?"

"I can't remember. Nick says he's Irish, so it's kind of a funny name. That's why I thought you two would hit it off."

"Because he has a funny name?"

"No, because he's Irish. And so are you. I mean, sometimes you sound Irish. You can talk Irish together. He just got off the boat."

"What boat?"

"He just arrived here from Ireland a few weeks ago.

Come on, let's go introduce ourselves. By the way, you can thank me later."

Emma caught the Irishman's gaze as she crossed the bar and he kept his eyes locked on hers as she approached. He leaned over and whispered something to Nick and they both laughed. He had a beautiful smile, Emma mused. A smile that hinted of a devilish sense of humor. His black hair was thick and long, curling slightly over the collar of his faded work shirt. He wore a brand-new pair of jeans and scuffed boots.

She held out her hand to him. "Hello, I'm Emma Callahan."

His smiled broadened, revealing even, white teeth. "Padriag Quinn. My friends call my Paddy." He took her hand in both of his and held it for a long time, rubbing the back of her wrist with his fingers. "I can see it," he said, his Irish accent thick.

"What is that?"

"Ireland. I can see it in your pretty face."

"My mother was born there," Emma said.

He grinned, his eyes lighting up. She was immediately caught by the unusual color, an odd mix of green and gold. "What a coincidence," he said. "So was mine."

Emma giggled. He really was quite handsome, and charming, too. "So, tell me, Paddy Quinn, why did you cross the big wide ocean? What brought you here?"

"I think it was you," he said. "I do believe that I came here to meet you."

Emma felt a warm blush creep up her cheeks. From any other guy, she'd consider the statement nothing more than a cheesy pick-up line. But from Paddy, it was devastatingly effective. "With charm like that, you should do very well with American girls," she teased.

"I'm starting to fancy American girls," he said. "One in particular."

Emma reached around him and poured herself a beer from the pitcher that Nick had bought. Her arm brushed against his and she felt her blood warm and her heart beat a bit faster. Yes, this man was handsome and charming. But she really wasn't looking for a boyfriend.

She glanced over at Diane and her friend winked. Then she and Nick wandered over to the pool table, leaving Emma and Paddy on their own. "What really brought you here?" she asked, sipping at her beer.

"Work. I'm starting a new business venture. I'm a commercial fisherman and I'm plannin' to buy myself a grand boat. Well, not so grand, but it will be once I've shined it up a bit."

"I like fish," Emma said.

"And I'll be catching fish. We're a perfect pair, we are." He held out his hand. "Would you care to dance, Emma Callahan?"

She glanced around the bar. Though there was a jukebox playing, no one was dancing. "Here?"

"Wherever," he said. "Do you know of a better place?"

Emma nodded. "There is a little club a few blocks from here. We could—"

He grabbed her beer and set it next to the pitcher. "Off we go," he said. He grabbed his jacket and shrugged into it, then helped her with hers, resting his arm around her shoulders as she buttoned it. Emma waved to Diane and Nick before they walked out.

They stepped outside to find huge snowflakes drifting down from the night sky. She turned her face up and caught a few on her tongue. "I love it when it snows," she said, turning around, her arms out.

He caught her and pulled her toward him, one hand around

her waist, the other cradling her fingers. Slowly, he began to move, back and forth in an easy rhythm until they were dancing on the sidewalk. "There's no music," she said.

He began to hum a Beatles tune, "I'm Happy Just To Dance With You." After one verse, he started singing and Emma found herself completely and utterly captivated. He had a beautiful voice, yet he made enough mistakes in the lyrics to keep their dance lighthearted and silly.

She began to sing along with him and before long, they were twirling down the sidewalk and screaming at the tops of their lungs. When the song came to an end, he dipped her back dramatically, and then pulled her body against his.

They stared at each other for a long moment, before Paddy leaned forward and covered her mouth with his. The kiss was perfect, just as she knew it would be, not too aggressive, not too meek, but passionate enough to let her know he was very attracted to her.

When he drew back, Paddy cupped her face in his hands and smiled. "I do believe you're the most beautiful girl in America," he said.

"You haven't met all the girls in America yet," Emma teased. "How would you know?"

"I have a good sense of these things," Paddy replied. "Trust me on this." He kissed her again, then took her hand. As they walked down the street, Emma couldn't help but wonder where this was all going. She'd never been so immediately attracted to man. And though some of her girlfriends had engaged in one-night stands and casual sex, she hadn't tried it herself.

Just the thought of taking Paddy Quinn back to her apartment, tearing off his clothes and throwing him onto her bed was enough to make her pulse start pounding again. But was she willing to waste this attraction on just one night together? Or was Paddy worth a second date?

"HOW DO I LOOK?"

Emma reached over and smoothed her hand over the lapel of Paddy's jacket. "You look fine. Don't worry."

Paddy glanced in the rearview mirror and reached up to run his fingers through his hair. He should have gone for a haircut. He looked like a feckin' hippie.

Emma had invited him home for Sunday dinner and though he'd thought about refusing, it was time to meet her mother. They'd been dating for nearly two months and this was the first clue that Emma might consider him an important part of her life. Paddy, in contrast, had managed to fall arse over tea-kettle just minutes after setting eyes on her.

He'd never thought that his first week in America would be so momentous. To meet the girl of his dreams so quickly was a bleedin' miracle, it was. He still couldn't explain the attraction on her part. She was beautiful and smart and could have any man in Boston. But she was with him, a regular guy with no means of employment and dreams enough to spare.

"I found a boat," he said.

"Where?"

"It's at a boatyard in Quincy. I've got enough saved to buy it, but I'm going to have to get a loan to refit it. I'm not sure how that will work considering I'm not a citizen. I'm thinking I could get the owner of the yard to invest and then give him a share of the first season's profits."

"That sounds like a good idea," she said. She smoothed the same spot on his lapel again. "Don't let my mother scare you, all right?"

"Why? Does she have a big wart on her nose and three eyeballs?"

"No," Emma said, giggling. "She can just be a little overbearing at times. She's always had this idea of how my life was supposed to turn out. Wealthy husband, big house in a snobby neighborhood, three gifted children."

"Is that what you want?"

"No," Emma said. "I just want to be happy."

"And could you be happy with a bloke like me?"

Emma nodded, then leaned over and kissed his cheek. "I am happy with a bloke like you," she said in her best Irish accent. "And you look very nice, by the way."

He'd bought the jacket at a second-hand store, but the fit was good and it looked nearly new. The tie he'd borrowed from Nick, along with a decent shirt. The trousers had been his only purchase, but it was worthwhile if it meant impressing Emma's mother.

Emma gave him directions through Marlborough and when they pulled up in front of her mother's house, Paddy began to get nervous. He was like a fish out of water here, unfamiliar with the customs and behavior expected at such a meeting. Back in Ballykirk, most of the families knew each other, so there was never a problem with formal introductions. If he was interested in dating a girl, he'd go down to the pub and meet her da, hoist a few pints and the way would be cleared.

Paddy parked the car at the curb, then got out and circled around to open Emma's door. But she was already out and closing it behind her. "Now what if your ma is watching? She'll think I don't have any manners."

From the moment Grace Callahan opened the front door, Paddy could sense that he wasn't the type she imagined for her daughter. With a tight smile, she invited them into the parlor. The questions began almost immediately—questions about his prospects came first, then his family, and then his own history with women. And this was all in the first ten minutes.

Though Emma had provided him with a drink, he'd left it on the table, determined to keep his wits about him. Paddy could see how uncomfortable she was with the direction of the conversation and made numerous attempts to change it. But her mother couldn't be deterred and Paddy reached out and gave Emma's hand a squeeze. Mrs. Callahan could lob grenades at him and he'd still find a way to kiss her arse, if that's what Emma wanted from him.

"Tell me more about this work of yours," Grace said. "Is this what you did in Ireland?"

"My father and grandfather were both commercial fishermen," Paddy explained. "But the living over there isn't quite as good. I've always been keen to try deepwater fishing. There's more money to be made."

"And you go out for the day and throw a line in, is this how it works?"

Paddy chuckled. "No. The boat goes out for five or six weeks at a time, into deep water, usually off the Grand Banks. We'll play out a long steel line with bait and numerous hooks on it. And then, a few days later, we go back and pull the line in. When the hold is filled with fish, the boat comes home."

"And you've never fished like this before?"

Paddy shook his head. "But I learn quickly. Fishing comes easy to a Quinn. In Ballykirk, they say we Quinns can hear the fish before we see 'em. I've got myself a spot on a longliner starting in July. And by next season, I hope to have my own boat ready."

"In July?" Emma asked. "You didn't tell me that."

Paddy shrugged. "I guess it just seemed so far off that I never thought to mention it."

"Well, let me go see to supper," Grace said cheerfully. "Emma, would you help me in the kitchen?"

Reluctantly, Emma let go of his hand and followed her mother into the kitchen. A few moments later, he heard the sounds of an argument, beginning softly at first and then growing in intensity.

"Oh, fuck," Paddy murmured. "This is going well." He grabbed the drink that Emma had poured him and downed it in a few quick gulps, then walked over to the liquor cabinet and poured himself another.

Back in Ballykirk, he'd been considered quite the catch. He was polite, didn't drink to excess, bathed regularly, and had a good income, the kind of bloke mothers were drooling over. But even in the short time he'd been in the U.S., he'd noticed how folks here were always trying to rise above their place in society. No one was ever satisfied with what they had, they always wanted more.

He gulped down another whiskey, then poured himself a third, knowing he'd need something more to get him through dinner. But a few minutes later, Emma stormed back into the room, her color high.

"We're leaving," she muttered, grabbing her purse from the floor next to the sofa.

"What about dinner?"

"You want to stay?" she asked, her voice rising in pitch. "You're welcome to stay, but I'm leaving."

"No, I think I'd rather leave with you," Paddy said. He downed the third whiskey, then reached into his pocket and grabbed the keys to her car. "Here, I think you'd better drive. I've had a bit too much of the drink."

"In five minutes?"

"Hell, I thought I'd have to sit through a whole bleedin' ten-course dinner with your mother. I needed something to calm my nerves."

She grabbed his hand and pulled him along to the front hall. When they got outside, she screamed in frustration, turning back to look at the house. "This was such a huge mistake. I am such an idiot."

"I take it she wasn't too fond of me," Paddy said. "And here I thought I was charming the pants off her."

Emma frowned at him, then burst out laughing. "My mother would have to be in a coma before anyone could charm the pants off her." By the time they got into the car, the mood had lightened considerably. "She really was awful to you."

"She wants the best for her daughter," Paddy countered.

"But shouldn't I be the one to decide what's best for me?"

"You should," Paddy agreed. She started the car and pulled out onto the street. He watched her silently as she drove back through town. "If you were making a list of all the things that were best for you, would I be appearing on that list?"

Emma glanced over at him and smiled. "You'd be at the top of that list," she said.

"Pull over," Paddy ordered, pointing to the curb. "Right there, pull over."

Emma did as she was told and the moment the car rolled to a stop, Paddy dragged her into his arms and kissed her, deeply and thoroughly. When he finally drew back, her face was flushed and her breath was coming in tiny little gasps.

"I love you, Emma."

She blinked in surprise. "You do?"

He chuckled softly, running his hand over her cheek. "Yes, I do."

Emma drew a quick breath and then hesitated. Paddy knew it was too soon, that he shouldn't have revealed his feelings so quickly. But it was bloody impossible not to. When he looked into her eyes, he wanted to say everything his heart felt, to babble on like an idiot until he was certain she understood how much he wanted her.

"You don't have to say anything," he murmured.

"No, I want to," Emma replied. She met his gaze, then gave him a soft kiss. "I love you, Paddy."

He'd heard the words before from other girls. But they'd never really meant anything to him until now. "That's good. That's very good," he said.

CHAPTER TWENTY-TWO

GRACE GLANCED UP AT AN unfamiliar car as it pulled up in front of the house. She rubbed her gardening gloves together, then pulled them off and got to her feet. She wasn't expecting visitors. In truth, the one person she'd wanted to visit had been avoiding the house on Poplar Street for over a month now.

Emma could be stubborn at times, but she'd never remained angry for this long. Grace wasn't about to pretend she approved of Paddy Quinn. The man had absolutely no prospects. His dream job required him to be away from home for weeks at a time. What kind of life was that for her daughter and her future grandchildren? Grace had seen more than her share of heartache when it came to love. She didn't want her daughter to experience the same.

She watched as a gentleman stepped out of the car and stood by the curb. He was quite tall, with a slender build and a full head of dark hair that was graying at the temples. He appeared to be about her age, if not a bit older. Grace slowly approached him. "May I help you?"

He stared at her, smiling. "You must be Grace."

"I am," she said. He spoke in a proper English accent, his words clipped and precise.

"Still as pretty as I remembered."

"Do I know you?" Grace asked.

The man shook his head. "No, we've never met. But I know a lot about you." He paused. "I knew your husband."

"Adam?"

"Edward," he said.

"Oh." Grace felt her knees go weak and she drew in a sharp breath, pressing her hand to her heart. "I—I'm sorry. It's just that—well, no one here knows I was married to Edward." She drew another breath, this one more deliberate. "It's been so long since I've heard his name. Or even looked at his photo. How did you know him?"

"We served together in North Africa. My name is Miles Fletcher." He held out his hand and Grace shook it. "Perhaps we might find a place to sit. I have a great deal to talk to you about."

"I'm not sure that would be a good idea," Grace said. "It's taken me a long time to come to terms with Edward's death. And I'm not sure I want to bring it all back again."

"Your daughter. Does she know Edward was her father?"

Grace frowned. "How do you know I have a daughter?"

Miles reached in his pocket and withdrew an envelope, then handed it to her. She recognized the handwriting as her own. Grace opened the flap and withdrew the letter. In an instant, she was transported back to the night she wrote it.

"I'm sorry I opened it," Miles said. "But I felt it necessary. I thought it might offer a clue."

"A clue?"

"To your whereabouts. I've had an investigator searching for you for a very long time, Grace. He found you last year, shortly after your husband died and told me about your daughter. I thought it might be best to wait for a bit before I contacted you."

She looked up from the letter, her mind filled with images of the past. "Would you like a glass of lemonade, Mr. Fletcher? Or perhaps a cup of tea?"

He grinned. "I'd like that very much. And you can call me Miles. I feel we've known each other for a lifetime."

"Miles," she repeated. "Come with me."

They walked into the cool interior of the house. Grace settled Miles in the parlor while she fetched the drinks and a light snack of cinnamon bread and butter. When she returned, she found him looking at the framed family photos that had been spread along the mantle.

"Is this your daughter?" he asked, holding up Emma's college graduation photo.

"It is. Her name is Emma."

"Emma. A beautiful name for a beautiful young lady. She must be…"

"She's twenty-five now. She just finished graduate school a couple years ago and has a master's degree in social work. She works in Boston running a youth center. Not the career I might have wished for her, but she's determined to save the world. Perhaps she inherited that trait from Edward." Grace picked up the pitcher of lemonade and poured him a glass. "So tell me, how did your investigator find me? And more importantly, why would you want to find me?"

Miles took the glass from her then shook his head when she offered him a piece of the cinnamon bread. "It's a very long story, so I think it best if I start from the beginning."

"All right," Grace said, sitting down.

He began at Harrow, where he and Edward had met as teenagers. He told her about the first time Edward had mentioned her name, when they were drinking in a small pub near his family's estate. And then he jumped to the war and North Africa and the second time he'd heard Grace's name mentioned.

"And then Edward went back to England for a time,"

Miles said. "He accompanied an officer back on one of the hospital ships."

Grace smiled. "That's when we were married. We met in Belfast while he was on furlough."

"He told me he was planning to ask you before he left. He also made me promise that if anything happened to him, that I would look after you."

"Geneva," Grace cried. "Oh, do you know whatever happened to his mother?"

"I do. And I'll get to that." Miles paused to gather his thoughts. "When we got word that his transport had been sunk, I went to his quarters to go clear out his things. I found your letters and some other personal items and put them in a box and addressed the box to you, so that it might be sent if something happened to me before I had a chance to deliver it personally. And then I carried that box with me for the rest of the war, knowing there would come a time when I'd meet you. Before long, that letter caught up to our unit as well, and I put it in the box."

"And you have this box with you?" Grace asked.

Miles nodded. "It's in the car. Would you like to see it now?"

"I would," she said.

When he left the room, Grace sat silently, wondering if she was really ready to open up this door to the past, a door she'd kept tightly closed for so long. Edward had been the first man she'd ever loved, and to some extent, the only man. She'd come to cherish Adam in their last years together, to respect him and care for him, but she'd never loved him with the same single-minded intensity that she'd had for Edward. She and Edward were opposite sides of the same coin. No one had ever known her better than he had.

Miles walked back into the room a few minutes later, a small box in his hands. He set it down next to her on the sofa, then returned to his chair. It was tied with string and wrapped in brown paper. As she removed the paper, Grace felt her heart began to beat a bit quicker, as it always had when Edward entered a room.

The box was filled with all the letters she'd sent him, a chronicle of her life at Porter Hall while Edward was at war. There were photos of her as a teenager and a young woman, photos she'd never known he'd had. She uncovered a thin leather string and she drew it out and found herself holding the gold medallion that had once belonged to her father.

One end of the leather string had broken and Edward must have put it with her letters. Grace's fingers automatically went to her own neck before she realized that she'd left her medallion in the stables the night she ran away.

"I didn't just come here to return these things," Miles said. "I've also come representing the estate of Lady Geneva Porter."

Grace looked up. "The estate?"

Miles nodded. "She died in 1961. She was eighty-three. I met her after the war when I came looking for you. Her husband was very ill, as a result of his drinking. He died in '46. She had been hospitalized after Edward's death but the doctors found a treatment that worked and she lived out her days quite healthy and happy. Malcolm was running the businesses and had inherited his father's love of the drink. Isabelle divorced him and took their son back to England in 1949 and he died in an auto accident in 1951, leaving the entire Porter estate in Geneva's hands. It was then that Geneva called upon me to help her with the businesses and to find you."

"She knew about Edward's child?"

"Yes. By then I'd opened the letter and I told her you were pregnant. But she never knew anything beyond that. I think she hoped and prayed that Edward had an heir out there somewhere."

"An heir?"

"This brings me to the reason I'm here." Miles reached into his jacket pocket and pulled out a thick envelope, then handed it to her. "This is just an outline of your holdings in Ireland. When Geneva died, she put everything in your name, with the provision that it be passed to Edward's son or daughter if that child lived."

Grace stared at the envelope, aghast at the news. "This isn't possible. How are we supposed to— Oh, my God, I can't believe this. Why would she do this? What about Malcolm's son?"

"Isabelle remarried shortly after the divorce. Her second husband is quite wealthy and adopted the boy. And she was very bitter, so I don't believe she'd want anything to do with Porter money."

"I know nothing about mines and mills," Grace said.

"I've been supervising those since Malcolm died. Though the holdings are not as extensive as when Lord Henry was alive, there is enough there to provide a comfortable living for both you and Emma. Mines and mills are a dying business in Ireland. But there are other investments that do quite well. There is also a family trust that provides for the care of the manor house and the employment of the staff."

"What are you saying? Do you expect us to return to Ireland?"

"I don't know. That is entirely up to you, Grace. And to Emma, I suppose. But Porter Hall is there for you both if you care to have it. If not, you can sell it. But the proceeds from any sale will go to Emma." He smiled, then reached out and patted her hand. "I know this is a lot for you to take in. So I'm going to leave you with this. We can speak in greater detail in the next several days. I'll be in the States for a week. My wife and I want to see New York and take in a few Broadway shows. We have tickets to see 'Fiddler on the Roof.'"

He stood, then reached into his pocket again for a business card. "My hotel phone number is written on the back. Ring me when you've had a chance to digest all of this news and I'll bring the paperwork by to transfer ownership of the estate to you and Emma." Miles held out his hand, then snatched it away, patting at his pockets. "I nearly forgot. I have some letters for you. From Sophie McCurdy, or Cook as you knew her, and John Dennick. When they heard I'd be paying you a visit, they insisted on writing."

"They're still at Porter Hall?"

"No, Sophie lives with her niece in Waterford. She's nearly ninety but in excellent health. And John Dennick is retired and living in Dublin. His son, John Jr., now runs the household and Grady helps him."

With a trembling hand, Grace took the letters from Miles and pressed them to her heart. "Thank you. Thank you for everything you've done." Tears flooded her eyes as she realized she didn't have words for what she was feeling.

"I'll show myself out. And I'll look forward to hearing from you, Grace."

Grace sat in the parlor for a long time, just touching the letters and twisting the leather cord from the medallion through her fingers. All of this seemed like lifetimes ago, and yet it was just twenty-five years passed.

She opened the envelope that contained the list of properties and slowly scanned the household inventory, recognizing many of the pieces of furniture and art that she'd become familiar with as a child. It was hers now, hers and Emma's.

A tiny smile touched her lips. No doubt both Malcolm and Lord Henry were turning over in their graves right now. But she knew that Geneva would be happy. Lady Porter had outlived them both, and had lasted long enough to outwit her husband and her son. Grace wished that she would have known her in the years since she'd left Ireland.

"Thank you, Geneva," she whispered. "Thank you for giving me back a piece of Edward, a piece of our life together."

THE DRIVE FROM BOSTON TO Marlborough seemed to go by much faster than usual. Emma was hoping for time, time to think about the conversation she planned to have with her mother about Paddy. They'd been dating for nearly four months now and he'd become an important part of her life.

At first, Emma hadn't taken the relationship very seriously. After all, she was a liberated woman and wanted nothing to do with marriage and commitment. But lately, she realized that sharing her life with Paddy would be the most wonderful thing she could imagine.

She reached over and turned up the radio, listening closely to the new Righteous Brothers song. The song had been playing on the radio last night when she and Paddy had gone for a drive, and he'd declared it their song.

The thought of being Paddy's soul and inspiration was an awful lot to live up to, Emma thought to herself. But it did speak to what they shared. On the surface, they were an unlikely couple, the working class Irish immigrant and the college-educated daughter of a formerly powerful family. But when they were together, all of that made no difference at all.

Paddy was a sweet and decent man, qualities that had been in short supply with her previous boyfriends. He treated her like a queen and with everything he did, Emma could see just how much he treasured their relationship. He'd told her not long ago that he felt like the luckiest man in the world when he was with her.

They'd said the words to each other. *I love you.* And Emma

was certain that Paddy had meant them. But she still struggled with her own feelings. Was this really love or just infatuation? She'd never had a very good example to follow. Or perhaps she had. Her parents had married because of a weeklong infatuation. And they'd both lived with that mistake until her father had died. And her grandparents marriage was more of a political alliance than true love. How was she supposed to know when love was real?

Diane had told her it would come down to choices. One day, she'd make a choice and then she'd know for sure. It might be something as silly as buying a dress in the color he loved or helping him scrape paint off his boat instead of going shopping with her girlfriends. Or it might come as an ultimatum, love me or leave me. But Diane was right. Relationships never stood still, they either moved forward or they ended.

Emma pulled her VW station wagon up to the curb in front of her parents' house. She sat in the car for a long time before getting out, gathering her resolve. Her mother owed her an apology and if she didn't get it, Emma intended to leave.

Things would have been so different had her father been alive. Adam would have loved Paddy. In truth, she saw a lot of her father in Paddy Quinn, his quick wit, his warm smile, and his unwavering affection.

She walked to the front door and let herself in. "Mom?"

Emma found her mother in the small breakfast room. She sat at the table, photographs spread out in front of her. She was staring down at one, a picture of a soldier. "Mom?"

Grace looked up, as if she'd been startled out of a daydream. She slipped the photo beneath some others and smiled. "Hello."

"Are you all right?"

"Yes," she said. "I'm glad you're here. I wasn't sure that you'd come."

"We have things to talk about," Emma said. "What is all this?"

Her mother scanned the surface of the table. "Memories. Sit down," she said, patting the place next to her.

"Mom, what is wrong? You're scaring me. You call me and tell me I have to come over right away. Then I rush over and you're looking at old photos." A sick knot twisted in Emma's stomach. Something was wrong. She could sense it.

Grace placed an old book in front of Emma and she recognized it immediately. It was the diary that her mother had shown her when she was younger. Her mother opened it to a page marked by a ribbon. "Read this for me," she said.

12 September 1847

Life has become a constant trial and I live from day to day, wondering when the end will arrive. Elizabeth is sick and there is nothing I can do for her. Disease is taking what hunger has not. Black fever has come to Wexford and entire families are found dead or dying on the roads. There are no coffins, so the corpses are thrown into mass graves. Those that aren't are left for the rats and the dogs. The potato crop has survived and Elizabeth and I will have some food for the winter. As for a roof over our heads, I barter with my landlord but it comes at a dear price, and one that I will not describe on the pages of this diary. I do what ever is required to keep my child alive and will bear no shame in it when this famine finally comes to an end.

"What does she mean by barter?" Emma asked.

Emma shrugged. "I suppose it means what we think it does. She did what she had to do to save Elizabeth, her daughter."

"She had no choice," Emma said softly. "I might have done the same thing."

"Then you do understand." Her mother picked up a sheaf of papers and placed it on the table in front of Emma. "Do you remember this?"

Emma paged through it. "It's the report I did on my family history when I was in high school. Why did you keep this?"

"Because I knew someday I would need to fix it," Grace said. She reached over and pointed to the branch on the family tree that included Emma's paternal ancestry. "This is wrong," she said softly, her voice almost a whisper.

Emma turned and stared at her mother, frightened by the strange look on her face. "What are you saying?"

"Adam Callahan wasn't your father, Emma. Not your natural father, though he was your father in every other sense of the word. And I will always be grateful to him for that. But you need to know the truth now." She pulled the photo of the soldier out from beneath the pile and held it out to Emma. "This man was your father. His name was Edward Porter."

Emma gasped, certain that this was some kind of joke. But her mother seemed to be dead serious. "No," she murmured. "This isn't true."

"It is," Grace said. "I was pregnant with you when I married Adam." She paused. "You might as well hear the whole truth of it because I know you'll probably hate me anyway. I needed your father. I was alone and pregnant and I had no other choice. He fell in love with me and I took advantage."

Emma stood up and walked away from the table, tears flooding her eyes. This couldn't be so. Adam Callahan was her father. Everyone had always said how much she resembled him. And she would have known, would have seen it in his eyes. He would have never loved her so much if he wasn't her—

She slowly turned and faced her mother. "He never knew, did he? You never told him the truth."

Grace shook her head. "I did tell him and he knew. And understood my choice. And he loved you anyway. You were his daughter in every way possible, Emma, and nothing will ever change that."

"How could you do that to him? How could you…trick him like that?"

"I did it to protect you, Emma. I had to protect you, just like Jane had to protect her baby. You were all I had left of the man I loved. And I gave you a father that you could love."

Emma drew a deep breath. Now that she knew the worst of it, she wanted to know all of it. "Why didn't you marry this other man? Didn't he love you?"

"I did marry him," Grace said with a tremulous smile. "We were married for one month. And then he was killed in the war and I was left alone." She took a ragged breath, as if the emotions were still very close to the surface instead of faded by time. "I was so scared. I had no family and Edward's family would never have accepted me. I was a servant in their household, Irish and Catholic and poor. They were very wealthy and powerful. And there were other reasons I had to leave that I will tell you about someday. I ran away to Dublin and I was sitting in a beautiful church and your father sat down behind me. He was so kind."

"And you decided to take advantage?"

"I gave you a future. I would have done anything for that."

"How am I supposed to feel about this? You've stolen my father from me. How can I think about him in the same way again?" She cursed softly, then crossed the room to stand in front of her mother. "Why would you tell me this? Why couldn't you have let me go on believing it was him?"

"Perhaps I would have," Grace said. "But now, you have choices. You're a woman of property now."

Emma ran her hands through her hair. "What are you talking about?"

"You're the heir to Lord Henry Porter's fortune. You have a manor house outside Dublin, investments, business interests. You have a legacy now, far beyond that diary. And I want us to go back to Ireland and claim it."

Emma's jaw dropped in bewilderment. "Are you crazy? I'm not going to Ireland. I live here. My life is here, my work is here. Why would I pick up and leave now?"

"You'll have something of your own there," Grace said. "Something to build a life around. That job of yours is going nowhere and your boyfriend, pleasant as he may be, will never be able to provide for you in the way that this estate will."

"Some*thing* of my own? What about some*one?*" Emma shot back. "You've lived these last twenty-five years without anyone to love. Can you really recommend it, Mom? Is that what you want for me?"

"No," Grace said. "But you'll find someone…better."

"You mean better than Paddy Quinn. Daddy would have liked him. He's smart and he's kind and hardworking. And he'll make a success of himself, you'll see."

"Don't throw your life away on a man who can't give you what you need," Grace said.

"He loves me, and that's all I need." Emma tipped her chin up. "And you can have it all. I don't want it. Have them draw up the papers and I'll sign them. It's yours. You go back to Ireland, Mom, and you live the life that you wanted for me. I'm sure you'll be very happy there." With that, Emma turned and walked out of the house.

Her mother didn't try to stop her. There was nothing left

to say. Her entire life had just been dismantled before her very eyes. Her past had disappeared and all she had left was the future. She glanced back at the house on Poplar Street as she drove away. Emma Callahan was still alive and well and the rest of her life began now. Her choices had been made and she'd chosen Paddy Quinn.

CHAPTER TWENTY-THREE

PADDY QUINN GRABBED THE BOTTLE of Coke and took a long drink, then gazed up at the hull of the boat. He could scrape from now until the end of the year and he still wouldn't be done. He'd have to rent a sander or invest the last of the money he had in proper tools. And there was still the engine to fix and the rigging to buy.

He walked around the stern of the boat, staring up at it as it sat in its cradle. He'd worked fishing boats his entire life, but he'd never thought to captain a boat as grand as this. He'd named it the Mighty Quinn, after the boat his father had run out of Ballykirk. But this was more than just a simple fishing boat. He had himself a long-liner.

He'd bought the boat for a good price and though it wasn't seaworthy yet, he knew he could fix that. Running his hand through his hair, Paddy took another drink, then set the bottle down on an old crate. He'd thought about sending for his younger brother, Seamus. Between the two of them, they could get the boat in the water and running in no time. But without Seamus, there was no one to help run their father's fishing business back in Ballykirk. Seamus had a wife to support and a baby on the way. Maybe after the boat was in the water, he might convince him.

Paddy glanced over at the entrance to the boatyard at the

sound of a car's tires on the loose gravel. A few moments later, he recognized Emma's VW station wagon. He grabbed his soda pop and started toward her. "Hello, there, Miss Callahan. Aren't you a pretty picture today."

She didn't greet him. Instead, she walked up to him, wrapped her arms around his neck and buried her face in his chest. Paddy returned the embrace, then realized she was crying.

"Hey. What's this all about?" He ran his hands over her hair, then gently drew her back. "Are you going to tell me or am I left to guess?"

"Just hold on to me for a bit longer," Emma said.

Paddy smiled. Whenever they spoke, he could hear a touch of Ireland in her voice, no doubt passed along by her mother. It made him feel like there was at least a part of home here in America. "If I've done something wrong, I'll find a big stick so that you can beat me senseless."

"It's not you," she murmured.

"Then what is it?"

Emma looked up at him, then cupped his face in her hands. She kissed him, her tongue dipping into his mouth provocatively, then sliding out again. The taste of her was so tempting that he didn't wonder at the cause of her sudden change in mood. He just enjoyed it.

"Take me to bed," she murmured as she dragged her mouth over his. "Make love to me."

"Here?" Paddy asked. Though they'd been seeing each other for four months, they'd always stopped short of full-on sex. Paddy had been happy to wait, knowing that he wanted the time to be right for her. And now, it seemed as though it was. "Emma, it's not very comfortable and it smells a bit musty."

She turned and walked away and for a moment, he thought his reluctance had spoiled the mood. But she pulled a blanket from the back of the car and then climbed the ladder up to the deck of the Mighty Quinn. Paddy followed her and when he stood on deck, he watched as she spread the blanket over the rough metal surface.

Emma knelt down on the blanket and slowly began to unbutton her blouse. Paddy watched, his heart slamming in his chest. He knelt in front of her and finished the job, smoothing his hands over her shoulders until they were bare.

She wore no bra and he reached out and cupped one breast, the feel of her flesh so familiar by now. He'd said it once, the very first time they'd met, and every time he looked at her he was reminded that she was the most beautiful woman he'd ever met.

Slowly, they stripped out of their clothes, tossing them aside until they were both completely naked. In the past, they'd always been sure to stay at least partially clothed. To let themselves go this far was too tempting. "Are you sure?" he asked.

Emma nodded, reaching out to stroke his cock. Paddy closed his eyes and moaned softly, the touch of her hand sending desire coursing through his bloodstream. He'd wanted to make love to her from the very first time he'd met her. But he'd known from the start that Emma was more than just a one-night stand.

Paddy slipped his hands around her slender waist and slowly drew her down onto the blanket. It was a beautiful May day, the sky blue and the sun warm. The gunwales of the boat protected them from the breeze coming off the Atlantic and from the eyes of anyone who might come into the boatyard.

His mouth trailed a path over her body and he licked at her soft skin as he explored each sweet inch of flesh. She writhed beneath him, murmured his name. And when he reached the juncture of her thighs, Emma held her breath. Paddy touched her there, first with his fingers and then with his tongue.

She had no inhibitions and opened to him, arching against his mouth as he licked and sucked at her sex. Her fingers furrowed through his hair and Emma gently tugged and twisted until she found the position that gave her the most pleasure. And then, she grew still, panting in short little moans, the tempo building until she cried out.

In an exquisite moment, she found her release, shuddering and groaning as he continued to taste her. And when she was spent, Paddy retrieved the single condom from his wallet and smoothed it over his shaft.

Emma guided him inside her, her eyes glazed with passion, her tongue flicking at her damp lips. He kissed her as he entered her and when he was buried inside her, Paddy drew her legs up around his hips. They fit perfectly together, as if she'd always been made for him.

He began to move, slowly at first, taking the time to enjoy each new sensation as it raced through his body. Emma whispered softly in his ear, telling him how she felt, how much she needed him, and Paddy soon gave himself over to the pleasures of her body.

Instinct took over and he didn't have to think, he only had to feel. Desperate to experience every bit of her, he rolled onto his back, pulled her up to sit on top of him. Paddy opened his eyes and watched her as she rode him, her skin gleaming in the sun, her hair tumbled around her face.

He tried to last as long as he could, but there came a point when delaying was more than he could bear. Grabbing her hips, he held her still but she moaned softly, refusing to stop. Paddy lost his grip on control and let himself erupt inside her. Wave after wave of intense pleasure washed over him and when it subsided, he pulled Emma down on top of him, burying his face in her hair.

"God, I love you," he murmured.

"I love you, too," she replied. She slid off his body and curled up beside him, throwing her leg over his hips and gently rubbing his chest.

"Did you come here to seduce me?" Paddy asked. "Or was there another reason for your visit?"

"I went to see my mother today," Emma replied. "I was summoned."

"What did she have to say for herself?"

"I didn't get an apology, if that's what you're asking. But she had some other very upsetting news."

Paddy heard the tears in her voice and he tipped her face up until he could look into her eyes. "It can't be so bad that telling me won't help," he murmured.

"It seems I've inherited a house and some business investments in Ireland."

"I thought your mother was an orphan," Paddy said.

"This is from my father's family."

"The Callahans."

Emma shook her head. "That was the news she was so anxious to discuss. Turns out I'm not the daughter of Adam Callahan. My mother was married once before, to a man named Edward Porter. He died in the war and she was pregnant with me when she married Adam."

"So your father wasn't really your father?"

"Adam Callahan *is* my father," she said. "I'll never think of him as anything else."

"So there is bad mixed with the good news," he said.

"There's worse. My mother wants me to come with her to Ireland and live there. To claim my inheritance."

Paddy sucked in a sharp breath. "Would you want to do that?"

"No," Emma said. "Of course not. My life is here. My job is here." She paused. "You're here."

"But I could be in Ireland, too," he said. "I could be anywhere you are."

"You'd do that for me?"

"Darling, I love you. I'd do whatever you asked of me."

Emma smiled, then reached up and touched his face. "I wish my father could have known you. He would have loved you."

"So you'll stay, then?"

She nodded. "That's my mother's life, not mine. If she wants to go back and live in the past, then she's welcome to it. My future is here."

"Will you marry me, then?"

Emma pushed up on her elbow and met his gaze. He smiled at her, then stole a quick kiss. "You don't have to answer right away. You can take a minute or a day or a week to think about it."

"I don't need to think about it," she said, tears swimming in her eyes. One dribbled down her cheek and he caught it with his thumb. "Yes, I will marry you."

Paddy drew her into his embrace as she wept. He slowly stroked her hair, speaking to her in soft, soothing words, telling her that he would make everything better. And when she stopped crying, he made love to her again, this time slowly and carefully, bringing them both to their peak together.

When he'd stepped on the plane bound for America, he'd thought he'd brought all his dreams with him. But now that he was here, he had discovered that there was so much more he'd wanted. He would love Emma and do everything in his power to protect her. And they would build a life together and a family.

And at the end of the day, he would look into her beautiful face and know that he'd been given a life that any man would envy.

EMMA STOOD IN FRONT OF THE house on Poplar Street. The sign in the front yard proclaimed that the property had been sold, but she still couldn't believe it. Her childhood home would soon be occupied by strangers.

She walked inside, surprised at how different the house looked stripped of everything that had made it a home. The furniture had already been cleared out and the pieces she'd asked for were tucked into a corner of the front parlor. Next to them were boxes marked with her name in big black letters.

"You're here." Her mother walked into the room, dressed in a trim pair of trousers and a neatly pressed blouse.

"I brought Paddy's truck. I thought I'd take some of the boxes and the smaller furniture with me. I'll have to make another trip for the bigger stuff."

"Is he with you?"

"No, Mom. He's no more interested in seeing you than you are in seeing him."

She raised an eyebrow, her customary reaction to Emma's sharp tone. But Emma was no longer a child and she was allowed to speak to her mother in any manner she chose. "I have nothing against the man, Emma. He seems like a perfectly pleasant fellow. I just don't think he's right for you."

"Well, you're wrong," she said. "And you might as well forget trying to convince me otherwise. We got married last week."

Her mother's jaw tensed and her expression went cold. "Why would you have done something so stupid?"

"I don't need to explain myself to you," Emma said. "You've made it abundantly clear how you feel."

"I think you've made a mistake, Emma."

"I don't care what you think. And I'm not going to take advice from you on how one should run their life. You made a pretty tidy mess of your marriage to my father."

"You know nothing about our marriage," Grace said.

"I know you made each other miserable for most of it. I was there. Don't you remember?"

"It was very difficult, and it took us years, but in the end, your father and I did manage to make it work. And now, I see you repeating all the mistakes we made. We barely knew each other when we got married. You barely know Paddy."

"How can you say that? You knew my father for a week. I've known Paddy for four months. That's long enough to know that I want to spend the rest of my life with him."

"Nothing I have to say really makes a difference to you, does it?"

Emma shook her head.

"I can't approve of this marriage," Grace said. "I won't."

"You don't have to. Go to Ireland, live the life you've always wanted. And I'll live my life. We both need to find happiness, but there's nothing to say we have to agree on where to find it."

Grace nodded. "When the house sells, I've asked the Realtor to forward the funds to you. You can do what you want with the money. Buy yourself some security because I don't think Paddy will be able to provide any. Put the money in the bank in case the marriage doesn't work. And when it does fail, you're always welcome at Porter Hall. It will be your home as much as this was."

With that, Grace walked out of the room. No goodbyes, no good wishes for the future. Emma swallowed the lump of emotion that clogged her throat. How could her mother be so convinced that marrying Paddy had been a mistake when Emma knew, with every ounce of her being, that it wasn't? How could they see things so differently?

She walked into the parlor and picked up one of the boxes. It contained all of her memories from high school, old corsages and yearbooks, awards and photos of friends. She stared into the box, then set it back down. She didn't need these bits and pieces of her past to remember her life in this house. She'd carry the memories of her father with her always.

For now, she needed to look to the future, to the life she'd build with Paddy. Emma turned and walked out the front door. That life had begun the moment she'd looked into his eyes and said "I do."

As she hopped into the front seat of Paddy's truck, Emma took one last look at her childhood home. Then she took a deep breath and started the truck. "Goodbye, Mother," she murmured. "I hope you find what you're looking for."

CHAPTER TWENTY-FOUR

THE YEARS HAD PASSED SO QUICKLY, Grace thought to herself. It seemed like just yesterday when three young boys, her grandsons, had arrived at Porter Hall. And now, she'd put three young men on the plane for America. Ian, Declan and Marcus had been in her care for over eight years and in that time, she'd come to love them as if they'd been her own sons.

Ian, Declan and Marcus were their father's boys. They were wild and headstrong, but at the same time they had a wonderful capacity to dream. For them, nothing had been out of their reach. Every day was an adventure, every hour a chance to discover something new.

As she'd grown to know them, she'd seen more and more of Edward in their personalities. Ian was the honorable one, always anxious to do the right thing. Declan possessed the charm and could talk his way out of any scrape. And Marcus, the youngest, was the sensitive one, his emotions always bubbling close to the surface.

Through it all, Grace had known she would have to give them back. There wasn't a day that went by that she didn't wait for the phone call, the call that told her that her daughter Emma had lost her battle with cancer. The Hodgkins disease had held on for eight long years but now, after a new treatment and almost a year of total remission, the doctors had declared her a cancer survivor.

She'd wanted to ring Emma and tell her how very pleased she was to hear the news. But Grace was afraid that her daughter would refuse to answer the phone, or that if she did, they wouldn't be able to carry on a conversation. Paddy had done his best to communicate Emma's condition throughout the years and for that, Grace was grateful.

It had been nearly twenty years since they'd spoken, twenty years since they'd last set eyes on each other. With each year that passed, it became more difficult for Grace to admit that she might have been wrong about Paddy Quinn. He and Emma were still together, despite Grace's dire predictions for the future of their marriage.

They'd had seven children. He'd nursed her through years of illness, staying by her side in the worst of times. He'd sacrificed everything to get her the medical care she needed. And now that they'd finally triumphed over this illness, they would have their family back together again.

Grace had stood in the terminal at Dublin's airport and watched as the plane pushed back from the jetway. She'd cared for her grandsons as best she could, but in the end, she wasn't sure whether she'd helped them at all. Perhaps it was an impossible situation, sending them here to live with her, a complete stranger in charge of three rambunctious boys. Grace knew how difficult the decision had been for Paddy and Emma to admit that they had nowhere else to turn.

One summer had turned into a year and then two and three. There were so many times that Grace had wanted to go to her daughter, to nurse Emma through her illness like only a mother could. But that was Paddy's job. So much anger and bitterness had passed between them that Grace had decided to leave the decision in Emma's hands. If they would ever meet again, it would have to be her doing.

"I'll miss them," Grady said from the driver's seat in the Bentley.

Grace turned her gaze away from the scenery as it passed by and caught Grady's eyes in the rearview mirror. "There was once a time when I would have been happy to be rid of them. But I grew quite fond of them." She swallowed back the tears that threatened. "I love them like they were my own."

"You did a good thing caring for them while their mother was sick."

"They hated every minute here," Grace said, "because it wasn't home."

"Maybe you could go visit them," he suggested.

"No," she said. "I've burned all those bridges long ago."

"Then build new bridges," he countered.

"I made my choice when I came here and Emma made hers. If she wanted me to come for a visit, she might have invited me. Lord knows, she's always had an open invitation to visit Porter Hall."

"Your grandchildren did," Grady said. "But did you ever invite Emma and Paddy?"

"Well, that was always implied. I just thought it would be better to show them that I wanted to get to know my grandchildren."

Grady shook his head. "The house will be awfully quiet, it will."

"Yes," Grace murmured. "It certainly will."

Fifteen minutes later, Grady pulled into the driveway of Porter Hall. "It looks like Mr. Fletcher has come to pay us a visit. I guess you won't be lonely for too long, then."

Grace shushed him, then smiled to herself, secretly pleased

that her good friend had come. Leave it to Miles to know when she needed him the most. He'd always been there, lending a hand, providing a shoulder to cry on or an ear to listen. Giving her good advice on how to raise boys. They'd become great friends and had grown even closer since his wife had died five years ago.

Grady beeped the horn and a few moments later, Miles walked out the front door. When the car pulled up, he opened Grace's door and helped her out.

"This is a pleasant surprise," she said, giving him a kiss on each cheek.

"I was told the boys were leaving today. I thought I might stop by and see if you'd like to have lunch. I could take you in to Dublin. And then, perhaps we might catch a movie."

"I've had a busy morning getting the boys off. I'd love to see a movie another time and I'd rather have lunch here, if you don't mind. Will you join me?"

"I'd love to," Miles said.

They walked together through the house and out into the rear doors. Emma had made several changes to Porter Hall, adding a small terrace that overlooked the courtyard. They sat down at a glass-topped table and a few minutes later, Cook appeared with a pot of tea.

Grace smiled at her. "Thank you, dear. This is exactly what I need right now."

"When would you like lunch?" she asked.

"In a half hour?" Grace looked and Miles for approval and he nodded.

Grace poured the tea, then set a cup in front of Miles, adding a lump of sugar and a wedge of lemon to the edge of the saucer. "How long are you in Ireland?" Grace asked.

"I thought I'd stay a week. That is, if you can stand having a guest."

"I need someone here to keep me company. I've spent the last eight years watching over the boys. I'm not sure I'll know what to do with myself now that they're gone."

Miles picked up his tea and took a sip. "I have a suggestion. Why don't you do a bit of traveling? I've been planning a trip to India. Would you be up to coming with me?"

Grace gasped. "Me? Go to India?"

"It will be a great adventure. It's one of the only places in the world I haven't seen yet. And now that I'm officially retired, I have plenty of time to spend touring the world. I've been thinking about adding Tibet to the itinerary as well."

Grace thought back to the promises that she and Edward had made, to live their lives as an adventure. She'd never really fulfilled that promise. She'd had to raise Emma and then Emma's sons. And in between that, she'd had a few quiet years with Adam in their house on Poplar Street.

She was seventy-two years old and still in excellent health. Miles was a few years older, yet had boundless energy. Why not have at least one adventure worthy of her promise to Edward? "All right," Grace said. "India it is. And then, on to Tibet."

Miles blinked in surprise. "You really mean that, then?"

"I do," Grace nodded. "I have money in the bank, money you helped me make. It's about time I began spending it. You know, I've always wanted to see Paris."

"Oh, it's a beautiful city," Miles said, his voice full of excitement. "The City of Light. And love. Very romantic, that. And I've heard they've resurrected the Orient Express. It now runs from Paris to Venice and it is supposed to be the height of luxury. Perhaps we ought to forgo India and try that first. After all, India doesn't make for much of a honeymoon. But between Paris and Venice, it's a tricky choice which is more romantic."

"What in God's name are you babbling about? What honeymoon? Whose honeymoon?"

"Ours," Miles said. "We've been seeing each other for a few years now. I think we ought to make it official. If we don't, then we'll have to rent two hotel rooms and you know how frugal I've become in my old age."

"So this is a proposal out of practicality?" Grace asked, laughing.

"No. I have a true affection for you, Grace. As I'm sure you do for me. We've both had our great love affairs. But it's not too late to have something smaller and more manageable. I'm an old man, so I can promise you that my days of chasing after young girls are long gone. I prefer my women experienced."

Grace laughed. "And this is how you propose?"

"I can't get down on one knee, my dear. I might never get back up again."

"Ask me properly and I'll consider your offer."

"Mary Grace Byrne Porter Callahan, will you marry me?"

Grace took a slow sip of her tea, then set the cup back in the saucer. "I believe I will, Miles Fletcher."

He chuckled softly, then leaned forward and pressed a kiss to her lips. "And I do believe you're blushing, my dear."

"What will your children say?"

"I don't really care," he said. "I plan to live out the rest of my years doing exactly what I want. I think I've earned that privilege, don't you?"

Grace looked across the table at the man who had been such a good friend to her over the past twenty years. She'd never expected that he might propose, but now that he had, she'd realized that Miles Fletcher would make an excellent husband. With Edward, she'd had passion. With Adam, she'd had respect. And with Miles, she'd have a great friendship.

EMMA PEERED OUT THE WINDOW of the car, watching as the signs for Logan International passed overhead. She glanced at Paddy and smiled. "I'm nervous. Why am I so nervous?"

"It's a big day for all of us," he said.

He'd been so calm. Emma hadn't been able to sleep for a week, not since they'd bought the plane tickets. "Maybe we should have brought presents or a sign. We could have picked up some balloons."

"The kids are putting together a big party at home. By the time we get back to Providence, they'll have the house decorated and enough food to feed an army. And I gave them some money to go out and get some things for the boys."

Emma reached over and touched her husband's shoulder. "Aren't you nervous?"

He nodded. "A little. It's been eight years. And it's been difficult to parent them over the phone. I'm not sure they'll even listen to me anymore. Ian is a man and Declan isn't far behind. Marcus is the only one who might need me."

"They'll all need you," Emma said. "You're their father."

"It's going to be tough, Em. There's going to be a period of adjustment. We can't expect it to go smoothly."

She closed her eyes and tipped her head back. "When we sent them to Ireland, it was only supposed to be for a summer. It's been so long. Was I selfish?"

"I think you wanted to protect them," Paddy said. "We both did."

"From what? From the realities of my illness? Sometimes I think it might have been better for them to see it, to know what I was going through."

"We can't change the decisions we made, Emma. We gave them a childhood, one they wouldn't have had at home. You know how hard this has been on the other kids, what an emotional toll it's taken. Every morning for eight years, they had to wake up wondering if this was the day you'd get worse, if this was the day the cancer would win."

"You're right," she said. "I just hope they understand."

A long silence grew between them, each of them lost in their thoughts. Emma couldn't believe how quickly the years had passed, how much of her sons' lives she'd missed.

"I think you ought to write to your mother," Paddy said.

Emma winced. He'd brought up the subject before but she had refused to consider it. Until her mother accepted her husband, Emma had nothing to say to her. "She owes me an apology. She owes you an apology."

"Don't you think this has gone on long enough? She took your boys in, Emma. She gave them what we couldn't. We owe her at least a thank you for that."

"All right," Emma replied. "I will write her a letter. But that's all. And if she doesn't reply, then I'm not going to write again."

"That's all I ask," Paddy said.

He followed the signs for the parking ramp and when they reached the airport, Paddy found a spot on the second level and pulled the car into it. He turned off the ignition and stretched his arm out across the back of Emma's seat. Emma leaned over and snuggled against him. "I wasn't sure this day would ever come."

"I was," Paddy said, kissing the top of her head.

"You got me through it all." Emma turned her face up to his and he kissed her gently. "I'm ready to go get my boys now."

Paddy got out of the car and circled around to open her door. They walked into the terminal, hand in hand, Emma's heart filled with a mix of emotion. She felt hopeful and anxious and insecure and exhilarated. For eight years, a piece of her heart had been missing, sent along with her boys to Ireland. And now, it was coming home.

By the time they got to the gate, the plane had landed and the first passengers were getting off. Emma wondered if she'd recognize her sons. Her mother had sent photos every year and Emma had watched them grow. But seeing them again would be different. She could touch them and hug them and listen to their voices.

Paddy stood behind her, his arms wrapped around her waist, his chin on her shoulder. "Are you ready?"

Emma nodded. A moment later, she caught sight of a trio of dark-haired boys, tall and lean and broad-shouldered. A tiny sigh slipped from her throat and tears filled her eyes. Declan saw them first and he grabbed his brothers and pulled them along to the spot where Emma and Paddy stood.

Suddenly, Emma found herself in the middle of a huge hug, all long arms and handsome faces and voices that had grown deeper over the years. She closed her eyes and let the tears come, her cheeks growing wet with the joy she felt. "I've missed you all so much."

The world was right again, and Emma's heart was complete. And no matter what the future brought, her sons would be here to experience it with her.

As they walked out of the airport together, she thought about the choices her mother had made. It wasn't always easy to do what was best for your children, Emma mused. Perhaps it had taken this long for her to fully understand. She looked at her sons. Tonight she'd celebrate their homecoming. And tomorrow, she'd sit down and write a letter—from one mother to another.

EPILOGUE

"HERE'S THE MAIL." YOUNG DENNICK dropped a stack of envelopes on Grace's desk. "There's a letter there from Providence. A big envelope."

Grace smiled and adjusted her reading glasses, then flipped through the stack until she found the envelope. "Would you like to open it?" she teased.

Dennick shook his head. "Would you like your tea in here or in the garden?"

"Is Miles working on the roses?"

Dennick nodded.

"Then I'll have it in the garden." The butler nodded and walked out of the room, and Grace turned her attention to the envelope. It was thick, as if there might be photos inside. Grace slipped her finger beneath the flap, breaking the seal.

The first letter had arrived a few weeks after the boys had left. And now, thirteen years later, they arrived every few months, full of news about Emma's children and grandchildren. Sometimes, she included photos and newspaper clippings and other times, the children added a short note to the end of Emma's letter.

It had taken a long time for them to repair the damage that had been done, but the boys had seemed to serve as a bridge, something they had in common. Grace had invited them all to visit, but every summer, Emma had sent her regrets. They were still paying off medical bills, she explained. When Grace had offered to help, she was politely refused and the letters had stopped coming for a time.

So she'd been forced to accept that this was her relationship with Emma, occasional letters and a phone call every Christmas. Though it wasn't all she'd wanted, it was what she deserved after her treatment of Paddy.

She slipped the greeting card out of the envelope and then realized it wasn't a card at all. She ran her fingers over the text on the front, the engraved type elegant across the cream-colored card. "Oh, my," she murmured, reaching for her handkerchief.

"Grace, there's tea. Are you coming?"

She looked up to see Miles standing in the doorway of the library.

"What is it?" he asked.

Grace held up the vellum card and smiled. "It's a wedding invitation. From Marcus. He's getting married next month."

"And why does it have you crying?"

"Because, I'd really like to go."

"Then we'll go," Miles said.

Grace brushed a tear from her cheek. "I'm eighty-six years old. I won't be flying across an ocean to attend a wedding."

"We flew across an ocean just last year, my dear, and you weren't any worse for it. In fact, I believe we flew across several oceans on our way to New Zealand."

"What if Emma doesn't want me there?"

He crossed the room and stood behind her, reading the invitation in her hand. "Isn't it expected that the mothers of the bride and the groom approve the invitation list? I seem to remember that from my daughter's wedding."

She reached up and patted Miles's cheek. "I can always depend on you to poke holes in my fears and insecurities."

"You don't have any fears and insecurities," Miles said.

"Oh, but I do," she murmured. "The older I get, the more I seem to discover. As for regrets, I have plenty of those."

"But regrets you can fix."

"I regret how I treated Paddy. And I regret that I've been so stubborn about an apology. But I regret my estrangement from Emma most of all. I want to see my daughter again and I want to look into her eyes and tell her how much I've always loved her."

"Then do something about it," Miles said. He took the envelope from her hand and pulled out the response card. "Do you have a pen?"

She plucked a fountain pen out of the drawer and handed it to him.

Miles bent over the desk and scribbled on the response card. "Mrs. Grace Fletcher accepts," he said. "As does her husband, Miles. There. Now we just need to post this."

"You really believe I should do this, then?"

"Absolutely, my dear. We have spent the last thirteen years traveling the world. Yet, we've never gone back to the States. I think you've deliberately avoided it, knowing that you couldn't go without at least trying to see your daughter again. But, now we have an invitation and I'm bloody ready to make the trip."

Grace rose and plucked the card from his fingers. She slipped it inside the envelope. "I'm going to give this to Dennick to post. And you can call for our plane tickets. I think we should leave as soon as possible. I'd like to spend some time in New York. I know you love Broadway shows. And I'd love to visit some of the museums and go to the opera."

She walked out of the library, her mind filled with all the

things she wanted to say to Emma. Grace climbed the stairs to her bedroom and sat down on the edge of her bed, then opened the drawer in the bedside table. She withdrew the diary and ran her hand over the worn leather cover. It was time to pass the legacy on to her daughter. Now Emma would preserve the story of Jane.

There was nothing more powerful than a mother's love, Grace mused. And though her own choices hadn't always been right, they'd always been borne of her need to protect her daughter, to keep her safe and happy. She opened the diary to the last page and smiled as she read.

31 December 1851

> I write this last entry in my diary and today will close this chapter in my life. A new year begins tomorrow and with it, a new life. The famine has eased and though Ireland will never be the same, those that are left will survive. Elizabeth is healthy and I have met a man who has asked me to marry him. He will give us a comfortable home and provide well for us. I never believed I could love again, but I was wrong. I still carry Michael in my heart and I see his face every time I look into my daughter's eyes. I will always bear a deep sadness and grief for all those lost to hunger and disease. I pray to God that Ireland will rise again and I will see it in my lifetime. Until then, I will read this story to my daughter and her daughters and they will know the true power of a mother's love.

Happily ever after is just the beginning...

Turn the page for a sneak preview of
DANCING ON SUNDAY AFTERNOONS
by
Linda Cardillo

Harlequin Everlasting—
Every great love has a story to tell.™
A brand-new line from Harlequin Books
launching this February!

Prologue

Giulia D'Orazio
1983

I had two husbands—Paolo and Salvatore.

Salvatore and I were married for thirty-two years. I still live in the house he bought for us; I still sleep in our bed. All around me are the signs of our life together. My bedroom window looks out over the garden he planted. In the middle of the city, he coaxed tomatoes, peppers, zucchini—even grapes for his wine—out of the ground. On weekends, he used to drive up to his cousin's farm in Waterbury and bring back manure. In the winter, he wrapped the peach tree and the fig tree with rags and black rubber hoses against the cold, his massive, coarse hands gentling those trees as if they were his fragile-skinned babies. My neighbor, Dominic Grazza, does that for me now. My boys have no time for the garden.

In the front of the house, Salvatore planted roses. The roses I take care of myself. They are giant, cream-colored, fragrant. In the afternoons, I like to sit out on the porch with my coffee, protected from the eyes of the neighborhood by that curtain of flowers.

Salvatore died in this house thirty-five years ago. In the last months, he lay on the sofa in the parlor so he could be in the middle of everything. Except for the two oldest boys, all the children were still at home and we ate together every evening. Salvatore could see the dining room table from the sofa, and he could hear everything that was said. "I'm not dead, yet," he told me. "I want to know what's going on."

When my first grandchild, Cara, was born, we brought her to him, and he held her on his chest, stroking her tiny head. Sometimes they fell asleep together.

Over on the radiator cover in the corner of the parlor is the portrait Salvatore and I had taken on our twenty-fifth anniversary. This brooch I'm wearing today, with the diamonds— I'm wearing it in the photograph also—Salvatore gave it to me that day. Upstairs on my dresser is a jewelry box filled with necklaces and bracelets and earrings. All from Salvatore.

I am surrounded by the things Salvatore gave me, or did for me. But, God forgive me, as I lie alone now in my bed, it is Paolo I remember.

Paolo left me nothing. Nothing, that is, that my family, especially my sisters, thought had any value. No house. No diamonds. Not even a photograph.

But after he was gone, and I could catch my breath from the pain, I knew that I still had something. In the middle of the night, I sat alone and held them in my hands, reading the words over and over until I heard his voice in my head. I had Paolo's letters.

* * * * *

HARLEQUIN® *Romance*®

From reader-favorite

MARGARET WAY

Cattle Rancher, Convenient Wife

On sale March 2007.

**"Margaret Way delivers…
vividly written, dramatic stories."**
—Romantic Times BOOKreviews

---

*For more wonderful wedding stories,
watch for Patricia Thayer's new miniseries
starting in April 2007.*

Rocky Mountain
BRIDES